I0760442

ENVY

A DARK ROMANCE

THE SEVEN PRINCES
BOOK ONE

C. L. BRIAR

Edited by Samantha | Radiant Editorial

Cover design: Artscandare Book Cover Design

Audiobook production:

Christian J. Gilliland, Rylee Kuberra

Identifiers:

ISBN: 978-1-956829-27-3 (ebook)

ISBN: 978-1-956829-29-7 (paperback)

ISBN: 978-1-956829-30-3 (hardback)

ISBN: 978-1-956829-31-0 (special edition)

CONTENT WARNINGS

The follow book contains:

- Violence, strong language, death
- Blood, injury, and gore depiction including gunshot wounds and knives
- Torture
- Physical and emotional abuse/manipulation
- Mental health struggles including depression, suicidal thoughts and imagined attempts (not acted on), cutting, and disassociation.
- Religious trauma
- Jealous and possessive MMC (I know, the title kind of gives it away)
- Abduction
- Child sexual abuse (recounted, not on page)
- Attempted sexual assault (drugged drink, not successful),
- Panic attack

- Detailed sex scenes including (but not limited to):

Dubious consent (she thinks she's dreaming but he's really there), Consensual non-consent (CNC), Exhibitionism, Voyeurism, Degradation, Praise kink, Cum kink, Anal sex, Choking and breath play, Virgin blood kink, Spitting, Dom/sub, Rough sex, Primal play, Somnophilia

For the good girls who wondered what would've happened if Eve finished the forbidden fruit and joined the serpent, this one's for you.

1

SILAS

Blood sprays as my fist collides with his face. The familiar *crack* of bone against my knuckles vibrates through my leather glove as the piece of shit falls to the floor. The concrete is new, the unimposing grey sheen of it glinting in the dim light cast from the single bulb overhead. We'll need to pour another layer after tonight. Bleach can do a lot, but it's always better to start with a fresh canvas. I wonder how dark the pools of blood will be. I wonder if I'll be able to capture the beauty of it later with a brush and palette.

"Please," he whimpers, scrambling away from the center of the ring toward the others. As if my brothers would let him leave. As if anyone escapes once we've decided their time is up.

Six figures clad in black, shrouded with warped skeletal masks, stare back at me, reflecting the demons inside. Morality is such a fickle thing. It plagues only those who have empathy, weakening them against the onslaught of the apathetic. I've had to silence the softer parts of myself, cutting and hacking away at the writhing soul inside to allow me to do what's necessary.

I was innocent not too long ago, before the harsh realities of this world twisted and bent me into my true form—just like my brothers—rising from the carnage into the personification of the Seven Princes of Hell: Pride, Erik. Wrath, Mavros. Gluttony, Bane. Greed, Adrian. Lust, Dominic. Sloth, Noctis. And Envy—me.

Feel no pain.

Grant no mercy.

Take no prisoners.

Tension radiates from the six of them, shoulders taut and hands clenching. They're itching for a chance to tear this asshole to shreds just as much as I am. We've been at this too long. Far too long. But my brothers hold back in respect for me.

"Who are your buyers, Tony?" I ask, stalking toward him. His left eye is swollen shut, bloated and discolored like a plum on the verge of bursting. Scarlet droplets coat the floor as he scampers back, searching the room for an escape. As if we'd be foolish enough to leave him an opening.

There are only two doors here. One leads to the showers, a necessary installment to wash away incriminating evidence once we're done. The other opens to the blistering wasteland of the Mojave Desert. Tony must realize this, because the pathetic bastard turns, his grimy fingers gripping the pants of the masked figure nearest to him. Big mistake.

Red thread is stitched across the skeletal smile, matching the Xs embroidered across the eyes. The sight is made all the more menacing by the snarling bear threaded along the temple. Mavros, Wrath incarnate, glares down at the bleeding coward pawing at his feet, pleading for mercy he won't find.

"If there's something wrong with the drugs, take it up with the boss," Tony cries. "I'm just the distributor. I swear!"

Mavros jerks his leg back and snaps his foot forward before Tony has time to blink. Agonized wails fill the vacant warehouse, reverberating off the bare walls as the sole of Mavros's boot connects with flesh. My lips twitch as the squelch of muscles tearing and bones snapping rings out. A few broken teeth fall to the ground, blood and drool dripping from Tony's mouth as his hands move frantically, shaking as he feels the mangled shape of his face.

My smile fades as I take in the fucked-up state of his mouth. That's going to be a problem.

"How is he supposed to talk if his jaw is broken?" I shoot Mavros a glare, one he feels even through the fabric of our masks. It took us months to track Tony down. Despite earning his death ten times over, the fucker is too valuable to lose. We need answers first. Then we can play.

Mavros lifts a bulky shoulder, shrugging as if the thought hadn't occurred to him.

"Don't blame the big guy," Erik says from behind me, sauntering into the ring. He'd say he's more easygoing than I am. I suppose all of my brothers would. We've each had our own battles, but unlike Erik and the others, I can't forget that I have to work for every inch I take, fighting my way through all the shit weighing me down.

Nothing is easy. Good things don't come to those who wait. That's just another lie the powerful want you to believe. Another pacifying notion they whisper to make you believe those who are deserving will receive.

I know better.

So do my brothers.

But somehow, each of them has managed to continue living —sometimes fucking or fighting through their pain—but they're *living*. They laugh and joke, eat and breathe, while every expansion of my lungs, each beat of my heart pushing another wave of blood through my veins, feels like a betrayal.

She's out there. My sister.

The world moved on—god, even Tempest, my little sister, is

thriving in college, set on becoming a doctor and shit. She was too young to remember. I don't blame her exactly, but Morana is stuck in a cycle of abuse, being passed around by fuckers like Tony, while everyone else just kept going. And knowing that fucking kills me.

Erik is the one person who comes close to understanding. I spare him a glance, noting the purple lion and matching stitches across his mask—Pride. The sewing is rougher than the others, with harshly dyed twine used instead of smooth thread. Just like mine. The imperfections of it are an eyesore, one Erik typically wouldn't tolerate—the cocky bastard—but some things are more important than perfection.

My fingers were stained for weeks after dyeing and stitching Erik's mask, the rich violet hue lingering long after I'd scrubbed my skin raw. It was nothing compared to the emerald green marring his own hands. It was a pact between us—the first two demons to claw our way out of the turmoil we'd been born into.

The rest of my brothers wouldn't dare speak during interrogations, not when I'm seeking answers like these, but Erik and I grew up together. We suffered through hell, fought our way out, and established a pack, collecting the others until our evil little club of princes was complete.

I'd kill for each of the Seven, as they would for me, but unlike the other princes, I know Erik would die for me. Erik was there when Morana was taken—the worst day of my life. He's been there at my side every step of the way as my death toll climbs. And fuck if I don't enjoy reaping the souls of the corrupted. Especially those involved in the world of buying and selling women and children. Like the fucker whimpering at my feet.

"He can still answer our questions," Erik says, sounding almost cheerful as he stoops, crouching on his knees just outside the growing pool of blood. "Can't you, pal?"

Tony lowers his shaking hands, face streaked with tears and snot and blood. "I didn't touch the drugs—"

His garbled protests are cut off by a quick slap from Erik, the force jerking Tony's head to the side. A surprised laugh scrapes the back of my throat, the unhinged noise sounding like something from a horror movie.

Keep it together, Silas. Can't lose your shit now. Not when you're so close to getting Morana back.

Erik would choose to slap someone rather than lay them out. The arrogant son of a bitch always thinks he'll be able to get answers—the true embodiment of Pride if there ever was one.

"Shh," Erik coos, gently tilting Tony's chin up until he meets the stitched-over eyes of Erik's mask. "We're not talking about drugs, friend. And I think you know that."

Tony stills, his face draining of color.

There it is, I think as a smile twists my lips. People always assume Erik is the kind one, but he's just as vicious as the rest of us.

"That's fucking right," I say, voice low as my pulse spikes. I've done this song and dance before. We're nearly done, and I can practically smell the mist of blood. Hear the *click* of metal. The blast of a bullet. And then—the blissful echo of silence.

"All this suffering is really unnecessary," Erik muses, shaking his head as if he's a disappointed parent. He sighs a moment before lashing out. Leather gloves wrap around Tony's throat, hauling him to his feet. Erik forces his chin up to meet my gaze, pressing Tony's back to his chest.

"All you have to do is answer the questions," Erik says, cutting off Tony's protests, "and the pain stops."

"I—I don't know..." Tony inhales sharply as I withdraw a Glock from my back pocket.

"Tsk, Tsk," Erik taunts in a playful rebuke just before he pinches Tony's distorted jaw. Bones grind, pulling a gut-wrenching whimper from his chest, but Erik's other arm has him bound, holding him in place. "You aren't lying to us now, are you, buddy?"

"Who runs the West Coast circuit?" I ask, glancing down at the gun in my hands. I rest my finger on the trigger, admiring the picturesque sight. It's new, lightweight, and easily disposed of. Just like everything else the Seven use. I raise a brow, surprised Tony isn't spilling all his secrets by now. "I have no need for you if you won't talk."

It's a bluff, one that Erik knows well, but he plays his part perfectly, stepping back as Tony crumples in on himself.

"Last chance," I warn, my pulse thrumming. I want him to give me a reason to draw this out. I crave the rush of adrenaline, the blast of power that comes from taking a life. Yes, pulling the trigger is exhilarating, but every time I disappear one of these fuckers, a child gets to return home to her family instead of being siphoned off into the game.

"They'll kill me." Tony shakes his head, muttering to himself.

Wrong. Fucking. Answer. Or right, depending on how you look at things. Because this means I get to play. I get to maim and punish and push. I get to create art with a gun and the flash of a bullet, coating the ground in red, as if his blood were my paint and the concrete floors my canvas. What a treat little Tony has given me.

The pain, the cries, the look of hopelessness that descends when they realize this mask—this black cloth with green twine Xs across the eyes and a skeletal smile stitched shut—is the last fucking thing they'll see before they die…

Fuck me, it's addicting.

A harsh chuckle vibrates through my chest as I tilt my head back, basking in the carnage to come. It's echoed by my brothers, the fuckers just as deranged as I am.

With a manic grin stretching wide beneath my mask, I pull the slide of the gun back, letting go as I take aim and fire. Tony jerks, crying out as the bullet connects with his leg. I wait until he curls over the blown-out mess of chipped bone and tendons that once was his knee before I adjust my aim a little to the left and shatter his other.

I cock my head to the side, allowing myself a moment to appreciate the sounds of his suffering before I remember all the shit Noctis dug up on him.

"You'll be praying for death before I'm through with you," I growl, barely suppressing the urge to put a third bullet between his eyes. "How old was she when you took her? Your *wife*."

I spit the last word, knowing she was nothing but a victim—just like my sister. Erik stills, his fist flexing, and I know he's contemplating reaching for his own gun.

Something about the situation must finally register, because Tony's pleas shift into unhinged rage, the kind that only surfaces when you know you have nothing left to lose. He glares, panting for breath as blood seeps from his wounds.

"I saved the bitch. Even told her she could buy her way out if she wanted."

"As if she'd be able to afford her exit fee," Adrian snarls, his voice channeling the golden dragon embroidered at his temple. "I may be a greedy, selfish prick, but stealing children? Getting rich off their suffering? It's something even the devil would condemn."

"Not just condemn, brother," Dominic says. Dark blue thread is woven into the demonic representation of Satan—the spiraling ram horns and vengeful goat eyes disconcerting for even the purest of heart. "Satan delights in eternal torture for assholes like him."

Dominic's mask tilts up, finding my watching gaze.

"Bullets are too quick, Silas. Switch to a blade. Carve off pieces of him until he no longer remembers his name."

Nodding, I make a show of putting my gun away.

"I don't know much about the girls," Tony pants, face growing paler by the second. There's too much blood.

Shit, I'm running out of time.

That's what you get for letting your heart make decisions, Silas. Minutes. I have fucking minutes to get him to tell me where Morana is—all because I couldn't control my feelings.

Dominic withdraws a knife, unfolding the blade as he strolls over looking like he doesn't have a care in the world.

"Here, use mine."

2

EVIE

The small silver cross hangs heavy around my neck, like a noose before the drop. My parents gave it to me when I turned thirteen, along with a lecture about rejecting temptation and remaining pure until marriage. I'd once worn it with pride. Only recently have I started to question why my worth as a person—a blessed child of God, as they would say—is determined by walking the line between modesty and temptation. I'm required to be attractive but never go too far. Be friendly and outgoing, but quiet and respectable. Everything is contradictory. And I'm beginning to think they made it that way on purpose.

Twisting the hair at the end of my braid, I glance through the smudged car window toward the unassuming house I'm parked in front of. The cement driveway is framed by bright succulents and smooth stones, complete with stretching palm trees swaying in the late summer breeze. Tendrils of warm air swirl through my cracked window, licking the beads of sweat trickling down my neck.

Where the fuck is my mother. She insisted on being here when I moved in, despite Tempest's offer to have her brother and his friends do the heavy lifting. Being that I'm horrible at confrontation and will do anything to avoid awkward social situations, I told Mother to meet me here four hours earlier than what Tempest had suggested. My new roommate agreed to leave the door unlocked, just in case I arrived before she returned from her morning hike—meaning I was hoping to have all my stuff moved in and my overbearing mother gone before anyone was the wiser.

Maybe if Tempest never meets a member of my family, the possibility of us becoming friends can still be on the table. College is my one chance to have a normal life, and I'm not about to let my fucked-up family mess it up. If my mother doesn't get here soon, I'll start unloading the half dozen boxes containing all my belongings myself.

I bite my lip just thinking about her reaction. *We agreed I'd approve of your living space, Evie. And this is simply unacceptable.*

My father's lecture follows close behind, replaying in my mind for the thousandth time about how inappropriate it is for a woman my age to live unattended. I should be at home, under their supervision, until I'm properly handed over to a husband. As if this were the 1800s and I a nineteen-year-old woman on the brink of spinsterhood.

I'm not sure what type of magic my mother worked to get my father and brother to agree to me living off campus, but I'll be forever grateful.

It's been nineteen years of pretending to be perfect. Of attending church every Sunday, kneeling at the pews and at home when my father insisted on extra sermons. Of forcing my eyes down and lips closed whenever my brother's blue eyes glanced my way.

Half-brother, I correct, as if that makes it any better. My skin crawls as memories assault my mind. My heart ricochets in my chest, cold sweat breaking out across my forehead despite the mounting heat in my car. I flex my hands around the steering wheel, resisting the urge to cover my body. To cower.

It won't help, I chide myself, but his voice comes anyway, blasting through the walls I've fought so hard to construct. *You're the damaged, dirty piece in the otherwise upstanding family portrait, Evie. No one will believe you.*

And no one did. Maybe that's why I'm questioning everything to do with God. Because how would someone all powerful, all seeing, all knowing allow so many fucked-up things to happen? If He is real, He's either abandoned us, or He's an unfeeling asshole—neither of which inspire much faith from me.

Shoving the shame-filled memories back into the pretty little box I keep them in, I unplug my phone from the dash and shoot my mother a text.

The screen flashes a second later, illuminating a thin, blonde-haired, blue-eyed woman who's had more than a few rounds of Botox and fillers. Groaning, I swipe to answer, wishing for once she'd just text back like a normal person instead of video chatting.

"Hi, Mother," I say, forcing a smile. "I didn't get out of the car. Promise. Are you almost here?"

The last thing I need is to upset her by being too independent and have her change her mind about letting me attend, but even as the words leave my lips, I can tell she's not on her way. Her heels *click* as she walks, her designer sunglasses perched above her plastic nose and pink-painted lips.

"I meant to call, sweetie, but I won't be able to make it. Can we push it to tomorrow?"

"Classes start tomorrow," I say, my smile faltering.

"Yes, I'm aware," she tsks, picking up her stride. Buildings constructed in the Mission Revival style come into view behind her, their expansive white arches topped with terracotta-tiled roofs that mirror those on my acceptance letter.

"Are you on campus?" I ask, the words spilling free before I can stop them.

She lifts a freshly plucked brow, glossed lips pressing into a thin line.

Immediately dropping my gaze, I mutter an apology as another piece of my hollowed heart dims. Mother is only this assertive when it's the two of us. She wouldn't dare pretend to be strong around my father or even my half-brother, Jonathan, but I know better than to pry into her business. After all, she's the one who taught me a young woman is meant to be seen, not heard.

"There are matters pertaining to your admittance that I must address with Dean Whitehouser," she clips. "Your father is needed at the church all day, but I'll call Jonathan."

"No," I practically shout, dread and disgust twisting my gut. I swallow against the narrow-eyed look she levels my way, forcing my voice to steady. "I mean, there's no need to bother Jonathan with this. I only have a few boxes, and Tempest just got here. She'll help me. The place is nice, Mother. And close enough to walk to campus."

My mother narrows her eyes as I wave to the vacant driveway, just out of the phone's camera shot. I swear she can sense the lie, but she sighs after a moment.

"Fine. But if your father asks, I was with you all morning." She pauses, her lips tilting into a brief smile, as if she sees someone behind her phone, before focusing back on the screen. "In fact, we went out for an early dinner after moving."

"Okay," I say, not questioning it. Whatever it takes to make sure I can get out of that cursed house and start my own life.

"But you will return every night for dinner and prayer."

"I—I can't," I stammer, nearly flinching when she removes her sunglasses and glares. Pressing on before she can punish me, I mutter, "I have evening classes every day."

Mother narrows her eyes, her lips parting. I have no doubt

she's about to tell me college was a stupid idea. That I'd be better off getting married and serving my future husband, just like Father wants. Forget about marine biology and conservation. "*Global warming isn't real anyway*," my father's voice echoes in my head.

"But I've already located the nearest church on campus to each of my classes and will go straight there," I rush on before she can protest. With this being a religious school, there were three main ones to choose from and a few smaller coves scattered throughout the grounds.

Despite what I just promised her, I wouldn't be attending prayer. God wasn't there when I needed him most, and the church decided on my damnation for simply being born a woman. But if my parents realize I'm no longer under their control—at least mentally—they'd never let me out of their sight.

"I'll return on the weekends when I don't have homework," I add, not liking the growing silence.

Another lie. I've purposely stacked my schedule with eighteen units, nearly double the standard course load, just to make sure I never have to enter that house again.

"Fine," she relents, clearly distracted by someone. Whoever it is, I hope they have a wonderful day. She pauses, tilting up her nose as she scrutinizes my appearance. Even through the phone, it feels like she's catching every wrinkle along my cardigan. The thin spike of her eyebrow lifts, as if she's able to see beyond the frame of the call—judging the tightness of my light blue skirt across my hips or the scuffed pair of white tennis shoes I chose instead of kitten heels.

"I'll see you Saturday morning."

"Thank you," I say, feeling like each lie I've told is inked across my skin.

"And Evie?"

"Yes, Mother?" I mutter, wringing my hands.

"Try to look presentable. Your brother will be bringing a friend, and I don't want to tarnish the family name with your disheveled state."

The edges of my forced smile crumple as her barb finds purchase between my ribs. *Tarnished. Corrupted. Damaged.* All things I've tried so hard to forget, and yet they still play through my mind on a loop.

The screen darkens before returning to the black-and-white picture of the *Cerebra odollam* blossom on my background. The suicide tree. One kernel from its fruit is potent enough to kill an adult. Despite the risk, I've discovered it's strangely popular in Southern California, especially in San Diego.

Unable to help it, my gaze drifts to the nearby greenery—swaying palm trees, flowered bushes, manicured lawns—but none of the trees I'm looking for. And god, the disappointment blooming in my chest is more telling than I care to admit.

Six months ago, I'd held the toxic seed in my hands. I'd intended to crush it, and then mix it into a tea. The toxin slows a human heartbeat within six hours, meaning I could go to sleep and just... fade.

The day I'd planned on taking it was the day I got my acceptance letter to Grace University. I'd thought it was going to be another form of the prison I was already stuck in, but then my mother suggested I live on campus—and despite Jonathan's protests, my father didn't object right away.

Being that I'm a transfer and technically at the sophomore level, I'm lucky I found a room within walking distance. For some strange reason, Mother hasn't pressed why I'm not in the dormitories. That's one of the perks of coming from a wealthy family: they didn't notice when a few thousand dollars went missing to cover tuition for online classes. I'd transferred the units I'd taken on my own with my family none the wiser. It made me wonder what else I could do without them knowing.

Starting today, I'll be living on my own. Away from

Jonathan, from the disapproving looks of my parents, and the endless sermons about how I need to beg for forgiveness for a soul that's already fractured beyond saving.

A smile tilts the corners of my lips—the first real flicker of happiness I've felt in years. Grabbing my phone, I open the car door. I inhale deeply, basking in the invigorating scent of citrus and salt as I step onto the sidewalk. The soles of my shoes heat from the concrete, the rays of the full sun potent enough to have me lifting a hand to shade my eyes as I gaze upon the modest-looking home before me.

For the first time in my life, I believe there could be a future without pain. Maybe I could erase all the corrupted parts of myself, scrub clean the blemishes, expunge the sin and start fresh.

I allow myself to believe in that future—in the lie—as I start unpacking. But in the deep recesses of my mind, in the haunting blackness of my soul, I know that if I succeeded in purging all my demons… there wouldn't be anything left.

3

SILAS

"No—fuck!" Tony trembles, eyes darting to the ring of masks surrounding him. "I took Ava five years ago. They said I could keep her as long as she met her quota each month."

My stomach rolls, but I have to keep my emotions in check. I need answers more than I need his death, at least for now.

"Who's in charge of the circuit?" I repeat, teeth grinding. "I won't ask again."

"Ray organized services when I was active," Tony pants, sweat breaking out across his brow. The pool of red around his mangled wounds expands with each beat of his heart. He's lost too much blood. I should place tourniquets, prolong the questioning.

"Last I heard, Ray caught a case about a year ago. Has two more years before he's out."

Mavros shakes his head in barely restrained fury, the red bear symbolizing Wrath catching the light. I feel his ire as if it's my own, disgusted by the fucked-up system that gives life sentences for drug dealers while rapists are out in months.

"Some new guy moved through the ranks—calls himself Lucifer."

"Where?" Erik asks, his normally light voice ringing hollow.

"I—I don't know," Tony sputters. "But the West Coast circuit is split. California breaks at San Francisco, the north continuing on to Portland, but the south... the south connects to Vegas and out through New Mexico. They say Lucifer has a place in Sin City."

Vegas. I've been worried Morana was wrestled out of the country, shipped halfway around the world, but maybe she was only a few hours away. This whole time.

"Who's your point of contact?" I ask, being sure to keep my voice low now that he's started talking. Tony doesn't realize it yet, but he has a few minutes, tops, before he bleeds out.

"Look, man, you don't want to get involved in this shit." Tony shakes his head, fingers stained red as he tries to slow the bleeding from his knees. "These bitches aren't worth it. Most of them were picked up on the kiddie stroll. They've only ever been whores."

The sharp, metallic scent of a bullet being fired registers a moment after the *click* of my trigger sounds. Blood plumes from Tony's shoulder, little more than a flesh wound, but it got my point across.

"Fuck!" he screams, hand gripping the torn leather of his jacket as his chest heaves. "Shane. Shane runs Baja up through San Francisco and over to Vegas. Another picks up from there. Lucifer has the circuits split into smaller regions. Says it'll help with cops."

I glance over to Erik, waiting to see what he thinks.

"Meeting time?" Erik asks, cocking his head. I can practically see his carefree smile back in place under the mask, but there's no hiding the anger burning beneath his words.

"The first of the month," Tony grits out. "And if I'm not there, he'll make what you're doing to me look like a fucking birthday party. Get me cleaned up and get me the fuck out of here."

"That's all I can think to ask." Erik shrugs. "Guys? Did we miss anything?"

Not waiting for a response from the others, I raise the gun, training it on the spot between Tony's eyes. My finger caresses the trigger, the familiar weight of the weapon confirming the state of my soul.

"See you in hell."

The blast of the bullet is followed by a crisp *ding*. Tony crumples to the floor, his lifeless body smacking into the blood-slicked concrete as another *ding* sounds. I turn, glaring daggers at Erik as he lifts his mask and pulls out his phone.

"Erik," I growl. "What the fuck are you doing? No phones at the warehouse."

Noctis assures me he has this location wiped from all databases and cloaked from satellites, but I don't take unnecessary risks. Especially not when I'm this fucking close to finishing it.

"What's wrong Silas?" Erik smirks, his icy blue gaze brimming with mischief. Blonde hair reaches his shoulders, grazing the collar of his dark T-shirt. "Feeling a little *envious* I'm getting all the attention? It's not my fault you smash and dash."

I yank off my mask, gripping the course fabric in my hand as I scowl. The rest of my brothers do the same, knowing we're done here.

Noctis withdraws his phone—the only permitted device in this location—and contacts the cleaners as the rest of the princes make their way to the showers. We'll leave all contaminated clothing here, knowing our masks will be washed and pressed while the rest is disposed of.

"If I wanted anything more than sex, I could have it," I snap, hating the way Erik's lips quirk. It's so fucking easy for him. Nothing is ever serious—not even death.

I could have a regular partner. Having options isn't the

problem. It's the emotions and entanglements attached to repeated hookups that I won't do. Love is a weakness. And if I did pretend, if I let a girl call me her boyfriend or whatever the fuck being in a relationship means, she would never really know me. I've spent so many years becoming what was needed to survive, most days I don't even know myself.

Erik laughs, thumbs darting across the screen. "Relax, Silas. It's just your sister. Tempest expects us at the house by four."

His carefree smile grates on my nerves. The truth is… I *am* envious of him. Of his ability to build trust with another person. I'm envious of all my brothers. Noctis for his ability to hack any computer program and make it his bitch. Sloth may fit his soul's personality with his quiet, assessing manner, but he's quick to action when it's called for.

Likewise, Mavros feeds on his wrath, while I'm controlled by mine. Dominic lets lust guide him, bouncing from partners without a care, but I grow colder with each woman I fuck. Their moans and whimpers of pleasure only highlight how detached I've become.

It's the same with the others. They each flourish under the title of their sins, like the punishing Princes of Hell rising from below, while I wither and rot, consumed by mine. Like a corpse being gnawed on by maggots. Trapped in the confines of my own coffin while everyone else has already hoisted themselves out of the grave.

"The new girl is arriving today, right?" Dominic asks, reappearing at the edge of the room, freshly showered. He tugs on a navy blue shirt and runs a hand over his cropped hair, kicking up the fresh scent of soap and leather. Tattoos cover dark skin, winding along his arms and curving up the sides of his neck the way mine do. His white smile flashes as he rubs his hands together with wicked anticipation. "I can't wait to introduce myself."

Erik snorts, glancing up from his phone. "As if she'll be looking at anyone else when I'm in the room."

"No fucking this up for Tempest," I cut in. "She wants to make a friend."

"She has us." Erik shrugs, glancing at his phone again as another text sounds.

"And Sloane, that girl with dark hair and gorgeous fucking eyes," Dominic purrs, licking his lips. "If only the two of them would give me a chance..."

Erik narrows his gaze for a moment before grinning. "My point exactly. Tempest has more than enough friends. Besides, the new girl is one of those uptight religious girls from the sound of things. She probably wears a cross and bathes in holy water. I doubt she'll last a week before I have her on her back."

"No fucking the new girl," I growl, stalking toward the showers as a team of men in hazmat suits enters from the left.

In most situations, I wouldn't give a fuck if they each took turns, but Tempest has been withdrawing. The princes are known for our ruthlessness and efficiency in getting shit done, collateral damage be damned. We accomplish what we set out to do and don't give a fuck how bloody our hands become along the way.

Most are afraid to look at us, the tattoos covering our bodies acting like a warning of sorts. Fear is necessary to win the game, but Tempest never wanted to be dealt a hand. It's true she's made a few friends at school, but nobody she felt comfortable enough to hang out with more than a handful of times.

"Tempest is more important than getting your dick wet," I say, tossing my blood-splattered shirt on the pile of clothes to burn as I head toward the showers. "Choose someone else."

"Fine," Erik whines as another *ding* sounds. "Tempest says she's expecting us before dinner."

Of course she is.

Ding.

"And we have to help the new girl move."

4

EVIE

My fingers flex as I lift the last of the boxes and start up the concrete walkway for what feels like the hundredth time. Late summers in the San Diego heat are no joke, but I do my best to ignore the beads of sweat trickling down my neck.

I find the single step that leads to the porch, unable to see the ground as I shift the box, my arms trembling with the effort of balancing it. Just when I think I've got it, the end of my skirt tangles beneath me, sending me toppling forward. The cardboard box crashes to the ground, books spilling out in every direction.

I let loose a string of curses that would earn me an exorcism from my father and repress the urge to scream. A sharp sting pricks along my knee, small drops of blood welling across the scraped skin. Great.

Moving would be so much easier if I didn't have to wear the cardigan and this stupid fucking skirt. If every inch of my body didn't have to be covered for modesty's sake. My entire closet is like this. Skirts and pants have to reach my ankles. Tops must have sleeves to the mid-arm and be loose. Some of the women in church enjoy the restriction, choosing to forgo everything but approved dresses. But me? I'd kill for a set of shorts right now.

Gentle caws of seagulls mingle with the boisterous noise of people along the sidewalks. Some are headed in the direction of the university, but most are wearing sundresses with swimsuits beneath, enjoying the afternoon without a care in the world.

How do they do that? I have the art of smiling and laughing down to perfection—the careful tilt of lips, the forced burst of breath at just the right moment—but these women aren't putting on an act. Most of the time I can pretend I'm normal, but there are moments like this where I realize other people are existing in real time. Walking and talking and breathing as if they genuinely want to *live*.

Is that something that can be taught? A fake-it-till-you-make-it type of situation, or are some of us just damned? Maybe I am one of the forsaken. Something was lost in translation when the Almighty God created me. Or He looked at the makeup of my soul and decided that was it. Before I'd even had a chance to live, I'd been cast out. No shiny light of peace and happiness for me.

That's fine. I'm better suited for darkness anyway.

I maintain the façade as best I can, fooling my family and the church, but the truth is I take after my namesake in the worst way. They tell me Eve is the ultimate sinner—the first woman, meant to be pure and good, expected to listen and obey, to heed warning and submit—but she fell.

They want me to hate her. It's been pushed down my throat so many times. Eve is evil. *Women* are bad, especially without a man to lead them. The awful things they say about her twist and tangle with my self-loathing and haunted past. But I don't want to believe them anymore.

I repeated the scripture each morning, the pages of my personal bible worn and stained from how often I was forced to read. I wore loose clothing—I still do—covering my body, keeping my dark red hair tied back in a single, simple braid or hair tie. And I stay as quiet as possible. But I never could stop my mind from wandering. From wishing for a way out.

The thin, scabbed cuts across the inside of my forearms are a testament to the shadows I couldn't leash. Just a scratch. Just enough to take the edge off. The way the sliver blade slices through my pale skin, the bright scarlet streaks—the pain and wrongness of it all—it calms the chaos of my mind. And yes, I know how unhinged that is, but those moments are the only spots of color in my otherwise grey world.

Brushing myself off, I grab the edge of the box and start tossing in the books that have spilled free. *Thank fuck this is the last of my stuff,* I think as I push the door open.

The cuts are tucked away beneath my oversized cardigan, and even if someone did happen to see them, I doubt they'd guess what they are. Because no one knows the real me. I'm nothing more than an oversized skirt and baggy top. A rule-abiding, meek little girl swallowed up in the big bad world full of things beyond my feeble mind's comprehension.

Just like I was raised to be.

But I'm almost twenty now, and by some twist of fate, I've been granted a reprieve from my sentence in hell.

My sneakers squeak across the terracotta floors as I shuffle past the brightly colored living room and toward the stairs. I glimpse the beginning of a kitchen at the end of the hall, along with a washroom, and what looks to be a bedroom.

Setting the box down with the others at the foot of the stairs, I tiptoe over to the door. There's a symbol of a serpent wound around the number seven across it. My brows furrow as I tilt my head, catching a glimpse of a dark green comforter inside and what appears to be an easel. I draw my lip between my teeth, knowing it's shitty of me to go through Tempest's things, but if I don't enter the room, it should be okay, right? I won't go through anything—just glimpse pieces of the person I'll be living with for the next year.

I nudge the door open a bit further. There's a green rug beneath the blank canvas, flecked with bits of colorful paint. Half-smushed tubes of paint clutter the desk beside it, clustered along the side of paintings of dark caves and serpentine eyes.

Odd decor choices, Tempest. She didn't strike me as girly, per se, but our conversations hinted at an optimistic, bright type of vibe. To each their own, I guess.

With a sigh, I return to the pile of boxes clustered together, glancing at the wooden stairs before crouching to inspect the bent one containing my books. The rest of my things were approved by my family, but my books are the only items I've been allowed to choose for myself.

Privacy isn't a right in my house—a lesson my father teaches often. Just last week, he entered my room while I was changing, demanding to go through my things. Jonathan hovered in the doorframe, a small bulge forming in his pants as my father dumped my underwear drawer onto my comforter, lifting each piece as if I'd be stupid enough to hide anything.

But he didn't think to look closely at my books. To him, they're just words. Reading is a humble activity, one I can do while staying out of everyone's way. What he'll never understand is that books offer glimpses of other worlds. They pierce the haze of my reality with pulses of electricity strong enough to keep me breathing until the next day. It's a precarious dance of staying grounded enough to know I'm alive, while remaining detached enough to not want that fact to change.

I lift the box, starting up the steps to where Tempest described my room on the second floor. Sweat pools under my arms, beads of it dripping down my chest. *Fuck*, it's hot. I walk through the open door on the left, a grin stretching across my face. It's easily half the size of my room at home, with mismatched furniture and a small closet, but the large window lights up the space. And most importantly, it's mine.

I set the box down at the edge of the bed, arranging the books on the desk as I check for damage. A small bookshelf will fit nicely beside the dresser, but this will do until then. I catch a glimpse of myself in the mirror hanging from the back of my door. More than a few curls have broken free from my braid, and I have no doubt there are stains under my armpits. I look ridiculous in my floor-length skirt and cardigan, sweating away —and for what?

Mother says modesty is a key pillar of being a woman. It's our duty to protect men from being tempted. Logically, I know it's all bullshit—it has to be, right?—but I still hear her voice reprimanding me, threatening eternal damnation if one man were to glimpse the embarrassingly white skin of my stomach.

Fuck it. I'm alone.

Making quick work of the buttons, I toss the cardigan into the laundry bin, leaving me standing in a thin white tank top before drawing up the edge of my skirt and tying a large knot, securing the fabric above my knees.

It's hard to unlearn a rhetoric I've been taught my whole life —harder still when I'm surrounded by the same nonsense daily. But I'm trying. And Grace University might have given me the perfect chance to break free.

Sweat drips down my neck as I trudge down the stairs once more. My arms feel like jelly with all the lifting, and the shallow scrape across my knee pricks with each step. I should've known there would be a catch with the low rent and prime location of this place. The A/C unit is shitty. It's arctic-level freezing in the main room, but upstairs feels like the gates of hell have opened and swallowed me whole. I'll need to have a talk with Tempest about the thermostat—or at the very least, get a few fans.

I take a moment to undo my hair from the dissolved braid,

twisting the dark red locks into a messy bun situated on top of my head. It's another small rebellion, and I lean into the surge of energy my defiance brings.

One of these days, I'll chop it all off, I think, choosing one of the lighter boxes as I turn up the stairs again. Mother would hate that. For years, I've allowed them to shape and mold and *use* me... but it's never enough. *I* am never enough.

"You're at college," I remind myself, muttering as I rip open the top of the box. It's filled with dresses—and smells like Jonathan. My stomach twists. Rather than hanging them up like I intended, I dump them in the laundry bin and pad down the stairs.

"Your childhood was fucked and you have no idea what a normal almost-twenty-year-old is supposed to be like, but you'll buy some new laundry detergent, wash *everything*, and figure it out."

The fine hairs on the back of my neck prickle as a shadow moves at the edge of my vision.

"Do you always talk to yourself?"

A scream tears from my throat as I slip and tumble down the last three steps. Fear threatens to take hold, my breaths coming in ragged gulps as my heart pounds against my ribs. There's a soreness in my ankle and a sharp spike of pain where I've bumped the back of my head on the step, but I force myself to move with unnatural speed as I scramble to my feet.

My pulse spikes, adrenaline tensing every muscle in my body. It's hard to think over the sound of blood rushing through my ears and the throbbing in my skull, but I do my best to focus and dart for the door.

A hulking man wearing biker boots and a motorcycle helmet rushes forward, trapping me against the wall with only a few scattered boxes between us. *Fuck,* he's fast—and nearly a foot taller than me, with pounds of muscle straining against his black T-shirt and jeans. Tattoos cover his forearms, extending down to his fingers—marking him as the predator he is. But I'm quick. All I have to do is find a way to slip past him.

"Don't get any ideas, little fox," the man growls, tugging his helmet off and tossing it aside. Piercing green eyes bore into mine, his dark strands of tousled curly hair perfectly framing thick lashes. The muscles lining his jaw flex as he drags his gaze over me, lingering on the swell of my thighs and peaked nipples pressing against the thin fabric of my top.

I fight the urge to cover myself, even as his green eyes find mine again, burning with something primal and far more dangerous than curiosity—desire. He cocks his head as if my idea of escaping him was amusing. And in the next breath, I understand why.

Two massive men appear behind him, wearing leather jackets and helmets just like his, followed by another four. The smell of gasoline and leather swirls in the air as my legs begin to tremble.

This is the part in stories when a brave knight or gallant price would arrive, sweeping in just in time to save the day. So, where are they? Devils surround me, live and well, but where are the angels? Where is the righteous fury of a god who protects the innocent?

A humorless laugh huffs from my lips as I back up, my spine pressing against the wall. There's no savior, because I'm no princess.

I could sprint up the stairs, maybe even make it to my room before they reach me.

The black gloves of the man with emerald eyes flex, his fingers curling as if anticipating a chase. His lips twitch, the tense set of his shoulders and slightly bent position of his knees making him look like he's preparing to hunt me down—like the little fox he'd called me.

I'm messed up in a lot of ways, but I'm no coward.

Lifting my chin, I stare into the dilated blackness of his eyes, pouring every drop of hatred buzzing through my body into a lethal look—and welcome death.

5

SILAS

School starts tomorrow, far too late in the summer for most students to still be looking for housing. So when I heard about Evie's application, I was curious. Surely, she was someone as diabolical as us. Someone who thrived in the shadows, who knew the only thing that mattered in this life was power. I hoped Evie would fit right in, but nothing could've been further from my expectations than the disheveled, sweaty girl rambling to herself.

"Do you always talk to yourself?" I ask, flinching at the scream that rips from her. Holy hells, she sounds like a cross between a pterodactyl and a hyena on death's doorstep. Thank fuck I still have my helmet on to muffle most of it.

I step forward to introduce myself, but the banshee slips. Cursing under my breath, I rush to the foot of the stairs, but Evie springs up, looking like she's ready to skin me alive.

"Don't get any ideas, little fox," I say, tossing my helmet aside as I block her exit. Large brown eyes stare up at me, her pupils dilating as she takes in the dark sweep of my hair, the angry gleam in my eyes. I wait for the fear to return, but it seems to be held off by something sweeter.

The scent of desire tints the air, and I allow myself a moment to appreciate the masterpiece in front of me. Thick hips fill out the bunched fabric, the muscles in her thighs tensing, her knees slightly bent as if she thinks she can out run me.

God, she's beautiful. Sweaty from moving, faced flushed with fear and excitement and the urge to put distance between the predator in front of her. And I know she's seconds away from risking an escape. If she'd just calm the fuck down and let me explain—but then my brothers file in behind me.

"You left the door unlocked," I growl, disapproval dripping from every word. I take her in—scattered boxes at her feet, hands trembling—and I see the moment she changes. Fear sharpens into determination, her spine stiffening as if we'd hurt her. *Maybe there's more fight in her than I thought.*

"Any threat could've walked in," I rumble.

Luckily for her, I'm the scariest monster in this city—but the sheer thoughtlessness is astounding. Her big doe eyes narrow even as the pulse in the curve of her neck flutters rapidly. I inhale her fear, drawing it deep into my lungs. It's raw and sweet, so like the naïve little fox before me.

Her white top molds to her skin, framing full breasts and the gleam of a silver cross between them. I bet she tastes like sugar with a hint of salt. Pure and clean—a sanguine dessert far too sweet for my appetite. The things I do to women, the kinky fuckery I'm into, isn't for a novice. And this girl has "virgin" written all over her.

As if hearing my thoughts, her nipples harden beneath the thin fabric. A few wayward curls slip free from the bun atop her head to frame her heart-shaped face. My eyes dip to her full bottom lip, then trace the length of her neck as she swallows.

She'd look so fucking pretty with my fingers wrapped around her throat, the brands inked into my skin forming a necklace just for her. Her eyes would widen, surprise and something darker staring up at me as I squeezed, just enough to leave her trembling.

Stop it, Silas. She's a fucking virgin. A bible-reading, never stays up past her bedtime, good little girl.

"Uh, are we interrupting something?" Erik asks, his cocky tone telling me there's an arrogant smirk stretching across the bastard's face.

"No," I reply, lifting a brow at the firm press of Evie's lips. The edge of her knotted skirt slips higher up her thighs as she bends her knees, hands balling into fists. She's going to run.

My lips twitch in time with my cock, and I fight the urge to groan. The only thing I like more than owning the women I fuck is the chase. And no, I don't mean that in a she's-playing-hard-to-get sort of way. I mean the physical act of setting a woman loose and hunting her down like the fucking monster I am.

There are places you can go, people you meet in my line of work, where nothing is off-limits. The princes and I ensure everything is consensual, of course. The women and men participating know what they're getting into, but it's been years since I've indulged in anything beyond a casual fuck. And even those have felt empty.

"You're not leaving, little fox," I say, stepping toward the door.

I shouldn't. I shouldn't be stopping her or coming up with stupid little nicknames. Or picturing the way she'd look with tears streaming down her cheeks as I fucked her pretty lips. But seeing my little fox preparing to fight back when so many others would've already bowed—it's like a shot of adrenaline jumpstarting the corpse I've been inhabiting. A burst of color in my otherwise grey world.

The painting flickers to life in my mind, and I can see the streaks of reds and browns slashing across brilliant greens, illuminating the murky haze that's consumed me.

It's almost enough to have me stepping back, my brothers be damned. Just so I can hunt her down. Evie would run for her life, her panic lingering in the air like a tantalizing trail for me to follow. A cat chasing a mouse, intent on devouring it. And when I caught her... *fuck*, the things I could do to that body. The supple curve of her hips, the swell of her ass—the way she would tremble with pain and pleasure as I broke her.

No, no, no. Bad Silas. What I should be doing is apologizing for being such an asshole, helping her get settled, and then never thinking of her again. She's scared of you. She's wearing a cross, for fuck's sake.

I don't know how anyone can believe in God with all the shit happening in the world. But then Evie takes a deep breath, the cross shifting as her chest rises. And now I'm think about her breasts again, the way I'd nip and suck her needy little nipples while my fingers trailed down...

"You can't make me stay here," Evie says, tilting her chin up as she attempts to stare me down. My lips twist into a grin.

"Nobody escapes me once I decide they're mine." I take a step toward her, my brothers backing up as Erik's laugh echoes behind me. I drop my voice, speaking the words just for her. "Mine, little fox. Mine to fuck. Mine to kill. Mine to break. It's all the same."

Those big brown eyes of hers widen, lips parting in surprise, but I catch the way her thighs clench.

"Then it's a good thing I'm not yours." She turns, darting up the stairs.

"Here we go!" Erik whoops, the purple lion of Pride glinting on his helmet as he bounds over the stair rail with unnatural grace.

Evie gasps, her footsteps faltering as she retreats. Subtle traces of wildflowers and fresh rain stir in the air as her back collides with my chest, her perfect ass pressing against my hardening cock.

"Careful, little fox," I murmur, my gloved hands gripping her trembling shoulders. "I like to hunt. And you're testing my limits of self-control."

Evie rips out of my grasp, shoving me back as her gaze darts between Erik and the rest of my brothers forming a semicircle around us. Her eyes swirl with hatred, burning with a rage I feel in my bones. Something that potent is only born from unfulfilled hopes and forgotten dreams.

What has my little Evie been through to grant her such ire? Courage doesn't come from a gentle life, and Evie has it in spades. In that moment, watching the dark flecks in her honey-brown eyes ignite with foolish defiance, I know her strength will only make breaking her all the more satisfying.

Her breath hitches, sensing the shift in energy as she takes a single step back. It's only inches closer to Erik, but a deep growl rumbles in my chest.

Mine.

6

EVIE

Tattoos cover his body—coating his fingers, hands, forearms, swirling up his neck—giving way to a face that looks like it was carved from marble. He's death incarnate, sin mixed with my darkest desires and given life.

Oh god. I'm so fucked. *Sorry, God!* I think automatically before chiding myself. If there is a God, and He really can hear my thoughts, I'm already condemned ten times over. Maybe there is, and this is the sick bastard's way of punishing me. Some cosmic karma for not being faithful enough—for questioning. But if I *am* going to hell, I want to go out swinging.

"Mine." The word spills from his soft lips, sounding like a snarl. A warning that resonates deep in my core. The towering man tilts his head, the movement like a predator toying with its next meal. My heartbeat skips, my breath coming in short, ragged bursts as I prepare—for what? They have me boxed in, and it's not like I could fight the two-hundred-plus pounds of stacked muscle before me.

"Easy," the one behind me says, tossing his helmet with a purple lion to the one in red below. I turn to glare at the blonde-haired asshole, but his blue eyes aren't looking at me as he takes a step back, moving further up the stairs. "No touching the new girl, right?"

"Enough, Erik," the one before me growls. But the others are already moving. My pulse spikes as the rest follow suit—retreating, conceding my life to the beast of a man still poised inches from me. Chest heaving, I turn, swallowing down my panic as I watch the dark-haired villain observe me.

His fingers flex, curling as if memorizing the shape of my face. The slight movement draws my focus to the tattoo along his neck: the number seven with a serpent coiled around it—exactly like the symbol etched on the door.

My pulse thrums in my ears, my knuckles white, nails digging into my palms. *Wait one goddamn minute.* Is this some shitty catfish situation? This bastard pretends to be Tempest to lure me here and… what? Kidnaps me? Sells me to the highest bidder?

"Is this about my father?" I ask, proud of the way my voice doesn't waver. "Because he's not the type of guy to pay a ransom. If you let me go, I'll go to the house and grab whatever I can—"

"We don't want your money, Evie," the one hovering on the stairs says—Erik. "Silas is being very dramatic at the moment, but I assure you, we're perfectly nice people."

"You're not leaving, little fox." Silas's deep voice rumbles, low and seductive, as he closes the distance between us.

"Not helping." The blonde one grins, extending a hand. "I'm Erik."

There's a snort to the left, from a man with dark blue, spiraling ram horns on the side of his helmet. He tugs it free, his deep cerulean eyes landing on Erik with playful disbelief. His black hair is cropped short, dark skin lined with tattoos like the others, and I realize his black shirt is actually a deep navy blue.

"And I'm Dominic," he says, batting away Erik's still-outstretched hand. A casually cocky smile tilts his lips, striking the perfect balance between confidence and flirtation. "Unlike Erik and his pride, I know casual introduction doesn't mean you're going to sleep with us."

My cheeks blaze scarlet as Silas's fists flex. A murmur of low chuckles rises from the rest as they each remove their helmets.

"Fuck off, Lust," Erik grumbles, shoving Dominic's shoulder. "I wasn't trying to sleep with her."

"Lust?" I ask, curiosity dragging the word from my lips as something dark stirs in the back of my mind.

"That's right," Dominic answers. "Along with Sloth and Pride and all the rest of the Princes of Hell."

"Stop, Dominic," Silas snaps. "She doesn't need to be bombarded with all this sin shit."

"Wait," I say, glancing at the three lingering behind Dominic —Lust. And Sloth and Pride… and the number seven displayed on their helmets.

My blood runs cold as a dawning realization takes hold. I thought luck was on my side when I found this listing—a single room within walking distance of classes and priced at half the cost. I swallow against the churning of my stomach, fighting the urge to run.

"What thoughts are swirling beneath those eyes of yours?" Silas asks, his voice a whisper along the back of my neck. It takes everything in me not to flinch, not to run. Lifting my chin, I force myself to speak the accusation out loud.

"I think this is the home of the Seven, the most ruthless motorcycle gang in Southern California. Images of them vanish within minutes of being posted—except for the ones with masks. All charges are dismissed on the grounds of insufficient evidence. Even crimes involving…"

"Murder."

Silas's voice rumbles behind me, vibrating through every cell in my body. The word should scare me. It's an admission as much as anything, but the heat of his breath on my neck, the scent of leather and spice filling the air, short-circuits my thoughts. My breathing hitches as his boots echo with each step he takes, bringing the predator into view.

"Erik's lion of Pride, Dominic the devil's goat of Lust," Silas continues, pointing to each of his brothers in turn. "Then there's Mavros, Adrian, Noctis, and Bane."

The others shift, moving to stand behind him. And I realize I know who each of them is. Mavros, with the red, snarling bear, must be Wrath. Adrian, with the golden dragon coveting treasure, is Greed. Noctis and Bane are harder to place. I glance between them before my eyes snag on the light-blue bull tattooed on the forearm of the one called Noctis.

"The Bull of Belphegor," I breathe, more to myself than to them. "I always thought his condemnation was harsh."

"Is that so?" Noctis asks, his voice almost encouraging me to work through my thoughts.

I nod. "He didn't partake in Lucifer's rebellion, but stood idly by. That was enough to get him banished to hell. But once he got there..."

"Keep going, little fox," Silas purrs, lifting Noctis's hand to show off the bull. "What was Belphegor's greatest sin?"

"Inventions," I reply, licking my lips as Silas drops Noctis's hand and steps forward. Striking emerald eyes pierce through me, compelling me to continue. "In hell, Belphegor created Pandemonium—the Palace of Demons. And for humans, he bestows the power of discovery."

"Discovery—questioning the world around us—should never be a sin," Silas murmurs, forcing me to crane my neck to hold his gaze. "Don't you agree?"

I swallow under the weight of his stare, sensing something shift between us.

"Answer me, little fox," Silas demands. "I don't like when my playthings disobey."

My eyes narrow, Silas's words echoing in my head as he mouths the word: *Mine.*

Mine. As if I'm not a full person by myself—with thoughts and questions and fucking dreams. I almost ended everything, preferring the possibility of an afterlife rather than spending one more second trapped in my current one. But college is supposed to be my chance to start over. And I'm not about to let a group of arrogant assholes fuck it up.

"I'm not yours."

I ram my knee into his balls, causing Silas to double over. I dart around him, aiming for the door as he spews curses behind me. Adrenaline courses through my veins as I reach for the handle—only to find it turning before I make contact.

"Evie, is that you?" A feminine voice cuts through the panic gripping my body. A short, curvy figure with long black hair framing heavily lined eyes and a flawless, makeup-adorned face pushes through the group. She's wearing shorts and a casual tank top, but they might as well be designer clothes by the way she moves in them. More importantly, she looks just like her pictures from online—Tempest.

Silence lingers for a moment before Erik speaks. "Yep. We were just welcoming Evie to the pack."

"Oh good," Tempest says, shutting the door before kicking off her sandals. "I lost track of time in the library and was worried Evie would have to move everything by herself."

The edges of her smile dip as her footsteps falter, taking in the slight swell of my ankle, the scrape on my knee, my disheveled hair, and the sweat coating every inch of my body. Her gaze shifts to the men around me, narrowing on Silas. "What did you do?"

"Don't be like that, baby," Erik says, throwing an arm around Tempest as he shoots me a lopsided smirk. "Your big brother would never do anything to upset your new friend. Evie is fine."

Brother? My eyes widen, darting from a narrow-eyed

Tempest to Silas, who looks like he's debating whether to kick me out of the house or pin me to the wall. I bite my lip, not sure which option frightens me more.

"Aren't you, Evie?" Erik prompts. The others shift, seeming to wait for me to give them a pass on everything that's just happened.

"Enough, Erik," Tempest says, shoving him off her. "Evie will be all right if you idiots back the fuck up and give her some space."

"No need to get all stormy." Erik smirks, barely managing to avoid a second shove.

"Take your boots off and set them by the door," Tempest orders, hands on her hips. "All of you. And why are your helmets tossed about in my hallway? Erik and Silas, help move the rest of Evie's things to her room. As for the rest of you, I expect the floors to be swept and mopped by the time we return downstairs."

A low grumble rings through the group as they heed her instructions, but my attention is fixed on Silas. His eyes burn with calculation and hunger, the blacks of his pupils dilating so wide that only traces of emerald green peek out around them. The fine hairs on the back of my neck rise as he holds my gaze.

My mother warned me against men like him—the kind who destroy worlds with sinful smirks and whispered promises.

Everything in my body is screaming for me to run, to hide from the monster before me, but that broken piece of my soul—the one that craves humiliation and pain nearly as much as it longs for love—wants to toy with the beast.

I wonder what it would be like to be kissed by someone like him. My tongue sweeps across my bottom lip, drawing the soft flesh between my teeth.

His jaw ticks, nostrils flaring as he takes a step toward me. The scent of leather and something darker swirls between us as the heat of his body brushes against mine. My heart pounds, unsure if I want him to make good on the punishment in his eyes, or if I'd rather disappear on the spot.

I'm saved from making a decision as Tempest loops her arm through mine and tugs me past him toward the stairs.

"Come on," she says, her teeth flashing as our footsteps squeak against the wooden floorboards. "We have to get ready."

I blink, my mind still half focused on the hulking figure following after us with a box clasped in his hands. "Get ready for what?"

Tempest looks me over with an assessing grin as we reach the second floor, raising a perfectly sculpted brow at my disheveled state.

"To celebrate your arrival. I took the liberty of stocking your en suite with a few things, seeing as how school starts tomorrow."

She leads the way into my bedroom, flipping on the lights.

"That's so thoughtful," I say, genuine warmth blooming in my chest. "Thank you."

"It's just shampoo, girl." Tempest laughs, heading toward the door. "Towels are under the sink. Silas and Erik will stack whatever's left in the hall. Come downstairs when you're finished, and I'll introduce you to the gang before we head out."

Something must shift in my gaze, because Tempest's smile stretches. "They really aren't as scary as they look."

"Of course," I say, forcing a smile back in place. "Wait—what do you mean by 'head out'?"

Tempest's lips tilt at the edges, and for a moment, the resemblance to Silas is nearly overwhelming.

"Have you ever been to a nightclub?"

7

EVIE

I tug down the hem of my dress as sweaty bodies writhe around us. Tempest suggested the long-sleeved dress with the high neckline, which I appreciated, but I hadn't realized how short it was. The silky black fabric is suffocating as it clings to the curves of my thighs, the pale skin of my legs on full display in the four-inch heels Tempest insisted I wear. Thank god for the three ibuprofen she had me take before leaving the house.

Under the bright light of my bedroom, it hadn't seemed all that scandalous. I declined heavy makeup and jewelry, thinking it would somehow make me feel more comfortable, but the lack of it only serves to highlight just how out of my element I am.

Tables fill dark alcoves, expensive bottles of alcohol resting on ice at their center. Women dance in cages suspended from the ceilings, black leather belts crisscrossing their bodies, breasts and asses on full display as they move.

The nearest one has her head thrown back, uncaring who watches as she trails her hands over her peaked nipples, pinching them before continuing downward toward the hem of her miniskirt. It's smaller than the width of my hand, and yet she basks in the beauty of her body—completely free as she twists and turns, feeling her sensual curves, enjoying the hungry eyes watching.

Jealousy steals through me as her dark eyes connect with mine.

This could be you, she seems to taunt. *If you weren't so fucking scared.*

"... having fun?" Tempest tugs loosely on my wrist, spinning me toward her.

"What?" I shout over the music. The bass rumbles against the walls, vibrating the floor and drowning out most of what she says.

"Are you having fun?" she repeats, louder this time.

"Yeah," I say, nodding a little too much.

Tempest frowns as the music shifts, sensing the lie. Weaving her fingers through mine, she drags me after her, navigating through swaying bodies as the next song starts.

"Where are we going?" I ask, doing my best to avoid those in her path, but I have my answer when the sea of bodies ends and a crowded bar appears.

"This is our first night out," Tempest replies, finally turning to me as we hit the back of the waiting crowd. "I thought this club would be modest enough—"

"Modest?" I sputter, eyes wide.

She offers me a pitying smile as my cheeks flame—one that has me wishing I'd worn the corset she originally picked out just to prove there's more to me than the prissy, uptight girl everyone sees.

"You need a drink," Tempest says. "So do I. It'll loosen both of us up. Maybe we can even find someone to dance with."

"I don't know," I say, worrying my lip as we're ushered closer to the bar.

It's not that I don't want to break out of my comfort zone, but I've only ever lived within the bars constructed for me. I was told I'm worthless if someone thinks I'm a slut—regardless of whether it's true. Rumors can be just as damaging as actions. More so sometimes. Even though I know logically that's bullshit, my stomach still twists.

Tempest wiggles through the last of the crowd, smiling widely and pressing her breasts out to get the bartender's attention. His brown eyes snag on the slope of her chest, and the mesh rhinestones glinting in the dim light.

He leans forward, and I watch, awestruck, as Tempest presses up on the bar to whisper in his ear. "I'll have a shot of tequila—the most expensive you have—and my friend will have..."

Her perfectly lined eyes land on me, waiting for an answer. I open my mouth, close it, swallow down the panic building in my chest, and try again.

"The same," I mutter, realizing I don't know the names of any drinks. Tempest's frown flickers for a moment as the bartender nods. "But not the most expensive," I add, thinking of the credit card tucked in my bra. "Just a cheap one."

The bartender looks to Tempest, lifting a brow. She shakes her head, handing over a heavy-looking card. "Two of the same, please. I can't have her suffering a horrible hangover on our first night out."

"Coming right up."

"You don't have to do that," I say, even as I take the first unencumbered breath of the night.

"Money isn't a concern," Tempest replies, flashing me a bright smile as our shots arrive.

My brows furrow as I take in the small glass rimmed with salt and topped with a lime slice. She grins, handing one to me before picking up the lime. "Lick the edge of salt, swallow, and then bite. Ready?"

"As I'll ever be," I say, steadying my breath as I mimic her movements.

"Cheers."

The bite of salt is cut with the burn of alcohol. It sears the back of my throat, causing me to cough, but I do my best to drink the entire thing. I make the mistake of trying to breathe before sucking on the lime, sputtering half the liquid as I bite. But then the bitter juice dulls the fire, and the lingering taste isn't half bad.

"They get easier the more you do." Tempest laughs at the grimace contorting my face, reaching to pick up the shot glass I'd just set down and finishing off the rest. She raises her hand to signal the bartender. "One more?"

I shake my head, already noticing a fuzzy feeling starting in my chest. I've never tasted alcohol before this, but I've heard enough to know I don't want to end up drunk or at the mercy of others.

"Even an alcohol novice won't get drunk off two shots. Tipsy, maybe, but not black-out drunk," Tempest explains as if hearing my concerns. "If you don't want it, I'll happily finished it for you, but you're safe here. Even if you were completely wasted or decided to hook up with someone, no one would dare harm you."

My eyes widen as I follow her gaze to a pair of men at the other side of the bar. The taller one is staring at Tempest with blue eyes and a cocky smirk. His light brown hair is shaggy, styled in an unkempt sort of way, and the dark tapestry of tattoos covering his forearms shifts as he takes a sip of beer. But it's the shorter, stockier man next to him who leaves me fumbling for words.

Hooded blue eyes a few shades darker than his friend's are fixed on me as he grins over a glass of amber liquid. His arms are ridiculously bulky, almost to the point of being obnoxious. A short nose and buzzed dirty blonde hair are offset by a wicked grin that has the girls around us giggling as he lifts his glass in our—my—direction.

"They seem... nice," I mutter, feeling self-conscious as the second round of tequila arrives.

"They seem horny," Tempest corrects, holding the glass out for me as a blush steals across my cheeks. "Don't feel pressured. Sorry if I'm way off here, but I get the feeling you've been forced into a certain lifestyle. But you're here now—free to be whoever you want."

Tempest peeks over her shoulder and squeals. "Oh my god, they're coming over!" Her voice pitches with excitement as she schools her features into a mask of cool disinterest. She holds the glass out, multicolored lights glinting off the rim as a song with a quicker beat starts. "Now or next time, Evie?"

Tearing my gaze away from hulking pair headed straight for us, I take a deep breath and toss back the shot.

8

SILAS

My hands rest on the back of the leather couch as the blonde licks up my cock, moaning like there's a camera recording. She's been at it for a while now, her jaw no doubt aching from the stretch. Snot runs from her nose as she gags, mixing with the black-stained tears trailing down her cheeks. She looks like a fucking mess—exactly how I like it. I should've finished twice over by now, but I can't help wishing it were someone else beneath me.

"Oh god!" the brunette across from me screams as Erik pounds into her from behind. His pale ass rocks, slamming into her as she stares through the one-way glass, watching the hundreds of people below find oblivion.

This nightclub was the first I opened, back when it was just Mavros and Erik at my side. Noctis found us not long after, lending his skills with electronics and security to make it our most profitable. It's where I go to feel good about the life I've built—knowing I own everything and everyone here. So why the fuck do I feel so empty?

"That's right, baby," Erik says between thrusts, glancing over his shoulder to throw me a wink. "I'm your fucking god."

I roll my eyes, doing my best to focus back on the blonde. She sucks harder, her cheeks hollowing as her hand strokes the rest of me. Nothing.

"What's the matter, brother?" Dominic asks, the picture of casual lust with his cock buried balls-deep in Adrian, while simultaneously finger-fucking a redhead impaled on Bane's dick. Lust, Greed, and Gluttony always did go hand in hand. Dominic's deep blue gaze drops to my swallowed cock, a wicked grin revealing a dimple. "My mouth is still free. I'd be happy to finally show you what you've been missing."

"Leave him alone." Mavros chuckles, appearing at the door. His shaggy dark hair, flat cheekbones, and broad chest embody the red bear branded across his back. Noctis follows close behind, the door to our suite clicking shut as they enter. I groan inwardly, knowing they've got something to report. I'm half tempted to tell the blonde to fuck off and call it a night—until Noctis speaks.

"Tempest is here, and she convinced Evie to join her." His tall frame, buzzed head, and pale blue eyes scream frat-boy entitlement, but Noctis is always watching. Calculating.

My eyes fly open, darting to the one-way mirror and the masses below as if I could somehow find my little fox among the hundreds of blissed-out bodies. I knew Tempest invited her, but I figured Evie would decline. She doesn't seem like the kind of girl who's ever set foot in a club. And I highly doubt she drinks.

But she's here. In my nightclub.

My cock twitches at the thought of her body swaying in time to the music, renewing the blonde's attempts to get me off. I'd almost forgotten she was there. Images of Evie's wine-colored hair and big doe eyes flash through my mind as I grip the blonde's hair, pushing her face down while my hips thrust up.

Evie would've borrowed something to wear. Maybe a low-cut top revealing the perfect slope of her breasts, the hard tips of her nipples begging for me to suck on them. I thrust again, forcing the blonde's head down in a quick pace.

No—too much. As hot as she'd look, Evie wouldn't wear something like that. It would be modest. Something formfitting, just enough to hint at her enticing curves beneath. Teasing and taunting.

I wonder, would her hair be up? Easy for me to grab onto as I fucked her face? Would she enjoy the taste of my cock, letting me use her pretty mouth until her lips were swollen and her pussy dripping?

A groan escapes me, my fingers tightening around the blonde's hair. It's the wrong shade, the strands dry and stiff from multiple rounds of bleach, but I use her like the placeholder she is, picturing my little fox as my body coils. What I wouldn't give to have Evie's thighs spread, her dripping cunt on full display as I took my time. As I licked every inch of her. As I branded her soul with my tongue.

"Fuck," I grit out, forcing her head down as I come—lost in the image of a virgin with wine-colored hair moaning my name.

The blonde staggers back, gasping for air as she swipes at the mess on her chin. "That was fun."

I push off the couch, tucking my cock away as I stalk toward the glass, scanning the crowd for the one face I need.

"Can I help you with anything else?" she asks, long nails scraping across my shoulder.

I stiffen, the slight buzz from the orgasm already fading. "No."

"That's right, baby. Come for me," Erik grunts to my left, pumping his fingers into the woman's ass as he splits her core with his cock. Her arms have collapsed, her head tilted, staring over the club as another wave of ecstasy crashes through her.

"I don't mind waiting," the blonde coos from behind me, her

hand drifting down my back. Her pupils dilate as she watches Erik pull out of the woman's pussy and enter her ass. "Whatever you want, Silas."

I know it's shitty of me not to get her off at least once. She's probably expecting a fuck-a-thon, getting passed around by the Seven all night, but I'm not in the mood.

"Dominic has a mouth free," I say, removing her hand as she pouts.

"Fuck yes I do," Dominic purrs, pulling his fingers from the woman with red hair still bouncing on Bane. "I've been missing the taste of pussy, and you deserve a reward for how well you sucked off my brother."

"He won't mind?" the blonde asks, looking over Dominic's shoulder to Adrian, but he's already living up to his title of Greed. Adrain kneels between Bane's thighs, spreading the redhead's legs on either side of his knees, showing just how stretched her ass is around his thick length.

"Fuck, you smell delicious," Adrian rumbles before leaning forward to feast.

"I think they're good." Dominic grins, murmuring filthy praises as he grips the base of his cock and ushers the blonde away.

Moans and heavy panting follow moments later, the blonde's cries of pleasure mingling with the others, but my attention is fixed on the crowd below. Mavros and Noctis join me, eyes scanning for the one who calls to me.

"Report," I say.

"We've confirmed Shane is the point of contact, and meeting times occur at the first of the month," Mavros begins. "We've also contracted women and set them up for discovery."

Jaw clenching, I nod once. Women are always underestimated, especially when the market in question involves selling their bodies. We might play the role of demons—meant to embody the worse types of evil—but we don't condone half the terrible shit humans do.

"Miles is in place, watching everyone who agreed to help," Noctis adds before I can ask.

Good. Miles doesn't fuck around when it comes to his girls' safety. They'll pose as victims for as long as it's safe. But if shit goes south, he'll get them out.

"Any sign of her?" I ask, voice low despite the increasing sounds of slick bodies and wanton gasps filling our suite. I sense more than see Noctis and Mavros share a look before the former speaks.

"There's been no sign of Morana."

I knew the answer before he said it. They'd have told me immediately. At least I stopped the bastards from taking Tempest too. My spine stiffens as I spot her in the crowd—my little sister—being pawed at by some fuckboy in an overpriced watch and jeans. He grinds against her from behind, and my fists flex as she presses back into him. I'm three seconds away from losing my shit completely when I catch sight of the person beside her.

Evie's head is thrown back with a wide smile, her hands in the air as she spins to face the bulky man behind her. The short, skin-tight black dress barely covers her ass as she stretches, locking her arms around his neck. My jaw clenches as he grins down at her, his greedy fucking hands wrapping around her waist, drifting lower to cup her perfect ass.

"Who. The fuck. Are they?" I grit out, chest heaving as tension radiates from me.

Mine. Mine. Mine.

But how can she be mine when she's looking at him like that —like she's ready to offer up her needy little cunt to the first taker? If she's that eager for a taste of darkness, I sure as fuck will be the one to give it to her.

"Tempest assures me they're good," Mavros says, following as I turn from the window and head for the door. "I checked with her and Evie before heading up here."

"Get dressed," I bark to the others, not waiting for them to respond. "We have work to do."

9

SILAS

The smell of sweat and expensive cologne fills the club as the bass vibrates through the floors. Bodies writhe, inhibitions loosened thanks to the mixture of alcohol and colorful pills circulating. Every one of them wants to forget something—bills, the interest on their loans, the unlikeliness of finding a job, of ever owning a house or car. But most of all, they want to forget themselves. To avoid the picture in their minds of who they thought they would be compared to the pathetic reality.

So they drink. And fuck. And try to forget. The daily drama, the petty fights and insecurities, the mundane gossip—all of it. Here, in this club, at this moment, with drugs pumping through their veins and strangers' hands touching their bodies, they are free.

How I wish oblivion were that simple for me.

People leap out of my way as I stalk forward, a perk of being one of the Seven. Men dip their heads in respect. Women eye us hungrily. With a snap of my fingers, I could have any one of them on their knees, legs spread and waiting for my cock.

But there's only one person I want to punish. One pair of full lips I want to use and fuck until they're swollen, until her jaw aches and tears coat her fair cheeks. *Fuck, this is a bad idea.*

It's just a passing interest. Never mind that last night was the first time I picked up a brush and painted beyond my usual shades of grey—with embers the color of her eyes and reds the same shade as her hair. Evie is too young, too naïve, too fucking good for someone like me. But fuck if that doesn't make me crave her all the more.

And right now, there's another man with his hands all over her.

"Silas…" Erik warns, having caught up to the three of us. His jeans are unbuttoned, cheeks flushed—but he's here. He's here, and he's warning me away. Erik's the type of man who can go for hours when he fucks, priding himself on his ability to wring orgasm after orgasm from his partners, but he left. For me. To stop me from doing something I'll regret.

"Let them go," Erik says, and I wish he'd said it with arrogance or malice or any fucking thing other than understanding.

"She doesn't realize what she's doing," I snap, fists clenching and eyes narrowing as I watch the four of them weave through the crowd. Tempest is unknowingly leading them in our direction, toward the back door she likes to use when leaving for the night.

"I think she does," Erik replies, following my line of sight. "You saw her at the foot of the steps. Evie thought we were going to murder her, and she still fought."

He claps me on the back with a sigh. "No one fucks the new girl, Sie. You said so yourself. Tempest deserves to have a friend…"

His voice trails off as he realizes where they're headed. Tempest pauses, arching her back as the man behind her licks up the side of her neck. His hands wrap around her, gripping the curve of her breasts from behind as she tilts her head and claims his lips with hers.

"On second thought," Erik mutters, stalking forward. They're only a few paces away, poised in the shadows, away from the gyrating bodies and rumble of music.

"I don't know, brothers," Noctis muses, the teasing tone of his voice telling me he knows exactly which buttons he's about to push. "Looks like the ladies are primed for an enjoyable evening. Would be a shame to cock-block them when both parties are willing."

My nostrils flare as I watch Evie glance between Tempest and the man beside her. She stares up at him, her gaze a mixture of tentative want and burning curiosity. Like she's realizing for the first time that she can do whatever she wants—with whoever she wants.

Her eyes dip to his lips, and all I see is green. A violent emerald haze of jealously erupts in my chest at that one glance. *Fuck*, not only is she practically shouting she's a virgin, but I'd bet the broken pieces of my soul she's never been kissed before. At least not like this. Not with want and hunger and sinister desire.

A low rumble starts in my chest as the fucker tilts Evie's chin up, her pretty lips parting for him.

"You did say Evie is off-limits," Mavros adds, nudging my shoulder.

"That was before I knew how quickly she'd throw herself at the first prick she met," I seethe, already moving. Noctis laughs as Mavros curses, but Erik is right at my side, matching my furious pace.

"We can't kill them here," Erik says, just as I grab the guy's collar, dragging him away from Evie before the fucker gets the chance to taste her. Erik's already at the door, holding it open as I toss the bastard through without a backward glance.

"Hey!" Tempest shrieks, her heels echoing in the dimly lit alleyway. "What the actual fuck do you think you're doing?"

"Sorry, little storm," Erik answers—not sounding sorry in the least—as he dodges a swing from the guy she'd been with moments ago. I catch the glint of Erik's smug grin, his fist splitting the skin over the guy's eye before he picks him up and tosses him into his friend. The two steady each other, squaring their shoulders as if they mean to fight us.

Erik cracks his neck, the crazed glint in his eyes igniting as a wicked smirk tilts his lips. "You'll thank me in the morning, Tempest."

"Like hell I will," Tempest snaps. "Jameson wasn't doing anything I didn't want him to do. Neither was Mark. Was he, Evie?"

My little fox shakes her head, but stops when I narrow my eyes. "You plan on fucking this guy, little fox?"

Evie pales, eyes widening as her attention bounces between us.

"You're not needed here, bro," Mark sneers, flexing his chemically enhanced arms as the sound of Mavros and Noctis's boots echo behind us. "And you're sure as fuck not wanted. Why don't you run along before I give security something to do."

His threat washes over me and the world goes still. The sound of the club fades, replaced with a dull ringing, drowning out everything except the smug piece of shit's flexing fingers and Evie's wide eyes.

"Fuck," Tempest grumbles, throwing her head back as she loops her arm through Evie's. She's pissed at me, and I'm fully anticipating a lecture in the morning about how she's a grown woman and capable of making her own decisions—albeit bad ones—but they're hers to make. But, she'd never side with some one-night-stand asshole over me.

Though, to his credit, Jameson looks a little worried, sensing the energy shift. While Mark… well, some of us don't get looks *or* brains.

I tilt my head, keenly aware of each shifting muscle in his body as I direct my command to where Mavros and Noctis are hovering. "No interfering."

10

SILAS

"Shit," Jameson breathes, eyes bouncing between Erik at my side and my brothers behind me. His gaze widens as he scans my tattoos, finding the coiled serpent at the base of my throat. "You're them, aren't you?"

"I don't give a fuck who they are," Mark retorts, licking his lips as his eyes drag down Evie's body. "He put hands on me and interrupted what was bound to be a memorable evening. That's a challenge of honor, and I'm not one to back down from a fight."

"Please," Jameson says, shaking his head as he steps forward, hands raised. "He's from out of town, visiting from Vegas. My cousin has no idea what he's saying."

"Like hell I don't," Mark cuts in, shoving Jameson back.

"Shut the fuck up," Jameson hisses beneath his breath. "Or you're going to get us both killed."

"Fucking pussy," Mark spits, shoving Jameson again before fixing his filthy gaze on my little fox. "Let's go, sweetheart. I'll have your knees trembling and my name rolling off your lips in minutes."

The snap of bone echoes against the narrow walls of the

alley as my fist crashes into his face. Pain blares across my knuckles, the sweet ache sending a burst of adrenaline through my veins, reminding me I'm alive. My heart pounds as I roll out my shoulders, relishing the way his arrogant smirk is wiped cleaned, delighting in the way his eyes roll back and his body crumples to the piss-covered ground.

There's a squeak of alarmed panic from behind me, and my eyes snap to her. To Evie. Her pouty lips are parted, brows lifted, and eyes wide as she stares down at Mark—the pathetic, roided-up smudge who tried to kiss her. And she's staring at his unconscious form with concern.

"Is—is he…"

"He's not dead," I growl. Though, now that she's mentioned it… "Yet."

"Fuck." Jameson seems to thaw from whatever held him in place. Without a backward glance, he turns, leaving his cousin at the mercy of the Seven, fleeing the alley toward the well-lit street in the distance.

"Noctis," I say, watching Jameson get closer to escape.

"On it," he promises, a wicked gleam in his eyes as he starts after his prey.

"This is your fault," Tempest seethes, her words dripping with loathing. I expect her venom to be directed at me, but when I look up, I find Erik pinned beneath her glare. "I can fuck whoever I want."

"Not when you're drunk," Erik counters, fire blazing in his eyes.

"We had two shots an hour ago," Tempest snaps, getting in his face.

Normally, I'd separate the two of them, but right now, I can't help being grateful Erik's bullshit excuses have Tempest distracted. Mavros is standing guard at the club's door, just in case Mark and Jameson had back-up, leaving my little fox and me alone.

As if sensing my intentions, Evie stiffens, her eyes snapping up to meet mine as I stalk toward her. Her plump bottom lip is drawn into her mouth again, teeth biting the tender flesh as her chest heaves. She takes a step back, then another, until her heels hit the wall behind her.

"Scared, little fox?"

"Should I be?" Evie swallows, lifting her chin even as her legs tremble.

"Yes," I hiss. My fingertips grip the edges of her jaw, wrapping around her neck with the lightest pressure. Her breathing hitches as I hold her there, not hurting, but stripping control from her all the same. I wait for the tart spike of fear, for the protest that will have Tempest rounding on me, demanding I leave—but Evie does neither.

She swallows, her throat bobbing beneath my fingers as her eyes dip to my mouth. Her pupils expand, that tongue of hers flicking out to lick her lips. A low groan builds in my chest.

"Careful," I warn, feeling her flickering pulse thrum in the soft curve of her neck. "If you keep teasing me like that, I'm going to shove up that little dress of yours and show you what it means to be mine."

There's the flicker of fear I've been expecting. My lips twitch into a cruel mock of a grin as I study the way her pale cheeks flame red. Unable to help myself, I tighten my grip, forcing her chin up further.

"Would you like that, Evie? To be owned. Cherished. To have me on my knees with my lips pressed to your pussy—licking, sucking, worshipping—until you forget to be afraid?"

Her eyes are wide, full lips parted—and fuck me, because she's too good. I've thought it before, but staring at her now, eyes glazed and my fingers around her throat, I see how full of light she is. Of life. But the most dangerous part is that my little fox has been caged for far too long. There's a hunger in her, a burning curiosity that has me leaning in when I should be pulling away.

"Do you want me to make this sweet little cunt of yours bleed all over my cock, Evie?" My mouth grazes her ear, and I inhale deeply, filling my lungs with hints of wildflowers and rain and a tinge of alcohol. With the heady scent of her, loving the way she trembles. "Afraid yet, little fox?"

"Yes," Evie admits, her throat bobbing under my palm. And then she leans into me, the smallest tilt of her mouth inching closer, begging me to claim her lips with mine. To erase all traces of Mark—the pathetic, unconscious sack currently working off a concussion at our feet—who dared to touch her.

I shouldn't. Pain is the only thing I can offer her. She stands still as I loosen my grip, something too close to disappointment flashing up at me, but it's for her own good. "You don't know what you're getting into."

"Don't I?" she challenges. I stare at her then, looking past the light makeup smeared beneath her eyes, ignoring the sliver cross at her throat, and peer beyond what everyone else sees. Because there's not just naïve curiosity—but pain. Vengeance. A thirst for the twisted and dark. All things I'll only make worse. But then a low groan sounds from the ground as the piece of shit regains consciousness.

And I break.

My mouth slams into hers, hungry and raw. The onslaught pulls a gasp from her, and I seize her surprise, exploiting the moment as I thrust my tongue inside, sweeping the length of her mouth as my fingers squeeze, tilting her jaw up for me. Her sweet taste, the feel of her full lips, her small gasps and needy sounds spur me on. I press my knee between her thighs, pinning her to the wall.

She's powerless like this. At the mercy of a merciless monster. Frozen as I take what I want. Her shock gives way in moments, and surely—surely—this is when she pushes me away. When she sees me and runs. I expect that.

What I don't anticipate is Evie's supple body melting into mine—like an angel yielding control to a demon. Fuck, if I don't want to reward her for being such a good girl.

I pull back, my tongue licking that sensitive spot above her racing pulse before my nose drags up the length of her neck. A shiver rakes down her spine as the warmth of my breath heats the shell of her ear, teasing my little temptress. I whisper my threat against her cheek as if speaking to a lover, soft enough to make a shiver run down her spine.

"If he ever touches you again, I'll kill him."

Evie draws in a sharp breath, and I withdraw completely. Her nipples are hard, pressing through the black fabric, begging for my attention. The hem of her dress is still hiked up from the position I had her in, and there's no doubt in my mind that if I lift her dress—even an inch—I'll find her soaked with need.

Her thighs clench as she tugs the dress back into place, stepping into my shadow and away from Mark. A warmth spreads through me as Evie crouches at my back, blooming in my chest at knowing she feels safer with me than him. I turn, brushing back a piece of wine-colored hair from her cheek.

"Mavros," I call, keeping my eyes locked on Evie's rosy cheeks and swollen lips. "Drop him at the hospital. I'm feeling gracious tonight."

11

EVIE

Silas is fucking crazy. They all are. And so am I. What the hell was I thinking, baiting him like that—especially after watching him knock Mark out cold? Sometimes the things running through my mind frighten even me.

Almost kissing Mark was a mistake, but I'm so tired of being the shy girl. I hadn't expected much, maybe something like the two boys I kissed in the back of church when we were supposed to be searching for extra bibles during Sunday School. Predictable. Underwhelming. Mark was decent enough to look at, but the entitlement radiating off him in that alley had been a wake-up call. Thank god Silas was there to stop me.

Silas… I can still feel the burn of his lips, the branding of my soul as his tongue swept in, claiming mine in a show of brutal dominance. He's the picture of sin—everything I've been warned against. I should be terrified. I should've pushed him away and run the first chance I got. But that dark, twisted part of me wants to know what it would be like to flirt with the devil.

One kiss, and I'm already signing my name in blood.

Which is precisely why I'm driving to my family home this

morning. I've managed to avoid Silas and the rest of the unhinged biker club for the past week. Tempest has tried to get me to hang out, especially when the Seven are there, but I've insisted I've been busy adjusting to classes. She knows I'm lying, but at least she hasn't called me out on it.

My phone dings as I turn off the ignition. Tempest's name and the selfie she forced me to take before going out flash across the screen, stirring a pang in my chest.

Tempest: We're heading to Sin again tonight. Want me to wait for you?

Looking through my windshield, I stare at the cold façade of my family home. Palm trees line the three-car garage and pristine walls at the top of the hill. The manicured lawn and freshly pruned tropical flowers are the picture of perfection.

You can't see it from here, but the massive windows at the back overlook the ocean, the glass-lined balcony the epitome of refined luxury.

Anyone else would kill to live in a house like this, to grow up with the kind of wealth and privilege I had. I've always known it was selfish and completely fucked up, even as a child. My family had so much while others struggled to eat.

I'd been brave enough to ask my father once why he took so much when we didn't need it. He told me God blesses the worthy, as if he'd somehow *earned* this obscene level of wealth. He hadn't.

No one who could afford three multimillion-dollar houses ever had. Bank accounts that size only came from deep-rooted selfishness, built on entitlement that allows for extortion of the less fortune—without feeling guilt.

Ding.

Tempest: I promise I won't make you take a shot.

Groaning at the thought of turning her down again, I get out of the car and start the long walk up the driveway.

Me: Can't tonight. My parents insisted on a family dinner. Maybe another time.

Even now, I can still feel the heat of Silas's lips on mine. The bite of his hand around my throat. His knee pressing between my thighs like he wanted to climb into my body. And I *let* him. I practically threw myself at him.

God above, maybe I really do need help. I may be questioning the church and religion in general, but I have no business toying with a serpent. And that's exactly what Silas feels like. Like I'm a mouse dangling above a den of venomous snakes, one wrong move from falling.

"There you are," Jonathan says, opening the door just before I knock. My entire body stiffens as his cold blue eyes drag down my frame, a frown twisting his mouth. "One week at school and you're already dressing like a whore."

I lower my head, double checking that the light blue sundress covers my knees. It's buttoned to the throat with a neatly folded collar and paired with modest white flats. My hair is braided back in a single plait, and I haven't touched a brush of makeup since the nightclub.

The only difference is the thin brown belt at my waist, vaguely hinting at the curves of my body.

With a mask of quiet submission firmly in place, I cross the threshold of my childhood home. The door shuts with an ominous *click* behind me, and a cold ripple of dread slides down my spine.

"You've been gone all week," Jonathan sneers, voice dripping with disgust. "Already spreading your thighs and condemning your soul?"

"No," I bite back, collecting myself a beat later as I round my shoulders and stay rooted to the spot. I'd expected a verbal lashing from my perfect brother—he never misses a chance.

One week. That's all it's been, but already I feel like I'm being shoved back into the box I've only just escaped.

I still don't know why my mother sided with me this time—why she allowed me to attend university—but I don't dwell on it. The security cameras have no doubt alerted my parents to my arrival. I only need to tolerate Jonathan's presence a little longer, until he puts on the perfect son act they expect from him.

I can do this.

His clammy hands pinch my chin, jerking my face up with cruel force. Flashes of Silas's sinful face invade my thoughts, so different from the repulsive, weak-jawed boy standing before me now.

"How dare you talk back to me, bitch," Jonathan spits, his fingers digging in painfully. "I'm your brother. It's my duty to make sure you don't embarrass the family."

"Half-brother," I mutter, even as tears prick my eyes.

Jonathan holds me there a breath longer, then throws me to the side. I stumble into the entryway table, the sharp edge catching me in the stomach. I double over, biting my tongue to keep from crying out. It won't help. My parents made it clear long ago which child they believe.

"Mother may think a semester of classes is acceptable, but a woman has no purpose in school." Jonathan grips my braid, tugging hard enough to send pain lancing down my neck. Spit flies from his mouth, flecking my cheek. "You were made to breed. To cook and clean. To open your legs, close your mouth, and do whatever your husband demands. You'll learn soon enough."

"Pumpkin, is that you?" Mother calls a moment before she peeks around the corner. Her blonde curls are topped with a wide-brimmed hat, the blue-and-white striped dress just modest enough for Father's standards. Smoky eyeshadow tints the corners of her lids, and a garish pink lipstick coats her over-filled lips. They twitch into what once might've been a frown. "Oh, sweetie. What happened?"

"She tripped over the rug, but I caught her," Jonathan says, yanking me upright. Revulsion curdles in my stomach like sour milk, but I force a weak smile.

"That's our Evie—clumsy as ever," Mother tsks, smoothing out my dress before beaming up at Jonathan. "I swear, sometimes I think the Lord sent me your father just so Evie would be blessed with a big brother to keep her out of trouble."

His white smile flashes as his fingers tighten on my ass. I flinch, bile rising in my throat as his dead eyes flicker with cold cruelty. Taking a deep breath, I retreat into myself, walling off anything vulnerable. Instead, I fixate on the pair of men's dress shoes near the door.

"It's nothing, Mother," Jonathan replies, his blonde hair and designer polo the picture of religious wealth. "I was just telling Evie how lucky she is to explore college for a semester before settling down. Truly, a modern woman."

There it is again—that idea that I'll only get *one* semester before being reeled back in. I risk a glance up, expecting Mother to gently correct him, but she just nods, the edges of her plastic smile tightening.

"Yes, Evie has always been the wild one in the family," she starts, but I don't hear the rest. A loud buzzing fills my ears as the fragile blossom of hope in my chest wilts, drowned by their polite chatter about my life. *My* future.

Knowing I'll break if I don't look away, I pull deeper into myself and refocus on the dress shoes. The shoes. Just the shoes. Father typically wears black, but these are brown, the leather more worn than usual. He prefers Oxford dress shoes, but these look like loafers with little tassels on top. One tassel is shorter, like it's been cut.

"I've already turned down two offers for Evie's hand," Jonathan informs us, throwing an arm around my shoulders. "Only the best for our Evie."

Mother laughs, the shrill sound snapping something inside me.

"I'm not getting married," I say, proud of how steady my voice is—until fear claws up my throat. Mother's smile fades as Jonathan's grip tightens on my shoulder.

"Don't be difficult, Evie," Jonathan reprimands, his voice adopting the cold, hollow tone that's haunted my dreams for years. "Mother is being more than fair."

"I can't finish a degree in one semester," I breathe, searching my mother's face. I'm her daughter, her flesh and blood. Surely she wouldn't be so cruel as to tease me with a glimpse of freedom before slamming the cage shut.

"Don't fuss, pumpkin," Mother chides. "You'll get wrinkles."

"Mother, please." This time the words come out thin and trembling, steeped in betrayal and loss. I really thought she'd meant it. That maybe some small part of her remembered what it felt like to be forced into something she didn't want. I should've known better. My happiness has never mattered.

"Oh, Evie." Mother offers a pitying smile as she lifts my chin, inspecting my face. "You really need to watch those frown lines, pumpkin. Nobody wants an old maid."

"You do look much prettier when you smile," Jonathan adds.

Mother chuckles softly, her eyes flicking to Jonathan as they share a laugh at my expense.

"Why don't you two head out to the backyard for lunch," she says. "I need to touch up my makeup, but Maria has the hors d'oeuvres out, and the shrimp should be ready soon."

Closing my eyes against the scream building in my chest, I force a breath through my nose and pretend I'm somewhere far from here. Just a ghost, hovering above her body. Watching as a young woman is led deeper into hell.

12

SILAS

The room falls silent as I answer the call and put it on speaker, ensuring my brothers hear every word. "Speak."

"Shane said he'll be here at the first of the month."

I lift a brow at Noctis, checking this is the same contact he and Mavros spoke with. A small dip of his chin is confirmation enough, but it's the lethal gleam in his eyes as he stares at the phone that has my body tensing. Noctis doesn't trust him.

"I want it moved up."

The cold edge in my voice makes my brothers roll out their shoulders, matching grins tugging at their lips as they brace for a fight.

"I tried, man, but he's transporting a large batch of bitches. Says he can't make it sooner."

My grip on the phone tightens as I tap into the simmering pool of anger always churning beneath the surface. The monster inside me stirs, perking up as if readying for a massacre.

"Robert Price. Thirty-four-year-old heroin addict with two children under the age of three."

There's a sharp intake of breath on the other end, but I keep going.

"Listen up, Bobby. Can I call you Bobby?"

"No."

"Because, you see, Bobby, this is the part where I'd normally threaten your family or girlfriend. But since you've abandoned the mothers of your children, refused to pay child support, or even apply for visitation, I'm going to threaten the one thing in your miserable existence you *do* care about—your drugs."

"Don't do that, man, come on," Bobby pleads, his voice rising. "Shane gets here when he gets here. I don't have anything to do with it."

"Tsk, tsk," I say in a falsely cheery voice. "Don't sell yourself short. You can accomplish anything with the right motivation. Lucky for you, I'm here to provide it."

"Fuck you," he snaps, and my demon smiles.

"Ah-ah. Don't mistake my kindness for weakness."

I enunciate each word, letting the haunting chill of my voice bleed through the line until I can practically taste the fear thickening the air around him.

"I don't give a fuck about Shane's current shipment or prior commitments. I expect a meeting with the head of the southern circuit by the end of the week."

"And if I don't?" he asks.

A deep chuckle rumbles from Erik as Mavros cracks his knuckles. Dominic, Adrian, and Bane stay close, their eyes gleaming with anticipation, listening, waiting for the green light.

I grin. I fucking *grin* like the maniac I am, because Bobby just made a fatal error—he questioned my ruthlessness.

I let the silence stretch. Long enough to hear Bobby's breath hitch and the *crunch* of gravel beneath his boots.

"I'm holding *you* responsible, Bobby. If Shane doesn't show, I'll come find you. Understood?"

"... Yes," he mutters, the bravado from moments ago long gone.

"Yes *what?*" I snap.

"Yes fucking sir," he barks. "But Shane's not gonna like—"

I end the call. My gaze shifts to Noctis. "Monitor him. Trace his calls. Once contact is confirmed for Shane—"

Mavros's grin spreads wide, looking every bit like the snarling red bear tattooed across his back. "I'll handle it."

I nod once, letting my gaze sweep over my brothers. Not for the first time, I wish we could move faster. Every second these trafficking circuits operate, someone is taken. Their bodies used over and over again until their minds break, their spirits shatter, and the drugs they're force-fed finally claim them.

If we *truly* were Princes of Hell, I'd craft a special place for men like that. I'd savor every method of punishment. Delight in the infinite ways I could bring their souls to the brink of insanity. Make them bleed. Make them *feel* every moment of terror they've inflicted. And when they think it's over—when death comes like a mercy—I'd heal them just to start again.

I've painted fantasies like that. Captured the blackness they leave behind. But the canvas I finished this afternoon is something else. Something unleashing the dangerous path my thoughts have taken. It's another slash of color across a black void. It started with the same routine strokes, the same dull tones I always reach for. Painting is supposed to be a release, a way to reflect the hollowness inside me.

But lately...

God, lately it's been *her*.

In each caress of my brush. In the pounding beat of my withered heart. In every thought—every fucking breath—Evie's there. She's slithered beneath my skin and taken up residence in my marrow. I feel her everywhere, always. Taunting. Tempting. *Fucking consuming.*

And the thought of one of these bastards *taking* her, stealing her light, and throwing her into that darkness—

Justice may be served in hell, but patience isn't one of my virtues. If God won't punish the wicked, I'll happily step in.

The back door clicks open. Tempest strides in carrying three bags of groceries and a small potted plant.

"Oh good," she says, kicking the door shut behind her as she enters the kitchen. Erik is the first to greet her, accepting the spiky cactus she shoves into his arms as she sets the bags on the counter.

"You're all here. Evie's coming back tonight, and I don't want a repeat of what happened last weekend."

Dominic and Bane exchange a glance with Adrian, the three of them smirking as they turn toward me.

"Yeah, Silas," Erik teases over Tempest's shoulder, a wicked gleam in his eyes. "No fucking the new girl."

A loud *crack* sounds from the pantry. A low curse follows as Tempest slams the door shut and stands, rubbing a spot on the back of her head while glaring at me. "What did he just say?"

I lift a brow, holding my sister's narrowed stare. "I didn't fuck anyone."

"My bad." Erik flashes a wide grin, slinging an arm around Tempest's shoulders. "A kiss is different than fucking—though one usually leads to the other when I'm involved."

Tempest rolls her eyes and shoves him off before stomping toward me, finger aimed at my chest. The rest of the Seven fall back, retreating to the safety of the couch for a front-row seat to the drama. Fucking cowards.

"You can't, Silas," she snaps, seeing straight through the practiced indifference I've mastered. "Evie's family is even more overbearing than I thought. They want her to attend church every day, meaning she knows all the alcoves on campus. Last weekend was her first time in a club—and probably the first time she's worn a dress that didn't touch her ankles."

Tempest's frustration gives way to pleading. She's begging me to understand how sheltered Evie is. How someone raised under that level of submission is naïve, impressionable, vulnerable. She hopes her words will turn me away. But all they do is flame the embers of desire I've spent the last week trying to smother.

She's not wrong. Evie *is* a grown woman—but she's never had control over her own life. She deserves the freedom to choose sin, to explore pleasure, to make mistakes. Tempest doesn't realize that I *felt* the way Evie leaned into me. I had my hand around her throat, and she didn't pull away—she parted her lips like she was *starving* for me.

And her taste—*fuck*. She tasted like the sweetest ambrosia. I wonder how sweet her cunt is. How addictive her breathy little moans will sound when I make her fall apart on my tongue.

"Silas," Tempest scolds, hands landing on her hips, like she knows exactly where my thoughts have wandered.

I tilt my head, ears pricking at the soft *click* of the front door closing. She's here.

Is my little fox actually returning when people are awake? I glance over Tempest's shoulder and spot the familiar shadow in the hall.

"Evie isn't like the girls you sleep with," Tempest continues, oblivious to her roommate's presence. I open my mouth to warn her, but she holds up a hand. "She can't play in your fucked-up fantasies. And she shouldn't have to. I know you all have some kinky little brotherhood where you pass woman around like drinks at a party, but I *won't* let you do that to Evie. She probably hasn't even had a boyfriend."

"I didn't say anything about being her boyfriend," I say, catching the soft hitch of breath from the edge of the kitchen.

Erik strolls between us, reaching for the six-pack on the counter. He cracks one open and leans against the island, clearly waiting for the next spark to light the fire.

"That's not the point," Tempest growls. "Evie is my friend. I'm not going to let any of you hurt her."

Porcelain skin and deep red hair come into view. She heard us, no doubt about it. I take in her rounded shoulders, the way she folds into herself like she wants to disappear.

And I'm *glad* she heard. I'm not the good guy. Not the knight in shining armor. I'm the monster heroes warn you about. I fuck hard. I don't go slow. I don't do nice. And I sure as fuck don't come back for seconds.

Evie, with her silver cross and sad eyes, is everything I need to avoid.

Her being a virgin doesn't bother me. On the contrary, it's the *only* thing I've thought about all damn week. I've imagined how her sweet little cunt would look stretched around my fingers. My tongue. My cock. Bleeding for me. I want to fill her, tease and suck and bite, graze her nipples with my teeth as I tear her reality to shreds. Force her to understand just how brutal this world is. And how beautiful pain can be.

Leaving her alone is the only option. Not just for her sake, but for mine.

But now she's standing there, hovering at the edge of the room. The heavy heat of summer lingers in the air, the shitty A/C doing its best to keep the place cool. It must be windy out, because her normally perfect braid is coming undone, strands sticking out in every direction. Her cheeks are flushed, and there's a hollowness in her eyes I haven't seen before.

One that makes me want to hunt down the fucker who caused it and rip them to shreds.

Tempest realizes the silence has stretched too long, and she turns to see who I'm staring at.

"Evie," she whispers, shaking her head before letting out a slow breath. "Shit."

13

EVIE

"I'm sorry," Tempest starts, but I hold up a hand, cutting her off.

"Don't worry about it," I breathe, forcing a smile. Everything she said is true—but it's not like I can tell them that. This is a room full of sharks. Showing them my bleeding wounds will only get me killed faster.

I let my eyes drift past the kitchen to the living room, where the rest of them are sprawled across the couch. Mavros—the one with the bear tattoo—is here, along with the sloth guy, Noctis. Adrian, Dominic, and Bane are crammed together on the cushions, while Erik lingers in the kitchen near Tempest, like he always is. He leans slightly in front of her, as if expecting me to snap. I wonder if they've ever dated, but then my gaze lands on the broody, six-foot-four asshole before me—Silas, with the snake at his throat, ink covering his arms and fingers—I doubt he'd ever approve of his little sister and best friend hooking up.

Silas's dark hair is tousled, a smudge of gold paint streaking through it. I flash back to the stacked canvases in his room from the first day, when I'd mistaken it for Tempest's, and wonder what he's painted today. Does he prefer realism? Capturing quiet, beautiful details others overlook? From the glimpses I've caught, I think he prefers impressionism, letting color flow and emotions bleed freely.

I almost ask him. But then I meet his eyes to find his pupils blown wide and the chiseled planes of his body coiled like a cobra prepared to strike.

"Is my little sister right, Evie?" Silas asks.

"Don't," Tempest snaps, but he doesn't look away.

They're watching, all of them already knowing the answer. Frustration rises in my throat. If I dodge the question, it'll only drag this moment out. I should've waited until they were gone to come back, but I had nowhere else to go. So, I lift my chin and stare into Silas's deep green eyes, before fixating on the forgotten splash of cobalt paint across his cheek.

"I am a virgin," I say. There's no point in lying. I'm not ashamed—not of *that*. What makes my cheeks flush and heat creep down my neck is the fact that it's never truly been my choice. Not really. Not when my family controlled every part of my life.

"My body is the only thing of value I can offer," I add, watching as the veins along Silas's forearms flex. The flicker of curiosity in his gaze morphs into fury. And for a second, I almost let myself believe he *cares*. "At least, that's what I was told. Being loud was the worst sin a girl could commit."

I meant to keep going, to pretend I'm unfazed by his anger, by Tempest's sharp breath, but haunted memories slash through my mind. Jonathan's hand on my thigh at lunch, his slimy fingers gripping me under the table while calmly discussing who my future husband will be with my parents.

All the while, Mother's voice rings out, criticizing my dress, my hair, my weight.

I'm a disappointment. A doll not quite pretty enough. A failed investment. And suddenly it's too much—all of it. My fucked-up childhood. The gnawing guilt tied to beliefs I don't even agree with anymore. The aching need to appease a god I still want to believe in, even as I claw at every barb of patriarchal control embedded in my soul.

And something inside me just… snaps.

"Nobody wants to hear what I think or how I feel. My dreams don't matter. What I want to do, who I want to be—who I am—*doesn't matter.*" A hysteric edge clings to my voice, and I don't know why I'm spilling all this to a room full of strangers, but if I don't get the words out, I'm going to scream. And if I start, I'm afraid I'll never stop.

"Evie," Tempest says gently, stepping closer. When I don't shy away, she wraps her arms around me, holding tight as soundless tears track down my cheeks.

"You do matter," she murmurs. "That's all I was saying. I just don't want them to be a bunch of dickwads to you."

A harsh laugh scrapes from my throat as she draws back.

"Tempest is right," Erik adds as the others rise from the couch to join us. "We mean well, but each of us has our own… vice."

The one with dark skin and striking blue eyes—Dominic—brushes a finger over the inside of his wrist, drawing my gaze to the tattoo there: the head of a demonic goat with long ears and spiraling ram horns, set before the number seven.

"That we do," he says, flashing a sinful smile. "I've never been great at controlling my lust."

Tempest rolls her eyes. "Dominic *is* always thinking with his dick."

"Hey," Dominic protests, half-hearted. "It's a real struggle sometimes."

"Don't act like you don't love it." The guy next to him chuckles. He has dark hair, tanned skin, and a strong nose—the one with the orange hellhound if I remember correctly.

"You're one to talk, Bane," says the one on Dominic's other

side. His golden eyes gleam beneath a tangle of thick russet hair. "Gluttonous to the end, this one. But I can't judge. I'm pretty greedy myself."

Laughter hums through the group and I smile along, knowing they're referencing the Seven. But even as the reminder stirs tendrils of fear in my gut, I refuse to make this night more awkward than it already is.

"Quit it, Adrian," Tempest says, shooting a glare his way.

Adrian holds up his hands in placation, pale skin splashed with freckles, covered in tattoos. "What about you, Erik? Anything you're proud of lately, or just your reflection?"

"I *am* fucking gorgeous." Erik preens, pulling out his phone and snapping a selfie as the others laugh.

"Ignore them," Tempest mutters, stepping in front of me and turning her back on the group. "Want a drink?"

Alcohol wasn't allowed in my house growing up. I once caught my mother pouring a generous glass of red wine before a church event. She claimed it was left over from service—Christ's blood was fine to consume, so long as she asked for forgiveness.

"Beer, please."

Silas huffs, shaking his head like I've said the most predictable thing imaginable. My cheeks heat as Tempest twists the cap off a brown bottle with a colorful artisan label and offers it to me.

"Something funny?" I ask, my tone clipped.

Silas raises a dark brow, eyes gleaming with challenge as he watches me accept the beer. "You don't drink."

"Yes, I do." My blush deepens as I glare at him, hating the certainty in his voice. "I drank last weekend."

"You had one shot."

"Two," I snap back.

"This is different." He smirks. "You don't even like beer."

"Why would I ask for one if I didn't?" I narrow my eyes, the audacity of him igniting something sharp in me. "In fact, this is my favorite kind of beer. Thank you, Tempest."

"It's nothing," she says, offering a smile, but there's a crease between her brows as she looks between the two of us. She knows last weekend was the first time I ever had a drink, but I can't admit that to Silas, not when he's staring at me with that smug grin plastered across his stupidly perfect face.

Silas glides across the kitchen, closing the distance between us in a few long strides. I straighten my spine and glare up at him.

"You're a rule-abiding, skirt-wearing, domesticated little fox who doesn't have the first clue what life is like without Mommy and Daddy to protect you," he says. "You've never had a drink in your life, let alone porter brewed in a whiskey barrel."

Biting the inside of my cheek, I force the sheen of tears not to fall. I hate that I cry when I'm angry. Hate that Silas sees exactly what everyone else does: a spoiled, sheltered girl with the perfect family and perfect upbringing. I'm not a real person to Silas, the Seven, or even to my own family. Just a puppet, dressed and pressed into an obedient servant.

Mother confirmed everything Jonathan said.

I have until the end of this semester to enjoy my life. One semester to experience everything I want before they lock me up again. No time to waste, right?

Holding Silas's gaze, I lift the bottle to my lips and take a long sip. Notes of bittersweet chocolate and malty vanilla roll over my tongue, mingling with the bite of alcohol that lingers at the back of my throat. It warms me, the heat smooth and sweet as I swallow. I lick my lips, savoring hints of toffee. And Silas's eyes dip, tracking my tongue with an emotion I can't quite place. Anger… or something darker. Something *wanting*.

"Delicious," I breathe, watching a flicker of desire spark behind his eyes. Is he remembering the kiss we shared? Is he imagining me pressed against the alley wall, his fingers tangled in my hair, knee shoved between my thighs as he fucked my mouth with his tongue?

He must be, because he's looking at me with want and need and… the openness in his gaze ices over with cool detachment. It's only then I realize I'm leaning toward him. Pulse racing, I jerk back, bumping into the counter.

"Okay, Evie," Erik says, nodding at me as he tugs Tempest against him. "I see you."

Tempest laughs softly, her attention shifting to Erik's playful touches as he leads her toward the couch with the others. But Silas's gaze stays locked on me.

"How was it?" he asks, studying me like he would a game, anticipating my next move.

"Fine," I answer, gripping the bottle tighter. "Like I said, it's my favorite."

Lie. And judging by the smug little grin tugging at his mouth, he knows it. But what really pisses me off is the look of triumph in his stupid, glinting eyes.

"You don't know anything about me or my *perfect* life," I snap. "Tossing back drinks and riding motorcycles doesn't make you tough."

Something shifts between us—something slow and coiled, like a python wrapping around a sleeping mouse. By the time the mouse realizes the pressure isn't comfort, but death—it's too late. I feel like that mouse as Silas watches every trace of emotion flicker across my face.

"Careful, little fox," he murmurs, lips twitching. "That almost sounds like you're asking for a ride."

My pulse spikes, heat searing through me from the look in his eyes. I know exactly what he means—and god help me, I *want* to know what sex with someone like him would be like. There wouldn't be a white dress or diamond ring. No sweet kisses or promises of forever. I was taught to expect a quiet softness… but what would it be like to lean into the chaos?

Would it be so wrong to yield to that twisted part of myself? The one that yearns to taste the forbidden embers of hell? The same cursed piece of my soul that finds release in the sharp bite of a blade across my skin. Would Silas cut me? If I asked him nicely and was a good girl, would he lick the blood that welled beneath his knife?

My thighs clench as desire coils low in my stomach, a gnawing ache I've never been able to quench. I bet Silas knows how to satiate me. I'd bet my soul he could take me apart, delivering me to hell's gates on a platter and leave me begging for more.

Silas's shoulders go rigid, and for a split second, I worry I've spoken my forbidden fantasies aloud. His pupils are blown, nearly eclipsing the green rings as he holds me there, transfixed. But before I can do something incredibly stupid, Tempest is there.

"On second thought," she says, glancing between us, "let's go out."

14

SILAS

"You shouldn't run off like that," I say, my lips brushing the crest of Evie's ear as she sets the empty whiskey glass on the counter. It's her third of the evening, the effects of the alcohol already visible in the way her supple body moves to the thrumming music of my club.

I love watching the way her spine stiffens, the way her breath catches when she realizes I've followed her off the dance floor. Someone had to. She's lucky I don't bend her over my knee and slap her ass until her porcelain skin glows red from my touch.

"You're not the boss of me," Evie retorts with a slight hiccup, spinning around to glare up at me.

Her body looks divine in the clothes I picked out for her. She probably thinks Tempest chose them, but the thought of anyone else dressing her, of imagining her skin and breasts and body wrapped in fabric is enough to have me seeing green.

When Evie reappeared in the kitchen thirty minutes later with her hair down, dressed in the clothes I bought, glowing with a look of excited determination in her eyes, my demon practically purred.

Mine.

The red lace top is modest enough with short sleeves and dark buttons down the front. The black miniskirt flares just right, giving Evie the freedom she needs to move without the entire club seeing her perfect ass. She'd normally find it too short, but the black heeled boots and thigh-high stockings leave only a sliver of exposed thigh.

I press my palms against the bar, caging her in as I lean down. "Would you like me to be?"

Evie swallows, her eyes dipping to my mouth. "What?"

"Would you like me to be in control, little fox?" My lips twitch as I run my nose up the length of her neck, inhaling her sweet scent.

Fuck, how I've been craving her. Needing another taste. She shivers as my tongue lashes out, my lips closing around the fluttering pulse along the curve of her collarbone.

"You could pretend you're a good girl who had her choice taken away."

"Why would I want that?" Her voice is breathy as she arches into me, her nipples hardening through the fabric as they brush my chest.

"Because then you wouldn't have to admit how much you liked kissing me." A small whimper escapes her, and I smile against her jaw, nipping the sensitive skin. I shift closer, one arm braced on the bar, the other trailing up her trembling thighs.

"If I forced you," I whisper, "you could pretend you don't dream about my hands on you. About my lips exploring every inch of your skin. Like a fresh canvas brought to life beneath my brush."

"Can I see them?" she asks.

My hand stills.

She bites her lip, cheeks flushing. "I saw some of your paintings. They're yours, right? I thought it was Tempest's room, but the snake on the door matches the one on your throat…”

“You looked through my room?”

“No.” She winces. “Well, I mean… I guess technically yes.”

People move around us, drinks and drugs exchanged freely, but I’m focused on her. On how she’s looking at me. Nobody sees my paintings. I sometimes paint at the house, but once they’re done, I lock them away in my studio, entombed in the dark.

It’s an explosion of demons, how I wash my hands of all the blood I’ve shed. They’re grotesque. Haunting. Confessions spilled in color and shadow, but Evie is watching me, her thighs parted, gooseflesh pricking her arms while my fingers trace invisible designs over her inner thigh. She’s waiting, wanting to know more… about me.

“I liked them. Your paintings,” she clarifies.

My heart hammers against my chest as warmth rushes through my veins. The urge to share those secret parts of myself—the pieces that even my brothers don’t know—is more dangerous than any weapon. And yet, my hand moves higher, spreading her legs wider.

“People will see,” she hisses, her fingers gripping my arm, pupils blown wide in those big brown eyes.

“You’d like that, wouldn’t you, Evie? Everyone watching while I ruin you.”

“No,” she says, but she tilts her hips up.

“Liar,” I whisper, leaning down to taste her lips as my fingers continue their ascent.

She whimpers against my mouth, and my cock goes hard at the needy sound. *Fuck,* I want her. I want to taste and touch and claim. I want to know she needs me just as badly as I crave her.

My knuckles drag across her underwear, her wetness already soaking the fabric.

“Look how wet you are for me,” I growl, slipping my fingers

beneath to rub teasing strokes along her pussy. "Do you want me here, little fox?" Her breathing is ragged as I circle that small spot that has her legs trembling. "I would get on my knees for you, Evie. Spreading you wide on this bar as I feasted on this sweet little cunt. All you have to do is ask."

Evie's cheeks flush, shame washing across her face as she shoves me back. The flash of lights catch on the inside of her forearm and I freeze.

"You're disgusting," she spits. It takes a moment, but whatever she sees on my face must terrify her, because she flinches, trying to hide her arm when she realizes what I'm staring at.

"What the fuck are those?" I grab her wrist before she can pull way, twisting gently to expose the thin, raised pink scars.

My stomach twists and I have an overwhelming urge to destroy everything. To pour gasoline over the world, strike a match, and watch it burn because what kind of fucked-up reality makes someone like her—a person who's met each of my asshole moments with nothing but kindness and her own subtle strength—feel like *this* is the only option?

"Nothing," Evie breathes, face pale even in the club's dim light. "It's just a scratch."

"Don't lie to me," I growl, low and lethal, but my grip is gentle as my fingers brush the deepest cut.

"Really," she says, swallowing. "I'm fine."

I shoot her a warning glare, then raise her arm and kiss the scarred skin, wishing to the hell that bore me that I could erase her pain with something as simple as a kiss.

"Give your pain to me, little fox." The dark flecks in her honey-colored eyes burn with tears as I lick along each scar, reverent in my attention. "The darkness and I are well acquainted. I don't fear it."

Another slow lap along the blue veins in her wrist. Evie's chest heaves, body shaking as I lower her hand, but I don't let go.

I can't.

I won't stop touching her. Not when she's staring up at me like she's trying to see what's underneath.

Her gaze drops to my mouth as I lick my lips and it's like she's peering beneath my harsh scales, wading through the poison pumping through my veins, and reaching past the armor. Evie is the sharp scrape of vines sprouting in the chambers of my heart, embedding their barbs in my soul—and fuck if I don't love the prick of thorns.

"Never again," I breathe, my words nearly swallowed by the pounding music and roar of the crowd. But I keep her here, suspended with me in a world all our own. The pads of my thumbs brush over the places I just kissed, feeling the raised, healing wounds. Evie shivers, her eyes locking on mine. With a deep breath, her chin dips.

15

SILAS

Tempest flags us down, shattering the spell and stealing Evie away. I shake my head, doing my best to clear it of her. Of anything that might distract me from my goal. We're so close to finding Morana, to rescuing my sister after years of searching. I can't afford to lose sight of the finish line now. And it's become glaringly clear that Evie is a dangerous distraction.

Ignoring the coolness left in the wake of her touch, I scan the roof for my brothers. Adrian and Bane retreated upstairs with three woman an hour ago, but I spot Erik and Dominic behind Tempest. Erik's blue eyes meet mine, and he gives a slight shake of his head.

No word from Noctis or Mavros. No confirmation on Shane. No movement on this fucking lead.

Dominic welcomes Evie into the fold, dancing at a respectable distance with her and Tempest as the bass drops, but Erik holds my gaze, the two of us having an entire conversation without speaking.

Need to blow off some steam? he mouths over the music,

nodding toward the two women in cheap jewelry and orange makeup grinding on him.

I shake my head, disgust rolling through me at the thought of touching someone else when all I want is to spread Evie's thighs and finish what we started.

Where did my little fox run off to?

My eyes narrow when I spot a familiar face. Mark is sporting the black eye I gave him, sauntering over to where Tempest and Evie are dancing. Evie greets him with a smile, because of course she fucking does. She even goes as far as gently touching the bruise shaped by my fist before Mark waves away her concern and offers her a drink. I'm seconds away from storming across the dance floor and throwing him out when Evie declines, turning instead to dance—with her ass against him.

My nostrils flare, fists clenching as I take two steps forward. My mind swirls will all the colorful, painful ways I could end Mark's life. Which bones I'd break first. How much I could make him bleed. And then Evie's eyes find mine.

She flashes me a tentative smile, making a show of swaying her hips. Mark's hands are on her waist, but her gaze stays locked on me as her back arches, fingers playing with her unbound curls—getting off on my jealousy.

Erik raises a brow at Mark, asking if he should interfere. He could have the fucker bleeding and broken in the alley in seconds with a black bag waiting, but my little fox is still looking at me. And she's enjoying herself.

I was told being loud was the worst sin a girl could commit.

Her confession comes back to haunt me, confirming everything I suspected. My Evie has been controlled and silenced all her life. Her natural desires have been used against her, twisted into something shameful. The religion her family sold her to claims sex is inherently evil. All because pleasure is a form of freedom—of power—the church can't control.

My dreams don't matter. Who I am doesn't matter.

Tempest leans in and whispers something that causes Evie to laugh. The sound is stolen by the pulse of the music, buried beneath sweaty bodies and devious acts. I want so badly to snap my fingers and clear the place out. To be the only one who makes her laugh just so I can devour the sound over and over again. To take and twist and break everything she knows about this world, unmaking her reality. Obliterating her god from existence and setting myself in his place.

Evie surrenders to the music, caught in the rush of the moment. All the while, her heated gaze stays fixed on me, drinking in every drop of my attention. Her doe eyes widen when they dip, realizing just how much her little dance is affecting me.

I see it then, the war waging inside my little fox. She's an angel falling for the demon, drawn to the darkness but still fighting the pull. Evie wants to please me. And punish me. So, I let her.

Bringing my knuckles to my nose, I inhale the lingering scent of her arousal as I watch her body writhe. Even as I imagine what type of knife I'll use to slice off Mark's hands for touching what's mine, I yield this moment to her—to whatever she needs it to be.

I'll make her pay later, of course. She'll wish she would've heeded my warning, but punishment is always better when it isn't rushed. When I can take my time painting her ass red.

The music shifts as the night wears on, and still, I watch. Erik flashes me a grin as he heads upstairs. Tempest dances with Evie a little longer, but Mark just can't seem to help himself.

Tempest signals to Dominic that she's leaving with the dark-haired jock she's been dancing with, before leaning into my little fox. She points to where Dominic stands, reassuring Evie she isn't being left alone. She nods, pretending she doesn't know I'm still here, tracking her every move.

But Dom does. I give him a nod once Tempest is gone, confirming he's off babysitting duty for the night, leaving Evie on her own. Blooming independence or not, I start forward, ready to throw Mark into a coma, when my phone rings.

A light blue sloth appears on the screen. Noctis.

He speaks the second I answer.

"We've confirmed Shane's number. I'm sending the information we have through the system to get a location and rundown."

"Perfect. Is he local?"

There's a pause. I narrow my eyes, my grip tightening on the phone as I watch Mark return with another drink for Evie, more insistent this time.

"Noctis," I press, dread coiling in my stomach. "Is there a local point of contact?"

"Yes," he says, his voice muffled by the sound of a motorcycle engine starting. "We've already met him."

16

EVIE

Tempest bids me farewell for the night, pointing out Dominic in case I need help. I smile and wave, pretending I don't know Silas is watching.

Everything is so fucked. I thought college would be my escape. My chance to get out of the hell my father planned for me. That was my first mistake: believing my life could ever revolve around me. I wasn't raised to have opinions or emotions or do *anything* other than keep my mouth shut until I was handed off to my husband. Then I'd be his to abuse. His to erase.

What's even worse is that I genuinely thought my mother agreed I deserved autonomy over my own life. But this—pretending to grant me parole only to realize the bars were always in place—is worse than staying locked up. Because I imagined what my life could be. All for them to rip it away.

The joke's on me.

What's the point of following the rules when all it earns me is a quicker death sentence? So I tilt my head back, swaying as the club pulses beneath me, feeling more alive than I am. The pads of my fingers graze my exposed thighs, dragging the edges of my black skirt up as I stare into a pair of green eyes.

I know what I'm doing is wrong, but I can't seem to stop myself. Mark is all over me, but I imagine the rough callouses of Silas's fingers, the flecks of paint streaked through his hair. The way he touched me. The tattoos covering his knuckles are the same ones that brushed over my pussy in a nightclub where anyone could've seen. And I didn't want him to stop.

Mark leaves but I keep dancing for Silas, imagining his hands on me, loving the way his eyes flare with angry jealousy.

Would you like me to be in control, little fox? His voice rumbles in my mind as my hands trail up my torso, cupping my breasts. I've lost track of Silas in the crowd, but I still feel his gaze on me, even when Mark returns with another drink sporting a small pink umbrella.

"You must be thirsty," Mark says, extending the drink to me with what he no doubt thinks is a charming smile.

"I'm good, actually," I reply, taking a step away. The edges of his smile tighten, and the twisting in my gut intensifies. "Thank you, though."

"I insist," he presses, holding out the drink once more. "I've already spent money, and I know you're not the type of girl who's rude about accepting a gift."

"Oh," I sputter, raising my hand to accept it, even though I don't want to. He stares at me, waiting for me to drink. Alarm bells go off in my head as I lift the glass, but Mark's phone rings before the liquid touches my lips.

One glance at the screen has him muttering an excuse and rushing away. The band around my chest eases as he leaves, the drink still clasped in my hands like a bomb about to explode. Looking for the nearest table, I realize I'm poised on the edge of the room, mostly cloaked in shadows. Mark must've been ushering us to the side, and I hadn't noticed.

"Bastard," I breathe, setting the glass down.

And then I feel *him*, pricks of intuition telling me Silas is nearby. A shiver runs down my spine, a lingering sense from some long-lost survival instinct humans once possessed, telling me to run. My heart kicks into overdrive, fear banishing the last hazy effects of alcohol as I search the crowd of writhing bodies for my hunter.

His fingers wrap around my throat, strangling the scream trapped in my lungs, tugging my back flush with his chest before I know what's happening.

"You've had your fun tonight, Evie." Silas's lips brush against my ear, the warmth of his breath leaving zaps of electricity burning across my skin. "Now it's my turn."

"I don't know what you're talking about."

His fingers tighten ever so slightly as I swallow. My breathing hitches as he holds me in place, his other hand trailing down my thigh. The pads of his fingers trace patterns along the exposed skin above my knee before bunching the fabric of my skirt and tugging it up.

I gasp as the hard length of his cock presses against my ass. Hundreds of people are dancing and drinking mere feet away, and the only thing separating us is the soft fabric of my underwear.

"Mark will be back—"

Silas's fingers force my head back, cutting off my words as his nose drags up the side of my neck.

"Do not speak another man's name when I'm touching you." His hand splays across the inside of my thigh, holding me there as his chest rumbles with the threat. Teeth ghost along my collarbone, licking over my fluttering pulse before his fingers inch higher. "Did it turn you on knowing I was watching you, little fox?"

A small whimper escapes me as he slips a finger beneath the thin cotton.

"This needy little cunt is dripping for me, and I've barely

touched you. Imagine how wet you'll be—how beautifully you'll scream—when I bury my cock inside you."

My thighs clench around him as he plays in my slickness. I should be horrified, but I love the way he commands my body, the filthy way he speaks as if I'm already his. And maybe that's exactly what I want.

Letting the last of my inhibitions go, I arch my back, wiggling my ass in time with the music as I grind my clit against his palm. The hiss that escapes him is carnal, and I can't hide the grin ghosting across my lips.

The world spins as Silas turns me, pressing me against the wall. His hand cups my pussy, the back of my hair tangled in his grip, tugging hard enough to make me wince as he tilts my head up to his.

"This pussy belongs to me," Silas growls, rubbing a finger through my folds, forcing me to stare into his emerald eyes. I swear there's a flash of vulnerability—he looks almost afraid—but then Silas's finger is pressing into me.

I gasp at the intrusion, the sound swallowed by his mouth as it crashes into mine. The kiss in the alley was stolen and rushed, but this—this is punishing. Claiming, in a way that has my legs trembling and delicious heat coiling low in my belly.

We are a clash of teeth and tongues, of panting breaths and needy moans. A new song starts, and his pace picks up. Silas slips a second finger inside, and the stretch has me throwing my head back, bucking shamelessly against him as his thumb rubs circles over my clit.

"Oh my god," I moan, feeling the tension spike like a wave cresting.

"Eyes open, Evie." His words are a low rasp, the command absolute. "Look at me as you fuck yourself on my fingers."

I blink my eyes open just as he adds a third finger, the stretch painful as his thumb flicks. My hands drape over his shoulders, holding myself up as I writhe, needing more. Seeking that unknown release.

"That's right, little fox. Shatter for me."

His fingers curl as I cry out, sending me over the edge. I'm floating and falling and soaring all at once as waves of pleasure crash over me. Silas doesn't stop. His fingers pump as I shudder, coaxing every ounce of ecstasy from my orgasm.

My heartbeat pounds in my ears as I settle back into my body, painfully aware of Silas's fingers still inside me as I try to stand on my own. He waits until I'm looking at him, his eyes bouncing between mine with something like wonder.

Forcing myself to stand on wobbly legs, I unclasp my hands and allow them to drift over the hard planes of his chest, hissing as Silas withdraws his fingers. Slickness coats my thighs, the evidence of my first orgasm glistening on his skin.

"I've never come before," I whisper, swallowing as he holds his fingers between us.

Silas's eyes widen, searching my gaze as if waiting for the punch line. I draw my bottom lip between my teeth, doing my best to ignore the flame in my cheeks and let him see the truth.

"Your first with a partner?" he asks.

I shake my head, and his cock twitches, his gaze shifting from me to his fingers, still wet.

"Such a dirty girl," he purrs, inhaling the scent of my arousal with a groan.

Shame stretches the blush down my neck even as want pools in my core, my body already wanting more. Silas brings his fingers to his mouth, a sinful grin tilting his lips into a lopsided smirk, then licks them clean like a starved man offered a taste of his favorite meal.

"So fucking sweet."

My breathing hitches as I stifle a whimper, but there's no hiding the quickening of my breath. My breasts ache, my nipples hard, wondering what it would feel like to have his lips on other parts of my body.

He smirks as if reading my mind, dragging me flush against him. His cock presses against me, a promise of what's to come.

"I'm not going to fuck you tonight, Evie. Not yet." The spark of life shining in his eyes dims. "We have a date to get to."

17

SILAS

Evie tastes like salvation. Like a splash of sunshine in a sea of infinite darkness. It took every ounce of restraint not to drop to my knees and feast on her right then, but I have business to take care of.

Evie's small shriek sounds from inside her helmet, ringing in mine, as I veer off the main highway onto a narrow road that parallels the beach. My larger frame cages hers in, not trusting her to hold on as we climb the side of the mountain at a brutal pace. Especially not if she knew why we were here.

Spindles of yucca plants and underbrush bathed in moonlight blur around us as we ascend the dirt path. The state park is secluded. There's no lights, no patrols on the trails at night, which makes it the perfect place to get answers. Answers I've spent years hunting down.

Ocean waves rumble in the distance as I cut the engine and nudge the kickstand into place.

"What are we doing here?" Evie asks, tugging off her helmet. She spots the two men leaning against the hood of a car a few paces in front of us, a frown forming on her pretty lips. I do the same, replacing my helmet with my stitched mask.

I give myself a moment to appreciate how fucking gorgeous she looks. Her skirt's ridden up, exposing her thighs spread around my motorcycle, and she's wearing the leather jacket I had custom made for her. An emerald serpent is embroidered across the back, marking her as mine. Evie won't know what it means, but my brothers will. And I don't fucking care.

"Don't you recognize the one on the left, little fox?" I ask as Mark grunts. Memories of her body dragging along him have my blood boiling, burning with envy. She swings her leg off my bike, and I capture her before she takes another step. My gloved hands press against the soft curves of her stomach, making sure she feels how hard I am. "You were rubbing your ass all over him only hours ago."

The hitch in her breath is audible, and I don't bother suppressing a malicious chuckle as I lean forward, my mask scraping her cheek.

"Stay put," I murmur, relishing the way Evie's pulse hammers. "Do as you're told and I'll consider lessening your punishment."

"P-punishment?" she stammers as I step around her toward our guests. As much as I'd love to soak up the fear emanating from my little fox, this next part requires concentration.

"Whoever you are, you better get the fuck out of here," the man next to Mark says, raising his chin with a hand in his pocket. "We have business here that doesn't concern you."

"Oh, but it does." I grin, cocking my head slightly as I listen. A whistle cuts through the darkness behind them.

"What the fuck," Mark mutters, scrambling back as his partner withdraws a gun and points it into the trees.

Mavros and Noctis emerge from the thick overgrowth, dressed in black. Their masks are firmly in place—red and light blue stitching crossing over their eyes and mouths, twisted into grotesque smiles.

"Clear," Mavros says, ignoring the weapon pointed at him.

The red bear embroidered on his jacket shifts as he cracks his knuckles.

"Only the two," Noctis confirms with a shrug. In place of a bear, his jacket sports a creepy-looking sloth stitched in light blue, almost teal. "Turns out Mark and Andrew thought they could handle the southern region without backup."

"That's right, motherfuckers," Andrew snarls, pointing his gun between the three of us. "I handle my own shit—"

Mavros may be big, but he's fast. A shot cracks through the air, and red stains white cotton a moment before Andrew hits the ground.

"Shit," Mark curses, pressing a hand to his friend's chest. But Mavros doesn't miss. It won't matter what Mark does. Andrew is already gone.

I lift a brow in Noctis's direction and nod once. He steps forward, disarming Mark and retrieving the other two weapons from Andrew's body.

"Did you get his phone?" I ask, not taking my eyes off Mark, but painfully aware of the silence stretching behind me.

Evie isn't screaming. We just killed a man, and there's nothing but the thickening quiet. And maybe that makes me a coward, but I don't turn to check on her. This is who I am. What I've been forced to become. If she doesn't understand that…

"Yes," Noctis confirms. "I took his wallet, as well. We have a cleanup crew on standby, already aware that both will need dental work."

I nod once. The bodies won't be discovered. There won't be anything left to find, but I still prefer to take precautions.

It was Noctis who first suggested removing the teeth of the men who've gotten in our way. It's become standard practice now. No loose ends and all that.

"Call when it's done," Noctis says before he and Mavros disappear down the unmarked path. I wait until their motorcycles rev to life and fade into the distance before turning back to Evie.

"What's going on?" she asks, voice shaking as she stares at the growing red pool around Andrew. She's pale and trembling, but she lifts her chin, eyes flicking from Mark's scowling face to mine. "Is this because of me? I wasn't thinking about him when we were dancing."

"We?" I growl.

Evie swallows, her voice barely above a whisper. "It was you, Silas. I was only ever thinking about you."

"I know, little fox," I murmur, cupping her face. She turns into my palm, leaning into the touch, and my foolish heart kicks against my ribs. "But this is so much bigger than you know."

I turn, boots crunching over gravel as I stalk toward Mark. He's standing, his body tense and covered in blood.

"You look ready to run." He straightens his spine, jaw clenching. "I might let you—if you tell me everything you know about the southern circuit."

Mark keeps his mouth shut.

"Tsk, tsk." I smirk, pacing with my hands behind my back, careful to avoid the mess Andrew left behind. My nose wrinkles as I glance down, noting how the stains on his pants mix with the blood pooling beneath his corpse. Humans really are disgusting.

"Pride will be your downfall. That particular sin has never been a problem for me, but do you know what has?"

Mark's nostrils flare. But I see the fear in his eyes, note the beads of sweat forming across his brow.

He lunges, swinging for my ribs. I let the punch land, laughing through the pain as I ride the high, living for the next hit of adrenaline. Too quickly, I have him crumpled on the ground at my feet. Blood trickles from a cut above his eye. The blow to his temple probably has him seeing stars, but I made sure to keep his mouth intact—for her.

"How long have you been running the circuit for Shane?"

Mark spits on my boots. My fist connects with his jaw before I have time to think. Bones *crunch* as the skin over his cheek splits. So much for keeping his face pretty.

"That was rude," I say, wiping blood off on his shirt. "Let's try this again, shall we? I wouldn't want to kill you before you've had the chance to beg for her forgiveness."

Panting, Mark glances toward Evie, perched in front of my motorcycle before glaring up at me. "You'll let me go if I do what? Say sorry?"

"When's the next shipment?" I ask, ignoring his idiotic question. Of course, I won't let him go. His death certificate was signed the moment he touched Evie.

"Not for another two weeks," he says, jerking his head toward her. "I didn't realize she was yours. She'll do well if you're looking to sell."

My fists flex, but I hold the rage in check. *Just a little longer.*

"Where?"

"L.A.," he answers. "At least, that's what I've heard. I haven't made contact yet."

Now that he thinks I'm just a pushy client, the tension across his shoulders loosens. I fucking hate that he thinks we're the same.

"I was sent from Vegas to investigate missing shipments, but supposedly Shane is out of the game. Yielded the territory to someone else."

"Who?"

"Someone named Jonah. I haven't seen or heard from him yet."

"Waiting on Shane?"

"I'll put you in contact as soon as I can." He nods, glancing over my shoulder. "If I were you, I'd break her in a bit first."

I follow his gaze to Evie, tilting my head like I'm considering it. Luring the fly into the web.

"You think so?"

"What is he talking about?" Evie asks, voice rough.

"If the little bitch just took a sip, she would've been mine," Mark says wistfully, clearing his throat a moment later when I don't respond. "I would've shared her with you. And the others. Jameson told me to stay away, but we could've been working together this whole time."

Mark's chuckle dies in his throat, eyes widening when he sees the gun in my hand. I turn, angling my mask toward Evie.

"Do you see?" I ask softly. "Do you understand the mistake you made, Evie? Toying with me is one thing, but using this pathetic bastard to ignite my envy..."

"I'm sorry," Evie breathes, chest heaving.

I circle Mark, kicking his knees out from under him. He drops, kneeling in the dirt as I raise the barrel to his head and lift my gaze to my little fox. "Don't lie to me. I saw your face. The freedom in your eyes. You loved making me jealous."

Her eyes glisten with tears, but she doesn't deny it.

"Did it make you feel alive?" I whisper. "Watching me lose my mind while you used him?"

"Yes," she admits, and I grin.

"She was asking for it," Mark spits. He makes to rise, but I shove him back down, dirt spraying as he catches himself on his hands and knees. "You heard her. It's not my fault for wanting a taste of that pussy."

"Is that what you want?" I ask her, remembering how wet she was. "To use him while I watch?"

Evie shakes her head, but I catch the flush creeping up her neck, notice the way her thighs press together—she's unraveling. Biting her lip, she looks around, searching for an escape.

"Ah-ah," I say, wagging a finger as my cock throbs. "Running will only prolong your punishment, Evie. And there's no point. We both know beneath the pretty exterior of the braided hair and long skirts, you're nothing more than a filthy little slut."

She whimpers, the needy sound undoing me. And then she's biting her lip again, teasing the plump flesh as her chest heaves. I want to crawl inside of her. To spank her until her skin is painted in pink. To bite those fucking lips of hers until they bleed, and then lick her wounds clean.

"Are you ready to give in, little fox? To be the good girl I know you are?"

"Yes," she breathes, eyes glazed.

"Walk to the bike, Evie" I say, knowing she needs the command. Needs to believe this is out of her control—so she doesn't have to admit she's just as fucked up as I am. "Lean against the seat and remove your underwear."

"No," she says with a shaky breath. "The club was different, but he doesn't want this."

"Was dear old Mark thinking about what you wanted when he tried to force that spiked drink on you?" My grip tightens on the gun, finger twitching over the trigger.

Her eyes widen, dropping to where he sits on the ground.

"Don't look at him," I growl. "Look at me. Do as I say, or I'll kill him right now."

Evie holds my gaze, her chest rising sharply in challenge. But I don't waver. After a beat, she snarls a curse and stomps to my bike, planting her ass against the seat as she turns to face me.

"Good girl. Now spread your legs and show me what's mine."

18

EVIE

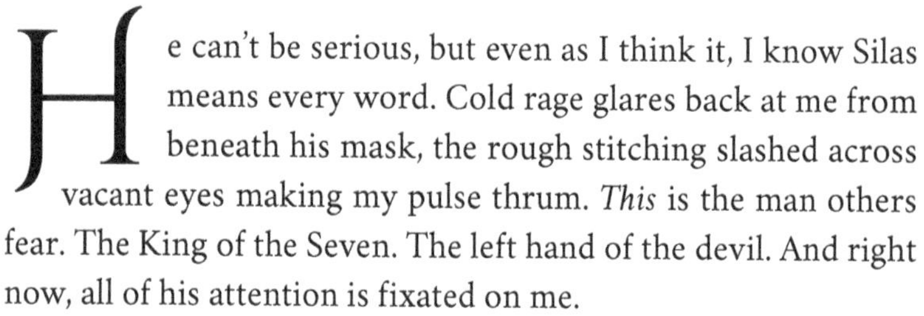

He can't be serious, but even as I think it, I know Silas means every word. Cold rage glares back at me from beneath his mask, the rough stitching slashed across vacant eyes making my pulse thrum. *This* is the man others fear. The King of the Seven. The left hand of the devil. And right now, all of his attention is fixated on me.

I steel a glance at the ground where Mark sits, brows furrowed as he tries to puzzle out Silas's plan. But I already know. Grinding my teeth, I part my thighs.

"Wider, Evie." Silas's harsh voice makes my heart flutter, my nipples hardening. "Show me how wet your needy cunt is."

Shame blooms across my cheeks, the blush deepening as I hold Silas's gaze—because he knows. He fucking knows how turned on I am. How being his dirty little slut feels freeing in a way nothing else does.

Not for the first time, I wonder what's wrong with me. I'm stranded on the edge of a canyon with no escape, being forced to tug my skirt higher, let my knees drift further apart—and all I can think about is how Silas licked every drop of me from his tattooed fingers.

"Good girl," Silas rumbles, staring at the soaked black fabric of my panties.

"Fuck," Mark groans, licking his lips. He's still on his knees, but the outline of his cock strains against his jeans.

"Yes," Silas muses, cocking his head to the side. "She looks fucking perfect—tastes even better. But you don't need to take my word for it."

"No," I whisper, my breath hitching as I catch his meaning. I feel the weight of Silas's gaze beneath the mask and bite my tongue.

"Yes, little fox." His voice is cold, hauntingly so. Mark flinches as Silas kicks his shoulder. "Mark needs to apologize for leaving without saying goodbye. Isn't that right? What better way than licking your needy pussy until you come."

"Silas," I warn, dropping my skirt back down and making to stand.

"Sit," he commands. "Or I'll make good on my threat."

To kill Mark.

Like an obedient dog, I sit, glaring up at my master with all the loathing I can muster. I can practically see Silas lifting a brow, his gaze dipping to my covered legs. Jaw clenching, I hold his stare through the mask as I resume the earlier position.

"Remove them."

My mouth falls open in protest, because fuck him, but then Silas fires. The bullet hits the dirt inches from Mark's hand.

"I won't ask again."

I slide my underwear down, doing my best to ignore the humiliation searing through my veins. That's exactly what he wants—control. Power. Unwilling to give him the satisfaction of waiting for orders, I settle back against the seat of his motorcycle and spread my thighs as wide as I can, being sure every part of me is on display.

"Fuck yeah," Mark says, wiping blood from his eye and lunging forward.

Silas stops him, shoving him back onto his knees. "Crawl to her."

God above, my body trembles at the violence dripping from his words. I should be terrified. I *should be* running, taking my chances racing through spiked plants and sharp rocks. But I'm panting at the thought of Silas watching me come undone by another man. Of him controlling my pleasure.

Mark looks like he might argue, until he glances up, finding my pussy drenched and bared to him. He's on me in seconds.

I stare into Silas's haunting mask, the manic grin stitched across it reaching into my soul as I feel the first swipe of Mark's tongue. The wrongness of the situation has me moaning as he licks up my center, Mark's pace increasing as he circles my clit.

"Such a good little slut," Silas murmurs, praising me as he steps closer, gun still trained on the man between my thighs.

Silas's scent of leather and spice swirls around me, and I whimper, gripping the motorcycle as I stare into the mask.

Mark laps at me, drinking me down like he can't get enough. He spreads my thighs wider, licking and teasing, brushing over my clit but never for long enough. My body is on fire, wound so tight I feel like I might snap. Wanton sounds fall from my lips, my hips undulating, chasing the release that stays just out of reach.

"Does it hurt, little fox?" Silas asks, amusement and anger coiled together. His leather-gloved fingers pinch my chin, forcing me to meet his masked gaze. Mark is still on his knees between my thighs, but my focus is only for Silas, aching for his approval, needing his command.

"Yes," I whimper. "Please."

A wicked, cruel imitation of a laugh escapes him, sending a shiver down my spine. "Do you think I *like* watching another man touch you? This is what you wanted, Evie. Me, burning with jealousy. And you—desired. Coveted to the point of madness."

"Silas, please—"

My pleas are cut short as Silas grabs the back of Mark's head and shoves his face into my core. He flails, palms bracing against my thighs as he tries to pull away—tries to breathe—but the struggle only spreads me further.

"You don't breathe until she comes," Silas snarls, jerking Mark's head up, repositioning his tongue over my clit.

I'm so close. So fucking close.

"Play with your nipples, Evie. Imagine my hands there."

I obey, slipping a hand inside my top, teasing and pinching as Mark's fingers dig into my thighs, his mouth sucking hard on my clit.

"Come for me," Silas growls.

I stare into his stitched green eyes as I come undone, shattering around another man's mouth. Mark's muffled pleas only intensify the orgasm, each vibration drawing out wave after wave until I'm shaking.

Until reality comes crashing back.

Silas yanks Mark away from me, tossing him aside without a second thought.

"Was it everything you dreamed of, little fox?" Silas coos, tugging his mask up enough for me to see his eyes. They're blown wide, devouring every flicker of emotion on my face. Each shameful truth. I swear there's a flash of tenderness, but it vanishes before I can be sure.

"Yes," I confess.

Whatever softness might have been there is gone. Silas only nods once and steps back.

"I warned you what would happen if he touched you again."

My brows furrow, the haze of the orgasm still thick in my mind. I don't understand what's happening until he raises the gun and points it directly at Mark.

"And I always keep my promises."

With no trace of hesitation, Silas pulls the trigger.

19

EVIE

Five liters doesn't sound that impressive. It's one and a half large milk containers. Fourteen cans of soda. My high school biology teacher made it sound formidable, though. I didn't understand why—until tonight.

Crimson sprays the ground as Mark's lifeless body drops, but it's the torrent of emotions trapped behind Silas's vacant gaze that has me leaping from the motorcycle and sprinting for my life.

Clouds roll across the moon, cloaking the rocky canyon in shadow, and it takes all my concentration not to slip on the jagged terrain. I don't know where I'm going, only that I have to keep moving. Keep running.

A crazed laugh pierces the night behind me, the *crunch* of Silas's boots giving chase pushing me faster. This is my fault—Mark's death, probably the other guy's too. I knew Silas was unhinged, could feel the truth of his promise the moment he uttered it.

If he ever touches you again, I'll kill him.

"Run, little fox," Silas shouts, his voice growing fainter. Holy fuck, I might actually have a chance of getting away. "It only makes the chase more fun."

I pump my arms, willing my boots to find purchase as I race downhill, the main road coming into view. And then the motorcycle engine rumbles to life behind me.

A scream rips from my lips as headlights blaze through the darkness. Shit. The valley's too steep for me to leave the trail, the underbrush too thick. One misstep and I'll slip down the side of the canyon, tumbling to the rocky shores below.

The beam of light of finds me.

Double shit.

I spot a narrow trail veering left and throw myself down it, sprinting for my life. Much too late, I realize what the stretch of black ahead means. This isn't a secondary path—it's a look out.

I try to stop and change direction, but I slip. Pebbles give way beneath me, gravel slicing into my thighs as I skid toward the cliff's edge. The ground goes out beneath my feet, the momentum carrying me forward finally slowing as my body stops moving. Terror propels me into action as I scramble back, clawing at the dirt, dragging myself back from the brink—only to be met with the blinding glare of Silas's motorcycle.

I stare through the light, chest heaving as he steps off, his helmet clutched in his hand. He lets it fall, stalking forward slowly, as if enjoying my alarm. His gloves are next, each finger peeled free with leisurely precision, the wicked grin tilting his lips suggesting he's going to enjoy this next part.

Shallow cuts burn along my palms and legs as I start to crawl backward, only to remember there's nothing but open air and crashing waters behind me. For a split second I contemplate hurling myself over the edge, embracing the razor sharp rocks and angry waves below. Maybe I'd survive. Unlikely. But maybe.

As if hearing my morbid thoughts, Silas pauses, his body coiling like a cobra poised to strike. The black mask is back in place, its haunting green stitching distorted in the harsh light. I move—only an inch—but that's all it takes for him to spring forward.

Silas lunges. His fingers close around my throat, halting my escape as he hauls me upright. He towers over me, the scent of leather and spice clinging to him like a storm, and something low in my belly burns. Heat. Want. Terror.

His knee wedges between my thighs, pressing against my exposed core, sending the fire pumping through my veins into overdrive.

"This virgin cunt is mine, Evie."

My pulse flutters beneath his fingers. But not from fear. I think I must be cursed. Or maybe my soul is just tainted, because I *want* him—the devil himself. Every nerve in my body is alive, primed and ready for his condemning touch. Silas just murdered a man after forcing him to go down on me, but that malicious glint in his eyes... god help me, it's intoxicating.

"Mine to taste. Mine to finger and fuck and defile in anyway I please." His other hand ghosts across my breasts, pinching and twisting my nipples through the red fabric as his jeans grind against me. I bit my lip, trying to suppress the rush of sensation, but a whimper breaks free.

"You love when I'm like this," Silas purrs, torturing my other breast before tracing patterns down my stomach. "Isn't that right?"

"No." I shake my head, the movement small beneath the grip he keeps on my neck.

"Tsk," he pouts. "You can lie to the world all you want, my Evie, but the beautiful way you're rubbing your cunt all over me says otherwise."

My breathing hitches as I look down, shame zapping through me when I realize he's right. I've been grinding against his knee. Silas jerks my chin back up, forcing me to meet his gaze. All the green is nearly gone, replaced by a blackness so cold I almost flinch.

"If I forced you into the dirt and spread your thighs, stuffing your cunt with my cock, would you beg me to stop?" His palm cups my pussy, two fingers sliding through the slick mess between my thighs before thrusting inside me. "Or plead for more?"

I cry out at the intrusion, hating how my arousal fills the air between us. A sick part of me enjoys the violation. Silas does something to me. Forces me to experience and acknowledge and fucking *feel*—to be awake in an existence that has only ever existed in my dreams. He pushes me to admit truths that I've denied myself, too fearful of the eternal evil promised should I succumb to their appeal.

The concept of morality may be one I'm trying to outgrow, but it's like teasing out the thorns of a cactus. Some barbs are so deeply embedded in my skin that it feels like I have to slice away pieces of my flesh just to be rid of them.

But Silas…

He has me welcoming the stab, craving the sharp points and bleeding wounds, because for the first time, my heart is *feeling* rather than simply beating.

Blood heats my cheeks as I rock against his fingers, searching for the perfect friction to grant me the salvation I'm so desperate for. His hold tightens around my neck, restricting air. My vision swims, hands gripping his forearm, but I don't pull away. Don't try to stop him.

"I could hold you here, suspended between life and death forever if I wanted to." Silas drags his nose up the curve of my throat, licking away the tears staining my cheeks. "I could use your sweet pussy or tight hole, fill up each with my cum, then make you lick my cock clean. And you would love every moment of it."

I want to deny it, to tell him he's delusional, but my pussy clenches around his fingers. The haze of reality tilts as he continues his punishing pace, causing my vision to grow dark.

I'm floating in a delirious cloud of ecstasy. Thoughts, sounds, feelings—everything vanishing except Silas's palm grinding against my clit, pushing me to the edge.

Just as I start to fall, he withdraws.

I stumble forward, gasping for air, but the relief of breathing is nothing compared to the painful need twisting between my thighs.

"You don't get to come, Evie." Silas looks down at me, the blackness of his eyes matching the color of his soul. "Not when I can still smell another man on you."

Tears prick my eyes, humiliation spilling freely down my cheeks as I drop my head. I shouldn't even want this psychopath. This *murderer*. From the moment we met, Silas has been honest about being a deranged monster. I just didn't believe him.

Silas may have the body of a god—bronzed skin and inked muscle—but he's a beast. A demon sent to show me how beautiful the darkness can be. And like a willing sacrifice, I laid my body upon the alter, desperate to be claimed—only for him to decide I'm not worthy.

Strong arms scoop me up, setting me on the motorcycle with a softness so at odds with the rest of him. I allow him to adjust the leather jacket that smells like him, zipping it up before tucking me in close. The engine hums to life beneath me as a cool detachment settles over my soul.

"Your punishment is done, little fox," Silas says through our helmets, a gloved hand pressing me back against his chest as we start down the canyon. But as we turn onto the highway, with my thighs trembling and pussy aching with need, I know my sentence has only just begun.

20

SILAS

Evie thinks I don't know what she's been doing, but my little fox isn't as stealthy as she believes. I hear her stirring in the early hours each morning, and then tiptoeing past my room when she returns. As if every fiber of my being doesn't know when she's nearby. I feel everything she does, am aware of her every passing second. Her fluttering heartbeat, the delicious spikes of fear and shame mixed with her cunt's sweet arousal—all of it *mine*.

She was so beautiful coming apart on my bike. Evie may look like a chaste angel, but I see the dark, twisted parts of my little virgin begging to be used. To be fucked and filled so thoroughly with my cum that she'll never be able to erase the scent of me. She's all I think about. Even now, with the moon high and the demons inside me at their strongest, she's all I see.

Chest heaving, I step back, studying the angry slashes of color, thick globs of paint splitting the canvas. A skeleton crafted of dark greens and midnight blacks wraps bony fingers around sparks of light. Caging it. I switch brushes, turning to the palette of bronzed reds and fierce yellows, and let the paint guide me. Each layer adds to her image, uncovering her soul trapped in the arms of mine. But when it's done, she's not running away as expected—she's gazing up at me.

The brush falls from my fingers, staining the rug beneath my feet, but I'm already down the hall, turning up the stairs. Stars shine bright, casting soft shadows across the wooden landing. And then I'm there, pushing her door open.

Cotton sheets ruffle, her perfect fucking leg peeking out as her body twists. Her mind is whirling beneath those closed lashes, her breathing coming in short bursts. I wonder if she's dreaming of me. Because she's been haunting every corner of my mind since the moment she showed up.

Her big brown eyes and wine-colored hair are seared into the back of my mind. The way her skin blushes when she comes, those needy little sounds she makes when she's close—I want to feel her clenching around me as she bounces on my cock, see the moment she realizes I own her, body and soul. I shouldn't still be thinking of her—shouldn't be standing at the edge of her bed watching her sleep—but I can't seem to get her poison out of my veins.

Evie mutters something too soft to hear. I'm moving before I can think better of it, brushing back the hair along her cheek, streaking gold paint through red strands. There's something insidious about her. The enticing shadows she tries to keep locked away call out to me, pleading for release.

She hasn't snitched. I murdered that fucker right in front of her, and she still let me catch her. Let me stuff her pussy with my fingers as I gripped her throat, yielding control of her life to me. Evie loves when I take her choice away—not that she'll admit it.

But I can't give in. Irritation pricks the back of my neck, warning me away from my latest fixation. That night in the canyon with Mark almost cost me everything. It was sloppy, killing him before Noctis confirmed the information. Turns out he was telling the truth, but if he hadn't been, years of tracking my sister down would've been for nothing. I could've lost Morana forever.

Evie is a sickness. An infection I need to eradicate. And the quickest way to do that is by fucking her out of my system. I will fuck her—hard and fast and brutal like I do all my conquests. That's all Evie is. All she can be.

Gritting my teeth, I start to leave, but then the clouds shift and a stretch of moonlight falls across her porcelain skin. Shallow scratches streak the white planes of her palms and thighs, still healing from our little trip. I frown, hating how the beast inside me wants nothing more than to lick every one of her wounds clean.

I don't like seeing my things hurt—not unless I'm the one doing the hurting—but Evie surprised me. She fucking loved me watching her, being envied and eaten by that piece of shit on his knees before her. All while jealously rolled off me in waves. The fucker couldn't even eat pussy right. It's not normally my thing either, giving instead of taking, but licking Evie's sweet juices from my fingers had me craving another hit. High off one taste.

And here I am. Watching my sweet little virgin toss in her sleep, the spike of her arousal growing more potent. Peaked nipples strain against her white cotton top, and I let my gaze trail down her body, landing on a pair of matching white panties.

I should leave. I should leave. I should leave.

But another low whimper slips from her lips, and it's my fucking name she whispers—a sleep-induced hallucination as she rolls, kicking the rest of the sheets away.

Her knees fall open, and fuck me, but I climb onto the bed, accepting the offer of Evie's parted legs. Slickness coats her inner thighs, and I drag my nose up the center of her. Inhaling her sweetness, letting it fill my lungs, breathing life into my withering soul as she unconsciously rolls closer to my touch.

"What are you dreaming about?" I murmur against her thigh.

If I didn't know better, I'd think my little fox has been touching herself. A low chuckle escapes me, the warmth of my breath fanning over her core as I realize she hasn't come since I denied her. I glance up her body, imaging how beautiful her nipples would look bruised from my teeth before brushing my tongue against the flickering pulse at the junction of her thighs.

"Would you like to come, Evie?"

A low moan rumbles in her chest as she twists, grinding against my mouth. The scent of her hits me like a primal pheromone, taking hold of my judgment and leading me down the familiar path of sin. I hook a finger beneath her underwear, tugging the thin fabric out of the way. Her pussy is fucking perfect, glistening with want, even in sleep.

"Fuck," I murmur, needing to sink my proverbial fangs into her soft flesh To have my venom invading every molecule of her being until she is utterly and irrevocably changed.

The first sweep of my tongue drags a guttural moan from her parted lips. *Just a taste,* I think. I've lost too much control already, but I'm diving back in, half-crazed by the way her sleeping body responds before I can stop myself.

Her hips undulate against the lashing of my tongue as her small fingers thread through my hair, holding me in place as I work her clit. Her thighs clench around my head, already on the precipice like the good fucking girl she is. Unable to deny her a second time, my teeth graze her clit, a gasp falling from her lips as her body coils.

Then, I suck. Hard. Her back arches as she cries out, and I hold her there, palm on her stomach, face buried in her cunt until the last of the orgasm passes and I feel her body start to relax. Start to wake.

Doe eyes, heavy with sleep, blink down at me as the edges of her blissed-out mind try to focus, but I'm gone before she has the strength to lift her head.

I don't allow myself to turn back as I pad down the stairs and slip into my room. My hard cock strains, aching from the scent of her still smeared across my lips and face. I shove my sweats down and grip the base, stroking myself in brutal jerks as I lick the edges of my mouth, imagining her riding my face. Her perky breasts bouncing as she grinds her pussy against my tongue, using me for her pleasure.

It's not enough.

The physical urge is only a reflection of my internal needs. And release won't find me until I've satiated both. With a growl, I tug my sweats back up, the grey fabric tenting over my massive hard-on, before reaching for a fresh canvas.

My fingers graze the textured surface, still smelling like her, and I want to capture it—*her*. My brush flies, color and chaos clashing as I think of her sweet taste, her smart mouth, and those needy little moans she just made for me. She's struggling with her faith, still wearing that silver cross, but I like the look of my fingers wrapped around her throat more. Of her mouth parted, tongue poised, waiting and ready for me.

Paint flies, coating the easel, the rug, my chest—but I don't stop. The picture is demanding, consuming, insisting—just like Evie.

I don't want to think about how alive I've felt these past few weeks. How Evie's presence has transformed not just me, but the world. Colors are more vibrant, sounds crisper. Touch… god, when she touches me—it's almost enough to make me question what's beyond this realm. This reality. This life.

My cheeks are damp with tears I don't remember shedding. I'm not sure if it's anger, envy, or something more sinister that has my fingers trembling, the brush falling from my grasp as I step back from the riot of texture and color.

Because as I stare at the piece before me, inhaling the heady mixture of Evie's arousal and acrylic paint, I wonder, for the first time since that cursed night when my sister was stolen, if maybe there's something beyond vengeance worth living for.

No. No, no. I've sacrificed too much. Come too far to go back now. Swallowing, I coat the edge of my brush in black, intending to hide the exorcism of my soul staring back at me.

Just as I lift the tip, my phone lights up with an image of a teal sloth.

Noctis: We've found him.

21

EVIE

I'm avoiding Tempest again, but not for the reason she thinks. Silas and the rest of the Seven have been at the house for the last few weeks. Music blasts downstairs at all hours, with different types of takeout cartons appearing in the fridge the next morning. Tempest knocks on my door each night after her homework is finished, but I always decline joining. Because what the actual fuck?

I've been consumed with thoughts of Silas, forced to admit to myself that I loved every moment of what happened. The terror, the hazy suspension of reality as his grip tightened around my neck. My body craves him to the point that I even tried to make myself come. He's the only person who's touched me like that, which has to be why I'm reacting this way. Surely, if I can figure out how to make myself come properly, I can move on with my life, get back to hating him, and focus on finding a way to stay in college after the semester is over.

At the very least, I should be reporting him for murder. But then I remember Mark admitting to drugging my drink, and all thoughts of turning him in evaporate. After the cliff, I spent all night in the shower, scrubbing my body clean but also desperately trying to dull the throbbing need Silas left me with. My unskilled fingers rubbed and flicked, but anytime I started to get close, embarrassment would crash into me, stalling the orgasm.

I wasn't upset he killed Mark. Not at all. If I'm honest with myself, I liked it. Delighted in the way Silas let me use him first—flipped the situation around so I was in control—before putting a bullet in the rapist's skull.

Those are the types of thoughts I normally keep locked away, even from myself. I know how messed up it is, realize that forcing Mark to go down on me at gunpoint is also rape, but being that the guy talked openly about delivering women and children—and how well *I* would sell—I don't feel one ounce of remorse.

And god above, the dream I had last week… It felt so real, like Silas somehow heard every wicked fantasy I'd had and fulfilled them. *I really need to see a therapist.*

Just like every day this week, I banish the shameful thoughts and wake before the sun, donning a boring long skirt and loose top. My fingers reach for the silver cross on my nightstand, skimming over the sleek metal. I've worn it every day since seventh grade. Mother said it would protect me. Jonathan claimed that's how people would know I wasn't a whore. But both of those things were lies.

Withdrawing my hand, I reach for the brush instead. Nagging doubts swirl in my mind, the cross glaring at me from its untouched position. If I manage to eradicate everything they've forced on me—submission, obedience, quiet compliancy—will I even exist? If I dig myself out of the grave they tossed me into, will there still be a life waiting for me? Or is it too late? Because it feels like all that I once was—everything I was meant to be—was killed long ago.

I reach for a tie to braid my hair back but pause, staring at my reflection. Sleep clings to me, my hair frizzy from the swift untangling as I stand in front of the mirror. I'm exhausted, but the haunted vacancy in my eyes that's been subtly creeping in over the last ten years is gone. Confusion and a morbid sense of curiosity stare back at me in its place, and it sure as hell beats the numbness I've grown accustomed to. I blink, tugging up my sleeve to stare at the thin silver scars on the inside of my arm. They're healed. More importantly, I haven't thought about making new ones since I started college.

Not allowing myself to linger on the reasons behind that—or rather, *who*—I creep down the stairs and pad toward the door. Walking to campus and studying in the library at ungodly hours of the morning has worked out well for reaching top marks in my classes—and for avoiding a certain someone. Today is no exception.

Thick textbooks filled with biology basics weigh my backpack down, all annotated with various tabs and color-coded notes. I admit Physical Geology wasn't what I had in mind when I decided on Marine Biology, but learning about the formation and evolution of Earth and all of its habitats has allowed me to appreciate Oceanic and Atmospheric Sciences much more. A few days ago, class was canceled in favor of a trip to La Jolla Cove to study tide pools in real life.

This is my first semester, but it's already been the best of my life. I know it will only hurt me in the end, but I can't help dreaming of continuing classes. If I had time for the prerequisites, I'd love to take a geophysics course to better understand how seismology, gravity, and magnetic fields affect animal migration and habitat selection.

It's a dream I can't let go of. And maybe that's why I allow myself to indulge in the daydreams of being a different person—of having the option of crafting a life of my own. One where I'd have independence, a career, and a love strong enough to burn through all of my baggage.

My heart skips as the stairs *squeak* beneath my feet. I can't help but glance up. Each morning I creep past his room wondering if his door will be open this time. Anticipation wilts as I find Silas's door closed, hiding the paintings I know he's crafting. Logically, I've made up my mind to let him go, but my body doesn't agree. Not in the slightest.

My phone rings, the screen lighting up with a picture of my mother. I ignore it as I head out the door and make my way to campus. The notification of a voicemail shows up moments later. I read through the transcript, not having the energy to listen to the disappointment lacing my mother's voice. She does, indeed, let me know it looks poorly on the family not to show up for lunch again. She expects me to attend this weekend. Apparently, Jonathan is bringing a friend I'm supposed to impress.

With a groan, I swipe and hit delete before I can think too much about it.

My guilty conscience leads me into the heart of the university. If a higher power does exist, I hope not for the first time, that they can't hear the turmoil of my thoughts as I stare up at the towering cathedral. It's beautiful, with vaulted ceilings and stained-glass windows stretching six feet high. Churches are meant to be places of refugee, of peace and acceptance. I've only ever known them as structures of oppression and pain, symbols of a woman's need to bow while men speak.

What I wouldn't give to be able to go back and believe the lie a little longer. To feel safe—just for a little bit. Even knowing it was unfounded. Maybe that's the real reason people don't change their views. Realizing everything you've held dear, the entire way you've lived your life is a lie… it's decimating.

I step over the threshold and onto hallowed ground, crossing my fingers that vengeful angels won't smite me on sight

A few students sit in pews, heads bowed, but the rest of the space is abandoned. Making my way to one of the alcoves, I close my eyes over the half-dozen lit candles and tilt my head back. Waiting. Standing beneath the opulence of the church, begging for a sign of something greater than myself.

I search for that sacred feeling, the one that will confirm I'm not alone in the universe. I want to believe I'm connected to a power beyond myself. An entity that is everlasting and accepting of who I am—not just the good, but all the messy bits as well. I hold the thought in my mind, seeking, searching for a soul that would find me in any lifetime. Love me in every form.

Flickers of darkness swirl through my mind. I lean into the image, inhaling the scent of incense and smoking candles as it condenses into two black pools with flecks of the richest emerald. My stomach flips, my pulse spiking as knowing awareness stares back at me. And Silas's wicked grin comes into focus.

I grip the edge of the alter as my eyes fly open, darting around the dimly lit space. The thundering of my heartbeat thrashes in my ears as I fight to ignore the chill sweeping down my spine. The cathedral feels colder than it did moments ago. Quieter. Peeking from around the alcove, I see that I'm alone.

Ding.

I flinch at the crisp sound reverberating along the walls. Jamming my finger against the silence button, I grip my phone and head toward the doors.

Ding. Letting out a deep breath, I glance down and find a text from Tempest.

Tempest: Finished bio test early. Lunch?

My thumbs start typing an excuse, but I pause. I have one semester to live life the way I want to before it all comes crashing down. Clearly, avoiding Silas isn't working. Maybe the best thing I can do is act like he doesn't bother me. Like I don't think about his fingers knuckle-deep inside me every night when I'm lying in bed.

Nope. I'm just a normal, well-adjusted girl.

Me: Lunch sounds great. Where to?

22

EVIE

We meet at the small burrito hut down the road. The once-red umbrellas are bleached from years in the sun, as are the multicolored flags, but they have the best food. I crunch on chips and freshly made salsa as Tempest slips into the chair across from me with our baskets.

"Thank fuck you responded to me," she says, sliding my burrito across the weather-worn table before digging into hers. "I was beginning to think I'd have to sit in on one of your classes just to get you to talk to me."

"I haven't been *that* bad," I protest, taking a bite. The sweet potatoes blend perfectly with rich spices and pops of cilantro, and I make a mental note to bump this place up on my regular takeout list.

"Girl, you disappeared. We had a great night at the club, and then you vanished." Tempest takes a sip of water, lifting her shoulder in forced nonchalance. "Did anything happen after I left?"

"Nothing of importance."

"Really? Not even between you and my brother?"

"No," I say much too quickly.

She lifts a brow. "It's okay if it did, but I want to warn you. Silas isn't a nice guy. He's the best big brother I could ask for and one hell of a friend, but he destroys women."

Yes, he does, I think, as I stuff my face with another bite to avoid answering.

"All I'm saying is... be careful." I make a noncommittal noise that seems to satisfy her before Tempest continues. "Oh, and if you *do* lose your virginity to him, I don't want to know the details."

The sip of water I'd been taking gets caught in my throat. I sputter and cough as Tempest looks me over with a bemused grin.

"Noted," I mutter around the blush creeping down my throat. Desperate to shift the focus of our conversation, I jerk my chin toward the stack of books crowding her half of the table. "How are classes going? Pre-med, right?"

"O-chem is kicking my ass." She groans. "Of course Erik is top of the class and has insisted we study together."

She wrinkles her nose, but I swear I see subtle hints of excitement in her eyes before she rushes on.

"Biochem and pathophys are easy, but then it all goes to shit in organic chemistry. Like, hydrophobic proteins can't pass through a hydrophilic barrier without aid—that makes sense—but o-chem is straight up memorization. How am I supposed to remember all the fucking proteins and their structures? It's completely ridiculous."

I shrug around a laugh. "Tell me about it. The memorization is endless."

"What *is* your major?" Tempest asks around a bite of her burrito.

The food settles in my stomach like a heavy rock. "I planned on majoring in Marine Biology."

"Oh cool," Tempest says, eyes going wide. "Wait, what do you mean *planned*? Are your parents making you switch or something?"

"Or something," I mumble at first, not wanting to admit that I have less than three months of freedom. But Tempest waits patiently until I'm ready to continue. "My parents are pulling me from courses after this semester."

Tempest lowers her half-eaten burrito, mouth open. It takes her a moment to find the words, but when she speaks it's with forced calm. "Is this a religious thing? I know your family is strict, but there are more churches on campus than any other university."

I shake my head, the action feeling like a lie. "Maybe in part, but they'd never deny Jonathan a degree if he wanted one."

"Your brother?" Tempest asks, her mask of icy control so similar to Silas's.

"Half-brother. The golden boy himself." My phone flashes from inside my bag. I glance down at the notification to find Jonathan has written a paragraph describing what he considers proper attire for family functions. After skimming the first few lines, I delete the chain and flip my phone over. "In fact, that was him confirming I'll be at lunch tomorrow."

"That's totally fucked," Tempest snaps, her anger breaking through. "They can't stop you from attending school."

A strangled laugh escapes me as I lean back in my chair, delicious food forgotten. "Yes, they can. They're the ones paying for this. Even if I tried to do this on my own, they're claiming me as a dependent, meaning I won't qualify for loans. I've priced it out, and I *might* be able to cover tuition if I worked full-time, picked up a second job over school breaks, and managed to get a scholarship, but then I'd have no time for classes. Let alone studying. And that's not even touching books, housing, or food."

"Shit, Evie," Tempest says. "You can stay at our place for as long as you need. Free of charge. And for all the rest of it… we'll figure it out."

"I doubt Silas would be okay with that. Or the rest of the Seven," I add.

Tempest waves off my concern before wrapping up what's left of her food to take back with us. "They're not as scary as they seem."

"I thought you told me to stay away?" I counter, wanting to know if I'm completely losing it or if there really might be more to Silas. I keep replaying that night in the canyon over and over again when I'm alone in my room and the house is quiet. I remember the way Silas used Mark's face to get me off. The way he hunted me down and could've taken me there, on the edge of the cliff. He could've let me fall—but he didn't.

Silas murdered a man for touching me, but he still gave me a choice in it all. Sort of. Which is more than any man has done for me. Or maybe I'm so far past the point of knowing what healthy looks like that I've romanticized a monster.

"I told you to be careful as far as dating goes," Tempest says, hands up in surrender. "The Seven are harmless when it comes to me, but they each have their demons. Erik's pride eats at him, pushing him to be perfect. Noctis likes to have all the information before committing to something, meaning he'll be single forever. Mavros has anger problems. Adrian is like a dragon weighed down by its greed, while Bane is more gluttonous—he doesn't covet items, but he can never seem to find a healthy point of stopping. Dominic will fuck any consenting adult, and then there's…"

"Silas," I finish for her. "Let me guess. He can be a little possessive?"

"Envious of everyone for anything," Tempest says, her piercing gaze seeing far too much. "Though lately, all his attention has been focused on you. Even his paintings."

I shift, fidgeting with my shirt as we push to stand. Tempest must glean something in my silence, because she links her arm with mine as we start back toward the house with leftovers for later.

"Ever been to L.A.?"

23

SILAS

"Mavros has him contained," Erik says as Dominic, Adrian, and Bane follow us up the abandoned dirt path snaking around the mountain. The arrival of fall has chased away the worst of the summer weather, but the fierce rays of sun lick along the black leather of my jacket, making the hike to the point of contact uncomfortable, to say the least.

L.A. doesn't allow for a lot of privacy, especially not when high levels of discretion are needed. It took Noctis a fair amount of time to establish untraceable security, but the abandoned cages and forgotten trails of the old Los Angeles Zoo serve as the perfect place to hold a person captive.

Graffiti and a few well-done murals cover the more accessible structures. The ground around them is littered with beer cans and cigarette butts, but we keep walking until the old bear exhibit appears.

To any passerby, it would look like a padlocked fence between towering man-made rock walls. Barbed wire links the two walls, closing the space off with a "No Trespassing" sign.

It'd be easy to overlook, but the small number seven etched into the side just above the ground indicates it's ours.

Erik steps forward, entering a code into the hidden keypad before turning to the right as the concealed door swings open. A well-lit passage comes into view, sloping beneath the City of Angels, leading down to where the demons play.

"He's talking," Noctis says once we arrive in the control room. He's focused on the one-way glass in front of us with a grim set to his shoulders. "But it's not what we want to hear."

I follow his gaze, finding the red Xed-over eyes and stitched mouth of Marvos's mask. Blood drips down the man's face, his nose twisted at an unnatural angle. Purple blooms beneath his left eye, the skin nearly swollen shut, and although his hands are bound behind the chair he's strapped to, the rest of his body appears unharmed.

"He must've started spilling secrets right away," Dominic murmurs, echoing my thoughts as he grabs a seat and swings his attention toward me. The King of Lust isn't really into torture, unless it involves some kind of kink. He, Bane, and Adrian normally defer to the rest of us when it comes to getting our hands bloody. He leans back, playing with his mask stitched with dark blue thread as he grins. "So different than our newest initiate."

I remove an invisible piece of lint from my black shirt, pull out my own mask, and turn a steely gaze toward Dominic. "Evie hasn't snitched."

I'd been waiting for the impact of that night to catch up with her, ready to throw her over my shoulder and drag her back home with me when she decided to run. But my beautiful Evie is still here. She's been avoiding me. Tempest too. But I've watched her from the periphery as she attends classes, studies in the library, and then returns home. *To me.*

"Wonderful," Dominic says with a mischievous smirk. "Since she's passed your little test, I say you fuck her."

"Agreed. Someone should," Bane adds with a laugh, his strong nose and dark features making the expression look more like a snarl.

Lust and gluttony. I'm not surprised.

"I volunteer," Erik chimes in, knowing it'll piss me off. He flashes me a grin before tugging the black fabric over his face, leaving only the purple-stitched eyes and mouth staring back at me.

"Enough," I say. They're assholes, but the approval of my brothers soothes something in my chest. Not that I would've let any of them convince me not to fuck my little fox. Evie signed her freedom away that first night in the alley when she leaned into my grip rather than away. I'm sure I'll get tired of her eventually. Being the type of fucked up I am doesn't allow for things like love to form, but I plan on enjoying her for a time.

"No broken bones," Adrian mutters, directing our attention back to the one-way glass as he flips a gold coin embossed with a dragon between his fingers. He joins Bane leaning against the back wall. "Mavros having an off day?"

Noctis shakes his head. "Shane claims he's out of the business."

"Bullshit," Erik says from my left. "Shitbags who can traffic humans don't ever leave."

I nod my agreement, but the tick in Noctis's jaw has me pausing. "What is it?"

"Apparently, he's never helped kidnap or transport," Noctis says.

"You believe him?" I ask, but the lack of violence inflicted against Shane already tells me the answer. Noctis nods anyway. I tilt my head, studying our captive. "Maybe a group chat can get things going."

The five of us file in with our masks in place, leaving Noctis at the control center monitoring the cameras.

"Shit," Shane mutters before fixing his attention on me. With impressive composure, despite his broken nose and swollen eye, he speaks calmly. "I only ever delivered cars to a country club in the hills."

I lift a brow, taking the seat across from him. "Continue."

"There's nothing more to say. I was approached by some holier-than-god asshole who offered me ten grand per car. Normally, people like him want luxury cars with more speed than space, but he insisted on larger seating capacities."

"You accepted a partnership with someone you only just met?" I ask, letting the venom in my heart coat each syllable.

"For ten grand in cash, on the spot?" Shane counters. "Fuck yeah, I took the deal. He didn't say anything about women or children. I assumed it was some low-level car peddling—or at the most, drug smuggling."

"Then why stop?"

A flicker of apprehension shows before he drops my gaze. "I arrived at the spot early one day. He was there, talking to some other rich-as-shit guy about all the ways he'd like to fuck someone, but you know those types of guys. I didn't think anything of it until he started spouting shit about the second coming and how avenging angels were already among us, reaping souls for heaven and a bunch of other unhinged stuff."

Shane swallows, seemingly at a loss for words. I wait, the others following my lead by letting the silence stretch until he continues.

"He said stealing women was the Lord's work. Whores needed to be used until they begged for forgiveness. Only then would they be granted absolution."

Erik growls as Mavros flexes his fists, both looking ready to crack Shane's skull.

"If I would've known the type of people I was helping, I never would've taken the job. I swear."

Shane's voice grows shrill as Mavros stalks behind him, but there's truth ringing from him. He may be an idiot for not realizing sooner, but I don't think he willingly helped. I level Shane with a look, cocking my head like a hawk studying its prey before ripping it to shreds.

"I need information."

Shane nods, eyes still glued to Mavros and the blood smeared across his knuckles—the same shade of scarlet as the thread woven across his mask. "I'll do anything to help. I want these fuckers stopped too. He told the old guy that the city was ripe for purging, and he had three women drugged and ready for transport as soon as the car arrived. That's when I ran."

"You said drop-off was at a country club?"

"The Blue Lagoon." Shane nods.

"And your contact?"

"Said his name was Jonah."

My pulse kicks as I catch the scent of a trail growing stronger, and I know Noctis is already putting two and two together on the other side of the glass. He's probably running another scan through his systems as we speak, hoping the new information will push the search for any mention of Jonah. "Who was Jonah talking to when you overheard him?"

"I don't know." Shane shrugs. "Some old guy with the same blonde hair streaked with grey and a neon-white smile. All those rich fucks look the same."

"Did you catch a name?" I press.

"No. I didn't want him knowing I heard." Shane's eyes grow distant. "I took a few steps back and was loud with my approach the second time. Told him that was the last car I'd be delivering as I was leaving town. We packed the next day."

"We?"

His jaw clenches, and for the first time since I started questioning him, I see his forearms shift, checking the bindings on his wrists. I lift a brow, sitting back in my chair as Erik lets out a low whistle.

"Maybe that's the real reason you left," Erik muses, suspicion gleaming in his eyes. "Found a girl, didn't want to sell her, and decided to make her your very own sex doll."

"Fuck you," Shane snarls, baring his teeth. "The only regret I have is not killing the rich bastards before I got us—me and *my daughter*—away from that shit."

Adrian's low, morbid chuckle cuts through the lingering silence, mingling with the flip of his coin. "I bet you feel like an asshole now, Erik."

Erik shoots him a glare but doesn't say anything.

"Jonah was the only person you met with?" I ask, trying to keep focus before my brothers fuck this up.

Shane nods, then levels with me. "Look. I want to help, but I can't risk my daughter. Her mother checked out years ago, and I'm all she has. Things are tough in L.A., but I've landed a steady job and decent apartment. If I hear anything, I'll pass it along. But as soon as I save up enough money, we're getting out of here."

I hold his gaze a moment longer. "Okay."

Shane blinks. "Okay?"

"Anything you hear in relation to boosting cars or selling people, I want to know. Noctis will set up a point of contact for you." The metal legs of the chair I'm sitting in *screech* along the broken concrete slabs as I push back and stand. "Oh, and Shane?"

He swallows as I let coldness seep into my tone. "If I hear one whisper of you supporting this organization again—cars or otherwise—I'll drag a blade through your stomach and have your daughter watch as I strangle you with your entrails."

His face pales for all of a heartbeat before he grits his teeth and lifts his chin. "That won't happen."

I meet his declaration with a tilt of my head, letting the chilling effect of the mask sink in. "I hope you're right."

24

EVIE

Most of my ideas about Los Angeles are images of Hollywood I've seen through movies and music. The city itself is a lot busier and, oddly enough, less romanticized than I imagined. We weave through heavily crowded streets passing towering skyscrapers sprouting between older 1950's-style architecture. We pass single-family homes lined with palm trees and bustling back alleys before entering the part of the city dedicated to universities and small overpriced coffee shops. Tempest assures me rush hour traffic has died down and this normal, but it still takes us far too long to reach our intended destination.

"Here we are," Tempest breaths, arching her neck to peer up at the brown crisscrossing beams that formed a hollowed, artistic structure above the entrance. She takes off her sunglasses before turning her excited gaze my way. "Isn't it beautiful?"

I stare at building's façade, marveling at the way modern art mingles with intricate stone and brick designs from another time. "Yes," I reply, letting Tempest link her arm with mine and lead us through the doors.

"In the late 1800s, this was a fairground of sorts, and then it became a science center in the early 1900s," Tempest explains as we queue for tickets. "There've been a few expansions since, with the rose garden being my favorite, but we'll go through the body exhibit first."

I glance at the science center before us, following where she points. When Tempest first mentioned L.A., I assumed she wanted to go on a shopping trip or wear triangle bikinis on the beach, and eye-fuck volleyball players. But her biochemistry professor offered extra credit to anyone who attended the exhibit featuring real human bodies—skinned, with muscles exposed.

Turns out, it was just as unnerving as I thought it would be. The preserved remains were set up in various poses, most in athletic displays. There were dancers and football players, both of which Tempest found fascinating. Even I could appreciate the intricate network of muscles and tendons linking together, admire the power and ingenuity of the human body, but then there were other displays. Like the wall featuring a human stomach, liver, and other bits of the digestive system strung up. *Gross.*

Tempest typed notes furiously as we sat through a film about medical marvels before we ventured through other parts of the museum, including photo galleries featuring microscopic creatures in bright colors.

"Thank you," I say, accepting the iced coffee from beneath a large umbrella. Retreating to the shade in the garden, I pick a bench near the roses and fountain, waiting for Tempest to get her drink. My phone buzzes for the tenth time today, and I already know who it is. I silence it and toss it into my purse, ignoring the dozens of texts and handful of messages. There will be time to deal with all of that later, after Tempest and I finish up at the museum.

"That was actually fun," I say, sipping my coffee as Tempest sits. Taking a deep breath, I close my eyes, lifting my cheeks to the sun as the sounds of water trickling over stone soothes me.

"Told you." Tempest nudges my shoulder with a smirk before glancing at my purse. My phone's flashing again with another notification. "Everything all right?"

"Not really," I reply, surprising myself. Tempest doesn't push, though. She sits quietly, posture relaxed, coffee loosely held in her hand until I'm ready. A heavy weight settles across my shoulders as I drop her gaze, choosing instead to focus on the bright pink blossoms framing the base of the fountain. "I'm missing a family lunch today, and my brother's a little upset about it."

Tempest lifts a perfectly sculpted brow as the inside of my purse lights up again. I tug it open, finding the screen flashing with an incoming call. "Did you tell him we had plans?"

"Yep," I say around a long gulp, letting the sweet taste of caramel roll over my tongue. "But he's probably using my absence to convince my father I'm 'slipping into sin.'"

A sharp snort escapes from Tempest before she realizes I'm not being sarcastic. "Holy fuck, Evie. All that over one day out? What happens when you have midterms? Or if you just don't want to go?"

"Nothing good," I mutter, crossing then uncrossing my ankles. "At best, my family views college as a distraction. At worst, it's a place of 'brainwashing.' As a woman, I'm meant to do whatever my husband needs. College only promotes the idea that I could live independently."

"You *can*," she snaps. "You can be a whole, happy fucking person without ever getting married and ripping your body apart for babies. Jesus fucking Christ, I knew they were a little off after lunch the other day, but this is starting to sound unsafe."

I flinch as my stomach clenches, because Tempest is right. I don't feel safe at home—or rather, the place I've been forced to call home. I'm not sure what would happen if Jonathan found out about Silas and all the filthy things I've let him do to me, but I know it would be bad. Honestly, it *is* bad.

I hate the rhetoric my family pushes. That I'm somehow lacking because I was born with breasts. It's exhausting to feel like speaking, thinking—*fucking breathing*—is an inconvenience for the people around me. And then they take all of that guilt and self-loathing and weave it into a religion that tells me I'm going to hell if I even consider an existence outside of their abuse.

No. I won't go back into the asylum my family raised me in, but that doesn't mean I need to throw myself at the first man I meet either. Though, technically, Mark was the first guy I met—and he's dead, so… Silas could be a possibility, right?

Get it together, Evie, I think, groaning inwardly. I don't need a boyfriend—or whatever Silas is. *Was.* Tempest is my friend, my first and only. It's only been a few months, but I know I can trust her with anything.

"You're right," I finally say, picking at my fingers. I grin, thinking of Mother's face if she saw the state of my chipped nail polish. "The house I've been raised in isn't safe. I'm only just starting to realize all the ways, but going back at the end of the semester might just kill me."

"Then don't go." Tempest holds my gaze this time, her deep brown eyes searching mine. "I meant what I said about the financial stuff. There are scholarships too. And we're roomies now."

"Okay," I say, relief washing through me the moment I make the decision. "If you really mean that. But can you and Silas afford rent on your own? I'll pay you back every cent. I swear."

Tempest holds up a hand, her face going serious. "I'm not supposed to say anything, because the Seven like to keep things close to the chest, but money isn't a problem. Besides, I know something happened between you and Silas."

My pulse spikes as I try and fail to keep my breathing even. Tempest nods slowly, as if I've just confirmed something, and grips my hand with hers.

"Did you know Silas and I had an older sister?"

I pause, my cup half lifted as I catch the hitch in her voice. *Had* not *have*. Not sure what to say, I lower my coffee and shake my head.

"Our mother was a drug addict and prostitute. I don't think she knew who our father was. Or fathers, I guess." With a long sign, Tempest continues. "Now that I'm older, I know our mother probably had an even shittier childhood than we did, but I'll never forgive her for letting them take Morana. Or for what Silas had to do to stop her from selling me."

"Oh my god," I breathe as horrific understanding dawns. "Your own mother tried to traffick you?"

"I'm not sure how Silas stopped them." Tempest weaves her fingers through mine, looking like she needs the contact to stay grounded. Her eyes are unfocused, voice nearly inaudible. "One of them grabbed me. He said a pair of sisters would fetch a higher price."

Bile sears the back of my throat, but I clutch her hand, offering what little support I can.

"Silas was thrashing—hitting and screaming—but he was too small to take on grown men. The one I was struggling against hit me. I must've been knocked unconscious because the next thing I remember is waking up to a room covered in blood. It was everywhere. Great arcs of it across the walls, puddles on the floor, and the ceiling—I remember thinking a pipe had burst, but the droplets raining down around us were scarlet."

Tempest straightens, blinking her eyes back to the present. "Silas believes Morana is still alive. For the past seven years, he's been following leads, convinced he'll be able to rescue her."

"I'm so sorry," I whisper, hating how trivial the phrase sounds.

"I'm telling you this so you'll understand." Tempest lifts her chin, watching for my reaction. "The people my brother and the Seven get involved with aren't good. If they... dispose of a few of them, I'm not sorry about it."

I meet her gaze, refusing to look away. Because hadn't I thought the same thing when I watched Silas put a bullet in Mark's skull? He killed a man in front of me without so much as blinking, and then I let him hold me by the throat and finger fuck me. The death of a man like Mark—of someone who would use, exploit, and abuse other humans—is nothing to mourn. On the contrary, ridding the world of true evil like that should be celebrated.

"Mark said I'd do well if Silas was looking to sell," I say, proud of how even my voice is.

Tempest flexes her jaw but waits for me to speak—for me to decide if I'm in this with her and the Seven or not. She doesn't realize I made my choice long ago.

"I felt safer with your brother after watching him kill a man than I have my entire childhood."

The harsh intake of breath is Tempest's only reply, but the silence that settles over us feels less like a noose and more like a comforting embrace. Dipping her chin toward my purse that's flashing once more, Tempest says, "Whenever you want to talk about that, I'll be here. No judgment."

There are so many pieces to work out—finances, school, my parents, my disgrace of a half-brother. But for the first time in a long time, it doesn't feel like I'm drowning.

25

SILAS

It's taken me years to get to this point, but all the fighting, torture, and fucking anarchy will be worth it. Morana is so close. I can feel it. This time—this fucking time—will be the one to bring my sister home. Once I have her safe with Tempest and Evie, the real work begins.

I'm not sure when Evie worked her way into my inner circle. I don't fall in love—I'm not sure love is something I can feel—but Evie fucking blinks at me and I want to drop to my knees and worship her. She's an addiction, one that has slithered into my veins, twisted inside my mind, coiled itself around my heart. But I can't afford another weakness, not when Morana is this close.

It's just an itch, I tell myself—not really believing the lie, but needing to all the same. Once I ruin her for all others, I'll be able to walk away. Evie will move on, marry some reliable nine-to-five type, and everything will be as it's supposed to.

That gnawing twist in my stomach returns at the thought of another man with her, hearing her deepest desires, causing that beautiful fucking blush to stain her cheeks, but I shove the thoughts aside and quicken my pace through the gardens of my brother's estate.

My boots pound along the water-stones beside manicured roses and European-style reflection pools as I approach the house—villa.

I don't have a house in Los Angeles, but Bane does. Staying true to his Italian heritage, he's built a villa in the heart of Bel Air, complete with soaring archways, intricate stonework, and wrought-iron balconies overlooking manicured lawns. The whole thing feels overdone to me, but Bane looks right at home with his tanned skin, strong nose, and short dark hair savoring a Chianti on the main patio.

I catch a glimpse of blonde hair and spot Erik restocking the outside bar with bottles of liquor. His cocky smirk is dimmed when he thinks no one's watching, softening the asshole vibes he usually gives off. Being there that night—when my mother ran out of cash and coke and offered her youngest daughter up —I know he feels the clock ticking as much as I do.

Each of my brothers has played his part well. Mavros is always looking for a reason to break bones—that crazy fucker is addicted to pain—and I'm pretty sure Noctis has a sick obsession with catching the bad guy. I'd say it's a hero complex, but it's not the saving people part that gets him off. It's the puzzle.

I wonder about the other three sometimes. Dominic is ruled by his lust, but Adrian's greed and Bane's gluttony can be twisted into drive if the settings are right.

The linen button-down and navy blue pants Bane wears fit him perfectly. He was born in Sicily, and even though he refuses to talk about it, we all know he ran from something.

"What's with the frown?" Erik asks, sliding a glass of amber liquid my way. I step between Noctis and Bane, joining them at the bar as Erik pours himself a matching glass. "We're celebrating tonight. Even Noctis turned off the screens."

"Correction," he says, his dark jeans and black T-shirt a

contrast to Bane's sleek style. "My program is analyzing all available information and compiling a list of our top suspects are as we speak. It feels different this time." Noctis lets out a low breath, teal-blue eyes cutting to mine.

"Like pieces are clicking into place," Erik adds, draining his glass in one swig before reaching for the bottle to refill it.

"I too am ready for this to be over and the next phase of our lives to begin," Bane muses.

Lifting a brow, I share a silent look with Noctis and Erik. Bane is the picture of self-control. He craves order, sticks to a strict regimen of meal preps, working out, and scheduled fucking. If one piece of his perfectly planned day is derailed… well, Bane doesn't just lose that mask of control—he shatters all traces of civility. Moving on to an unexpected future would normally have him spiraling. I wonder what's changed.

"We haven't found Morana yet," I breathe, fingers flexing around the half-empty glass as my brothers turn to face me. I drain the rest of it before meeting their stares, wishing Mavros, Adrian, and Dominic would hurry the fuck up already.

"Where's Noctis?" Tempest's voice calls from inside the house. She passes through the open glass doors, strolling toward us, but my gaze slips past her and lands on Evie.

Her hair is pulled back in a high bun, and there's a splash of freckles over her pale cheeks, slightly pink after spending the day in the sun.

"Right here," Noctis says, offering my sister an easy grin as if we weren't just having a conversation that could change everything.

"Good." Tempest beams before jerking a thumb behind her. "Evie needs your help blocking an asshole who won't leave her alone."

26

EVIE

My brother chooses that moment to call. Again. The screen lights up as my phone vibrates, drawing eight pairs of eyes to me before I can silence it.

"See," Tempest says. Her sandals pad lightly over the river-stoned patio as she joins them at the bar. I follow, admiring the sprawling mansion that looks like it's been plucked from the western coast of Italy, while also trying to look unbothered by Jonathan's incessant calls. Truth is, I'm starting to get a little freaked out.

"That level of obsession is not healthy," Tempest adds, reaching across Erik for a bottle of tequila. Silas's eyes find mine, and I swear his pupils expand as his jaw flexes. "You really should block him, Evie."

"I-I can't," I stammer, following Dominic and Adrian toward the bar.

The Los Angeles skyline stretches before us, spotted with palm trees and glittering lights in the early evening. The sky still retains hints of purple and pink, softening the harshness of the city. It's beautiful, like all of Southern California, but I find myself wondering what it would be like to travel the world if I had the chance.

"You *can*," Tempest insists. She shakes a mixture of alcohol and ice, then pours me a fresh margarita with sugar on the rim instead of salt. "Noctis is unrivaled when it comes to technology. I'm sure there's a way he can fix it."

"He'll know," I reply, shaking my head. "And that will only make things worse."

"Who is this *he* you're speaking about?" Silas's voice comes out smooth as silk and dripping with venom.

I swallow under his scrutinizing gaze, my heart racing. With just his voice, I'm back on the cliff, my thighs slick with a need he won't fulfill. One that haunts me even now.

"Her brother," Tempest answers, oblivious to the blush staining my cheeks and the spark of fury igniting in Silas's dark green eyes. "Or half-brother, right?"

"Yes, but—"

"He's called her at least a dozen times today, all because she skipped one family lunch."

"Tempest," I warn, not wanting to get the Seven involved, but it's too late. Noctis cocks his head, assessing me after sharing a loaded look with Silas. I hate the way they can have entire conversations with a glance.

"I can set up a forwarding number," Noctis offers, holding out his hand. "It'll only take a moment."

"Perfect." Tempest beams, finishing up her own margarita with extra lime. "Your creepy brother won't know, and you won't be bombarded with his constant hounding."

"I don't know," I say, swallowing against the nerves twisting in my stomach. Because even if Noctis blocks Jonathan without his knowledge, my half-brother has ways of keeping me quiet—secrets and shame that have kept me complacent for years.

"You don't have to," Tempest murmurs, her brows softening.

"But you're also allowed to live, Evie. You're not alone anymore."

Daring a glance around, I'm surprised to find each of the Seven staring back at me, silently showing their agreement. Something twists in my chest as tears prick my eyes. I swallow them down before any can fall, but hold on to that foreign feeling of belonging.

For nineteen years, my family tried to erase everything that I am, cutting off parts of me until I fit the image of what they wanted. But here—surrounded by a group of people I've barely known for more than a few weeks, all of whom have done reprehensible things—I feel seen and heard and valued.

Unlocking my phone, I place it in Noctis's waiting hand. My mouth runs dry as I watch him give Silas a silent nod before disappearing inside. The others ease back into smooth conversation. All except Silas, whose gaze I can feel searing into my back. Bane—the Italian one with the orange hellhound tattooed along the inside of his wrist—makes a call inviting a "few friends" to join us.

"I'm not sure a house party is a good idea," Tempest protests, and I hate the way her worried glance cuts to me. "Maybe we should go out instead."

"Agreed," Silas rumbles.

The scent of leather and spice swirls from behind me as pricks of electricity tingle along the back of my neck. It's intoxicating being this close to him. Silas is the serpent in the grass, the dark voice whispering in my ear to give in to my wicked fantasies. And just like my namesake, I'm not strong enough to resist temptation.

"Worried you'll see other women throwing themselves at me and finally be forced to admit you're jealous?" Erik asks, looping an arm around Tempest and ignoring Silas.

"In your dreams." Tempest rolls her eyes and shoves him off.

"Not everyone wants exhibitionism or voyeurism, you savage brute."

"You've never minded before," Erik teases, his smile faltering only after Tempests whispers something too soft for me to catch. His eyes flick to me, and I force my smile to be a little brighter.

"I'm fine with it," I say with forced bravado, trying to recall what they're referring to. I'm pretty sure it's sex in public, which isn't something I'd want to be a part of. At least, I don't think I would, but this place is huge, and Tempest already showed me the guest suite we'll be using tonight. If anything gets out of hand, I'll go to bed early and enjoy what's sure to be a comfortable bed with silk sheets.

"No, you're not fine," Silas counters, trailing his fingers down my spine until his hand rests just above my ass. He's barely touching me, but I feel his possession as if I've been branded.

"They've already been invited." Bane grins, orange hellhound flexing over his forearm.

"Then uninvited them," Silas growls through clenched teeth. His shoulders tense, the gentle caresses across my lower back stilling as he stares down his brother.

"How about this," Adrian chimes in, holding up a golden coin etched with a dragon's head. "Heads we stay and party. Tails we'll go to a local sex club and leave you two lovebirds here."

Silas's nostrils flare, and Tempest looks like she's about to protest, but Adrian flips the coin before either of them speaks. He snatches it from the air as it begins its descent, pressing it to the back of his hand with his palm. He looks down, Bane and Erik leaning in to see which side is staring back.

"Tell me, Evie," Adrian says, grinning at me, "do virgins like watching things they've never done?"

27

SILAS

No fucking way am I going to let any of these assholes have sex with Evie watching. They might catch a glimpse of her perfect blush or wide doe eyes and think of her while they're thrusting into someone else. And then I'd have to kill them.

I nearly ripped Dominic's heart from his chest when he suggested we join them. As if I'd ever let another person hear those sexy-as-fuck little moans my Evie makes when she comes. No, when I finally sink my cock into her sweet pussy, it'll be just the two of us. When I can bleed and fuck and destroy her over and over again until her orgasms are painful, her body too weak to stand.

I don't mind the occasional orgy, but my brothers know I don't like to share things that matter to me. And somewhere along the way, Evie joined that list, climbing the ranks and perching her pretty little ass at the top.

"Easy, brother," Noctis says.

After threats of violence, Bane finally agreed to make the west wing of the house designated sex rooms, leaving Tempest, Evie, Erik, and me—along with any other guests who weren't in the mood to fuck—the bar areas. Noctis has only just returned, his teal eyes and tanned skin flushed with post-sex warmth. He follows my line of sight to where Evie is being preyed upon by some polished fuckwit.

"She's only talking," Noctis adds with a grin. "And I'd rather not have to call the cleaning crew tonight."

My fists clench as the dark-haired, smug-faced Italian leans forward, whispering something in her ear. Normally, I don't mind Lorenzo. He's one of Bane's more reasonable cousins. Methodical like Noctis with a sex drive to rival Dominic's. But that combination won't do when his charming gaze is locked on Evie. Absolutely fucking not.

Evie throws her head back in a laugh, nearly falling over in her half-drunken state. His hand catches her around the waist—*touching* my little fox. My blood boils as his palm lingers far too long, rage blurring my vision. I don't give a fuck if he's Bane's cousin. The pads of his fingers graze the white sequins of her dress, caressing the material warmed by her body, clinging to her curves, while he eye-fucks the shit out of her.

And I can't help but imagine plucking his eyes from his skull, severing each vein and tendon connecting his hands to his forearms until every part of him that's held my Evie is erased.

"Shit," Noctis mutters. "Don't kill him."

But I'm already moving. I don't bother to hide the coldness in my eyes as Lorenzo raises his head, his cocky-as-shit smile faltering for the first time tonight.

"Not trying to make me jealous again, are you, little fox?" I purr, wrapping my arm around her waist and tugging her to my side.

A small yelp escapes her, but she doesn't pull away.

"The last man who touched you ended up with a bullet in his skull—*after* I made him eat your sweet pussy."

Evie's cheeks flame a brilliant scarlet as she turns in my arms, glaring daggers. "What is *wrong* with you?"

Lorenzo lets out a low whistle, his lips quirking. The fact that he's smart enough to take a large step back is the only reason I allow him to continue breathing.

"I didn't realize you were taken."

"I'm not."

"She is," I say over her, the cold warning in my voice snapping Lorenzo's gaze back to mine. He stays a moment longer, seeing the depth of that statement. I don't have girlfriends. Or even fuck buddies. I've never been good at sharing my toys, but I haven't cared if someone used them after I was finished.

But Evie is different.

"It was nice to meet you, Evie." Lorenzo offers her a small smile.

Evie softens, murmuring some polite bullshit. My hand wraps around her front, pressing her body flush against mine as she stares after him. A small gasp escapes her as my semi-hard cock presses into her ass.

"Do you want me to fuck you in his blood?" I whisper against her ear, relishing the way her body trembles. "Bane wouldn't be happy—but let another man touch you again, and I'll cut off his hands and lay them at your feet while I fuck your mouth until you gag."

I'm prepared for my little fox to run. Or scream. She does neither. Of course she fucking doesn't. Evie's breath hitches, but her body leans into mine, seeking comfort from the very demon haunting her.

And that display of trust unravels something inside me.

"You'd like that, wouldn't you," I murmur around a low chuckle. I grip her throat, tilting her head back. "My twisted little fox."

She shakes her head but I can scent the spike of arousal, feel the quickening of her pulse beneath my fingers. My other hand glides down, slipping beneath the hem of her dress.

"Silas," she breathes. I'm sure she means it as a warning, but the sound of my name from her lips is pure seduction.

I spin us, backing her into the adjacent hallway and pinning her to the wall. She's done something with the makeup around her eyes, the darkness highlighting the flecks of gold in her heavily lidded gaze. Her wine-colored hair is unbound, fanning around her shoulders in soft curls. Her white sequin dress is modest for the most part, reaching the base of her throat, but it shows off the softness of her thighs—thighs that clench together beneath my hungry gaze.

"What have you done to me, little fox?" I whisper, tilting her head as I drag my nose along the length of her neck. "You've invaded my every thought. When you're gone, I crave you. And when you're here…"

A low growl scrapes my throat as I thrust my knee between her legs, forcing them apart. My fingers glide over the thin fabric of her panties, the slickness I find there making my already hard cock twitch.

"Fuck, Evie. When you're here, I want to bend you over and fuck you in front of everyone, so they know you're mine."

Pushing the fabric aside, I run my knuckles through her heat.

"The thought of this pussy being tasted by anyone else makes me *fucking insane*."

"Silas," Evie repeats, but her hips rock against my palm, seeking friction.

I stare down into her eyes, realizing she's far more sober than I thought—sober and staring at me like I might hold the key to her salvation. Evie looks at me like a bird who's been forced to fly in daylight, only to realize her wings are webbed and the night far more enticing.

Holding her gaze, I slip a finger inside her, feeling her needy cunt clamp down as I begin to pump. I cover her mouth with my other hand, muffling the wanton sounds spilling from her lips as her body writhes beneath me.

"Careful, little fox," I warn, adding a second finger. She gasps before my mouth closes over hers, claiming the moan as my tongue lashes against hers.

"If you keep grinding on my fingers, I'll have to show you what it means to be fucked so thoroughly you won't be able to breathe without feeling me."

Her pace increases, her body seeking a release I won't let her have. She must realize what I'm doing because she twists beneath me, breasts heaving and nipples straining against her dress, as her fingers find my cock through my pants. This angle lets me go deeper, her sweet pussy wrapping so tightly around my fingers as I memorize the way her pupils dilate.

"Anyone can see us. Tempest, your brothers..." Her inexperienced hands tease me just as effectively as I'm doing to her, working my length while her words tap into my never-ending pool of envy. Evie bites her bottom lip, a blush blooming across her cheeks as my grip on her waist tightens. "I want you, Silas."

"You don't know what you're asking for," I grit out, using every ounce of control I have. Because for some fucking reason, I don't want to hurt her. Sinful darkness rises inside me, the beast within purring as my little fox flicks the button of my jeans open.

"Don't I?" She rises, impaling herself on my fingers and snapping the last shred of sanity I've been clinging to.

I add a third finger, punishing her ruthlessly as my other hand pinches her nipple, kneading her breast. My mouth is over hers, swallowing her cries as her pussy clenches, the inside of her thighs soaked.

"I'm going to ruin you, little fox. Your cunt is going to bleed all over my cock, your body splitting as I fuck you hard. And you're going to enjoy every moment like the good little slut you are."

My other hand finds her neck again, tattooed fingers looking so beautiful around her throat. Her eyes go wide as my fingers curl, those sweet little moans pitching as I grind my palm against her clit. Then her body detonates, strangled cries escaping her parted lips. And I wonder how good she'll look down on her knees, cheeks flushed and coated in tears, mouth stuffed full of my cock.

Soon, but for now I savor the sight of her blissed out, riding the orgasm I won't let end. A deep laugh rumbles through my chest as I tease every last ounce of pleasure from her, holding her suspended between this life and the next.

By taking her will away, I'm returning her voice. Offering her the choice to give in to her natural desires, including finding power and fulfillment in sex. Evie hasn't been allowed to explore, but she's risen to every challenge life has thrown at her beautifully.

And I won't be satisfied until she's screaming beneath me.

"Get ready, little fox. We're just getting started."

28

EVIE

By the time the last waves of my orgasm ease and I can breathe again, Silas has me slung over his shoulder, ass in the air and halfway down the hall. Slickness coats my inner thighs, evidence of how much I enjoyed being treated like a whore. I've long since accepted there's something seriously wrong with me, but whatever it is, Silas doesn't seem to mind.

I've tried to suppress it—to deny myself every taboo thing that makes me feel alive—but when Silas touches me, it feels like I'm being reborn. He's the serpent in the garden, whispering that a bite of the forbidden fruit will be worth it. And god help me, but I think I might just be falling for him.

The phantom touches, the shame and belittlement, the urge to drag a blade across my skin just to feel something other than the anguish twisting inside me—it all fades in his presence. Maybe I'm being led into sin, lured down to hell with only eternal suffering waiting. Silas warned me. Told me he'd destroy me if I didn't run. But maybe I'm just as addicted to the lick of the devil's flames as I am to the burning of his gaze.

Silas kicks open a door, smacking my ass as I jump at the

sound. The room illuminates as he switches on the lights, my upside-down view revealing olive-green silk sheets and ornate finishes throughout the large space, with what appears to be an en suite off to the side. A laugh escapes me as Silas flips me over and sets me on the edge of the bed.

"You should've run, Evie." His emerald eyes meet mine, swirling with longing and something far too close to guilt as he unzips his pants. He takes his time, hooded eyes blazing into mine like he's waiting for me to stop him. To change my mind.

"I'm not going anywhere," I say, because I don't like the haunted glimpses peeking out from beneath the well-constructed mask Silas wears. He has secrets, a haunted past filled with unmentionable pain... But so do I. Maybe that's why I'm not afraid to yield to whatever this is. Why I choose to walk into the fire knowing it'll rise up and ignite our splintered hearts. We'll blacken and burn, but at least we'll do it together.

"I choose you, Silas." *Just as fiercely as you choose me.*

Licking my lips, I sit up, bringing my hands to his where he started to push down the waistband of his dark jeans. His body goes unnaturally still, and for a moment I swear a primal beast stares back at me—a glimpse of the murderous serpent I know.

"I'm not on birth control," I murmur, anticipation and fear mingling together. Any form of contraception wasn't tolerated by my family, but staring into Silas's eyes, at the thin ring of emerald nearly eclipsed by smoldering onyx, I finally understand the difference between obligation and choice.

"It's too late for second thoughts, little fox."

My pulse races as I ease his hands away from his pants. Silas allows it, but there's no sign he's changed plans for the night.

"Even if I don't fuck you now, you're mine, Evie. Tonight. Tomorrow. And every fucking day after."

My heart clenches, splitting open and bleeding for the man before me.

"I'm yours?" I ask as I drop to my knees because I want to hear him say it again.

"Yes," he hisses, voice lowering into a growl. "Mine."

Maintaining eye contact, I guide one of his hands to the back of my head as I work his jeans down over his knees. Silas lifts a brow, nostrils flaring when he realizes what I'm doing.

"I suppose that makes you mine," I say in a breathy whisper I barely recognize.

His cock springs free as he steps out of his clothes, and I fight the urge to do the one thing I swore I wouldn't: run away. There's no way that thing will fit inside of me—mouth or otherwise.

"That's right," Silas purrs, nodding down at me as his fingers tighten in my hair. He tugs gently, forcing my neck to arch as his thumb drags along my bottom lip.

"Are you going to let me fill this sweet mouth, little fox? Are you going to suck and gag on my cum as I fill you up?"

"Yes," I breathe, wrapping my fingers around his thick length.

This is more than him using me. More than me poised on my knees, lips parted, mouth open and waiting for him. It feels like I'm accepting communion for the first time—finally choosing my own god.

And it's not the one I was taught to fear.

His body tenses as I explore, trying to get my fingers to touch as I stroke him from root to tip. He lets out a sharp breath as I do it again, cock twitching as I coax a glistening bead from his slit. My tongue darts out, capturing the salty taste of him as Silas's fingers flex in my hair.

"Fuck," he groans, holding himself in place. Waiting for me.

That small show of restraint has me guiding his tip to my mouth. I lick up his length before swirling my tongue around his swollen head, along the flared edge as I lap and tease, letting intuition guide me.

The guttural sounds Silas makes under my ministrations have my heart pounding, my thighs squeezing. I gasp for air, trying to take him further, to swallow as much of him as I can, but I gag, my teeth scraping the sides of his cock.

"Easy," Silas hisses, and I swear he grows harder. "The pain heightens my pleasure, little fox, but you're not ready for that side of me. Not yet."

I start to pull away, embarrassment heating my cheeks, but his hand twists in my hair, pinning me in place as his other hand caresses my jaw.

"Relax your mouth," he murmurs, his thumb stroking the edge of my jaw. "But keep these lips wrapped around my cock."

Nostrils flaring, I do what he asks. He starts to move, gentle at first as he works himself deeper.

"Hollow your cheeks and use your tongue. That's it. Such a good girl, sucking my cock like the little slut you are."

I whimper at the praise, something warm blooming in my chest. I take him all the way, jaw aching as the lingering scent of soap and sex fills my senses. My fingers curl into the edge of the bed as I suck him deeper, trying to find a way to breathe as his grip on my hair tightens, as his hips begin to thrust.

I want to please him—to make him forget about anything, everything, outside of this room. Outside of me.

"Eyes on me," he commands, tugging roughly to arch my neck further. "I want you to know who's fucking this pretty face."

I moan as he unleashes himself, thrusting between my lips. Tears spill down my cheeks, mingling with spit and drool.

"You cry so beautifully, Evie."

Silas thrusts deeper, forcing me to open wider as I gasp for air through my nose. I should feel sick, degraded—but the twitch of his cock as I suck, the tightening of his stomach as his gaze turns black—it fills me with a power I've never known.

"I'm the only one who gets to see you like this." Thrust.

"Who gets to see you on your knees." Thrust. "Being treated like the fuck doll you are."

My nipples strain against my dress, breasts heaving as my pussy clenches.

"I own you," Silas pants, his pace growing erratic.

My jaw is aching, but his words burst through the broken parts of my soul, soothing a sting I've held for years. Because in this moment, being owned feels a lot like being loved.

"Look at me, baby."

I blink through the tears, fluttering my eyes open. Silas caresses my cheek, tenderness clashing with the ruthless way he fucks my mouth. And then the truce cracks, and something shifts between us.

"Fuck," he groans, slamming into the back of my throat as his balls tighten. He holds me there, gagging around his length as spurts of cum fill my waiting mouth. I swallow reflexively, choking and drinking and sucking until he drags me off him.

I stare up at him, chest heaving, and realize he's breathing just as ragged as me. He swipes a thumb along my chin, gathering what's spilled before holding it in front of me.

"Swallow all of me, little fox. Every drop."

I close my lips over the pad of his finger, swirling my tongue until it's clean, feeling closer to heaven in this moment than I ever did in church.

Maybe this is what religion is supposed to feel like.

Maybe worshiping him—worshipping *us*—this magical connection weaving around our souls, is what God wanted us to know. To rejoice in. To feel. And know we're alive.

His finger pulls free with an audible *pop*, the salty sweetness of him coating my tongue.

"Good girl."

29

SILAS

The fresh scent of soap and the aroma of bleach fills my helmet as I speed down the freeway. My brothers follow close behind, the seven of us leaving the old zoo and messy remains of our latest victim to the cleaners. I much prefer the desert to the city. It's more secure, as Noctis keeps mentioning, but with the number of leads we've been burning through, L.A. will have to do.

"Another dead end," Mavros growls into our connected helmets.

"Literally," Erik chimes in, and I can hear the smirk in his voice. Crazy bastard. In his defense, all of the men we've questioned—and then disposed of—have been guilty of associating with the southern circuit. As far as I'm concerned, we're just weeding out the garden before setting it on fire.

"I'll run the search again," Noctis grumbles, weaving around a pickup truck to pull ahead.

"Aww, don't be like that," Erik mock-whines. "We all make mistakes."

Noctis strings together a colorful slew of curses before switching off his mic, leaving the rest of us chuckling. In all seriousness though, I'm fucking gutted we're back to square one.

"Dominic, Bane, Adrian—make sure he makes it home safe." My brothers acknowledge the request before their motorcycles chase after Noctis, leaving Mavros, Erik, and me.

Part of me wants to join them. It's been a week since Evie got her IUD placed, two since I almost spread her thighs and fucked her in that little white dress at Bane's place. *Craving* doesn't even begin to describe what I feel. Obsession. Addiction. Driven to the point of fucking insanity. I'm lost—strung out and bleeding with only one cure in sight.

My grip tightens on the handlebars as I remember the way her tongue ran along the underside of my cock. Tentative at first, then curious. My little fox might be new to the darker side, but she thrives in the shadows.

I set up the appointment at the campus clinic for the next day, assuming she'd come back with brochures on safe sex and a paper bag full of condoms. But Evie showed up at the house green in the face with sweat beaded across her brow.

Apparently, the doctor insisted on placing the IUD that day, saying something about "the consequences of her actions" and how an IUD was "less painful than childbirth." As if he had any fucking clue.

After carrying her upstairs, tucking her into bed, and demanding a shit-ton of pain-killers, I had Noctis run a full profile on the doctor in question. Turns out, he's a regular at the church Evie's family attends. I had him begging for his god in seconds and granted him the mercy of meeting Him shortly after. He's finding out now whether his god is more forgiving than I am.

"Are we following?" Erik asks, pulling up alongside me.

"Not yet." I switch off comms with the others, leaving just Erik, Mavros, and myself. The Seven's locations always remain open. It's a safety thing Noctis insists on, but I've got a hunch I need to follow before returning home.

We've interrogated six suspects in the last two weeks, none of whom knew where Morana might be. Despite our failure, my gut says we're getting closer. Shane might be lying, but after confirming his story about his daughter and absent ex, I believe the bastard didn't know the depth of the shit he was mixed up in. And then there's Mark. That poor fuck had no reason to lie. And they both named Jonah. Shane knew him as a drop point, and Mark claimed he took over operations.

Noctis searched the Blue Lagoon thoroughly with nothing to show for it, which isn't unusual if it's just an exchange point, but…

"Are you two up for a detour?"

"Anytime, boss," Erik says. "There's a new taco place just before Del Mar I've been dying to try."

"No," I cut in before his stomach derails the entire day. "A work trip."

There's a beat of silence before Mavros speaks. "You got an itch?"

"Something like that," I answer, splitting lanes between two cars and picking up speed. They follow me, the three of us sliding into the flow of traffic, pushing the boundaries of the speed limit.

"No word from Shane?" I ask.

"No," Erik confirms. "I touched base with him this morning. He's keeping his head down. Still swears the only person he met with was some asshole named Jonah."

"Only at the golf course?" I press.

"Pretty sure," Erik says slowly, like he's digging for the memory. "Want me to call him?"

I almost say yes, but we're an hour outside of L.A. and only twenty minutes from the golf course. "If this is another dead end, we'll follow up tomorrow."

"Noctis won't like us doubting his intel," Mavors rumbles, but there's amusement in his tone.

"Which is exactly why we're doing this now."

Sirens blare to life a few cars behind us. Instinctively, we drop speed and change lanes before they catch up. My speedometer reads three over the limit, not enough to draw attention, but my shoulders still tense as they get closer.

"Fuck," Mavros growls as the cops shift into the center lane behind us. "Noctis would've had a scanner running."

True, I think, signaling to the slow lane and hoping they'll pass.

They don't.

"Are you fucking serious right now?" Erik snaps as the blue and red lights flash behind us.

I flip comms back on, hoping Noctis and the others are still in range.

"I'll go over everything tonight, Silas," Noctis grits out. "I'm almost back—"

"We'll deal with that later," I interrupt, watching as the cops close in. "Right now, we've got a problem."

30

SILAS

A beat of silence rings from the other end before Noctis is all business.

"Where?" he asks. I hear the hum of his engine dull into a low thrum as he pulls over.

"Fifteen minutes outside of the Blue Lagoon on Highway Five," I say, glancing in my mirrors as the officers exit their cars. "Two cop cars, lights on. Hands on their guns."

"Cause?" Noctis asks.

"Officially? Probably speeding." I rush the words, already knowing we're not getting off with a ticket. "Unofficially, they look ready to shoot."

"Comply," Noctis barks.

"Like hell we will," Erik growls.

"They want a reason to kill you," Noctis insists. "Our interviews have been clean. All tracks covered. They can't hold you on anything unless you give them cause."

"Thank fuck," I breathe, my mind flashing to the gore we just left at the old zoo.

"Keep the mic on as long as possible." Noctis's voice takes on a slight echo, and I can hear the faint tapping of fingers on a screen. "I'm sending locals to distract and occupy the precinct. Then we're coming to get you."

"Good afternoon, officers," I say, keeping my hands on the handlebars. "What can we do for you?"

"Put your hands where I can see them," spits the shorter, stockier man with his palm hovering over the open holster at his waist.

"Can't get more exposed than this," I say. I hear Noctis curse, but I keep my breathing steady as I wiggle my gloved fingers. "Can you tell me what we're being stopped for?"

"Turn the motorcycles off," says the taller one with a buzz cut.

"They have to tell you why they pulled you over," Noctis chimes in.

"Why are we being detained?" Erik asks through clenched teeth.

The shorter one wrinkles his nose as he looks Erik over. "I gave you a command. Put your hands in the air and step away from your vehicle."

"Jesus fucking Christ," Noctis snaps. "These two idiots have no fucking clue about proper procedure. I'll be able to get you out, but you have to be alive long enough for me to do it."

As badly as I want to rage, I swallow my pride—something Erik is struggling to do—turn off my bike, and step to the side. The moment I'm clear, the tall fucker tackles me, slamming his elbow into the back of my neck. My helmet's the only thing keeping my face from being smashed as he yanks my arms behind my back.

The cold kiss of metal clamps around my wrists, and my fists flex.

"Motherfucker!" Erik yells.

I catch a glimpse of him on the ground, helmet off and visor smashed. He throws his head back, connecting with the officer's face. Blood streams from the guy's nose as Erik scrambles to his hands and knees—until the barrel of a gun presses into the back of his head.

"I should shoot you right now," the officer says, sending pricks of fury burning along my spine. Because I know that sound. I've felt that cold detachment that settles in before a kill. The difference is, I end monsters who prey on the innocent, while this fucker gets off on the power trip.

"Erik," I warn, needing him to get a grip. "Tempest will kill me if you don't come home."

"Got yourself a girlfriend?" the officer sneers, pressing the gun harder into Erik's skull.

Red clouds my vision as I'm hoisted up and shoved against the cop car.

"Say the word, Silas." Mavros is still seated on his bike, fingers flexing like it's taking everything in him not to snap. This is a fight, after all. And there's nothing Mavros enjoys more than letting wrath take the reins.

"No!" Noctis shouts through the mic. "I need you fuckers to live. Do you hear me? We're forty-five minutes out."

I size up the asshole holding Erik at gunpoint, hiding behind a costume of justice. People like him take one look at my brothers—the tattoos, the piercings, their skin tones—and think we're worthless because we don't look like them. We have accents and the ability to comprehend more than one fucking language, and instead of embracing our differences to uplift society, pieces of shit like them say we're the problem. All to distract from their own self-loathing.

They promote hatred because they can't stand their pathetic existence. So, they lie to themselves. They scream and slander, categorizing human beings into subclasses to fan the flames of fear—all to justify the disease inside of them.

The epitome of weakness.

The self-righteous cop kicks Erik to the ground, brandishing his weapon because he knows he'd be dead in seconds without it. My fingers are tingling from the handcuffs, and I bite my tongue hard enough to taste blood as Mavros steps forward.

"No killing," I say, nodding toward the officer as the red bear on Mavros's helmet gleams.

He disarms the cop over Erik, dismantling the gun in seconds and tossing the pieces into the heavy brush beside the freeway. The tall one reaches for his weapon, but I'm faster—kicking the gun across four lanes of speeding traffic.

The stocky officer abandons Erik and launches himself at Mavros, wailing on him. My brother just stands there, absorbing blows to his stomach and ribs—and laughs, an off-kilter unnerving sound that rings through the chaos.

"Can you open the door for me?" I ask, tilting my chin toward the back of the cruiser, drawing the partner's attention before we really do get killed.

The tall one stands there stunned for a moment, chest heaving.

Erik pushes up, lips pressed into a hard line and holds his wrists out. "Make it quick."

The officer swallows, finally snapping out of it, and pulls out a second pair of cuffs.

"You have the right to remain silent—"

"What are we being arrested for?" Erik cuts in as the metal clicks around his wrists.

The officer glances at his partner, who's still beating a laughing Mavros.

"You're under arrest for the suspected murder of Mark Rothchild."

31

EVIE

"My mind feels like mush," Tempest grumbles, slamming her laptop shut. We're sitting on the couch in the front sitting room beneath the wide window. Sheer curtains block most of the night from view, but the air feels heavy somehow. "If I do one more practice test, I think all the information is going to melt right out of my brain."

"Want to talk things through with me?" I ask, closing my own screen. "I know going over the processes sometimes helps you more than quizzes, and I've been staring at the same paragraph of my essay for the past fifteen minutes."

"Are you sure you don't mind? I'm going over sugar structures."

"I love sugar." I grin, taking her offered computer and flipping the screen open. I blink, finding a series of H's and OH's stacked around vertical lines and connected across it with perpendicular lines. "Uhhhh…"

"Read the name at the bottom, and I'll describe the structure."

"D-Ribose," I murmur, squinting at the small label.

"Thumbs up," Tempest says, raising her hand. "Double-bonded oxygen on top, all OH's on the right."

"D-Mannose," I call next, not understanding what she's saying.

"Pew-pew," she says, mimicking a gun with her pointer and middle finer. "First two have the OH's on the left, and the last two on the right."

"Yes," I answer, starting to catch on. "D-Glucose."

She holds up her middle finger with a grin just as the back door flies open. Noctis rushes in, shoving his helmet off as the others file in behind him. My brows furrow as I scan the group for the emerald serpent, but come up empty.

"Silas, Mavros, and Erik have been arrested," Noctis says, his voice lethally quiet.

I blink, my gaze sweeping the room as my mind tries to process his words. Teal sloth for Noctis. Orange hellhound for Bane. Gold dragon for Adrian. Navy blue devil goat for Dominic. My pulse picks up as I look again, hoping I missed something.

"How?" Tempest whispers.

"Her," Noctic snarls.

My brow furrows at his pointed finger, not comprehending why it's aimed at me. I glance at Tempest, hoping for clarity, only to find confusion mirrored in her eyes.

"What are you talking about, Noctis?" Tempest snaps, slapping his hand away and pinning the others with a glare as she pushes to her feet. I rise too, having her back as a gnawing sense of dread coils in the pit of my stomach.

"I've gone through everything in the last hour," Noctis mutters, shaking his head as he begins to pace. "The cleaners were there within minutes, and nobody else knew the location."

"I don't understand," I say.

"Mark," Adrian answers, pulling out his gold coin and giving it a flip. It whirls, spinning end over head until he snatches it from the air and slaps it against the back of his palm. He cocks his head, studying the result before lifting golden eyes to mine. "You're the only person outside of us who knew about Mark's death—specifically, the location of his justified end."

My throat goes dry as understanding finally dawns. "You think I gave Silas up to the police?"

"Are you saying you didn't?" Bane asks, and for the first time I see the ruthless glint of his Italian lineage.

"Of course she fucking didn't," Tempest snaps. "She's half in love with the idiot."

Blood rushes to my cheeks as my heart flutters. God above, am I in love with Silas? No. He's dangerous. Devious. Completely unhinged. I couldn't possibly—

"Really?" Dominic asks with a smirk, his deep voice smooth and full of intrigue.

"There's no one else, Tempest," Noctis insists. "The cleaners are loyal to a fault, and even if they weren't, I've got too much shit on them to risk defection. Next thing I know, Silas is calling me saying there are two cops taking them in."

"You weren't with him?" Tempest bites.

"I needed to get back." Noctis lifts his chin. "Erik and Mavros stayed."

"A lot of fucking good that did," Adrian adds, pocketing his coin. "We heard Erik running his mouth and Mavros cackling while getting the shit kicked out of him."

"Crazy bastard," Bane mutters with a shake of his head.

"Cops are crawling all over the canyon," Noctis says, fixing me with a dark stare. "And bail is set at three times the norm. If you didn't rat us out, then you told someone what happened."

Something about the ringing silence and loathing in Noctis's eyes finally shatters the last remnants of disbelief. I stiffen, clenching my fists as I straighten and meet each of their gazes.

"I didn't breathe a word of what happened. To anyone," I add before Noctis can accuse me again. He grits his teeth, but

Tempest loops her arm through mine, daring him to challenge me.

"I believe her," Adrian says, drawing Noctis's attention.

"She does seem to be telling the truth," Bane muses, his gaze sharp as it seems to pry into every corner of my mind. "Dominic?"

"The two of them have insane chemistry," Dominic says, titling his head as he purses his lips. "And I don't think they've fucked yet, so I believe her."

"Jesus fucking Christ," Tempest mutters. "Now that you lot have pulled your heads out of your asses, can we focus on the problem at hand? How the hell are we going to save Erik, Mavros, and my brother?"

My heart thunders in my ears as I watch each of them dip their head. My palms start to sweat as the silence stretches, making it clear there are no easy answers here. No quick fixes that can put everything back together.

"Even if I post bail," Noctis says finally, his shoulders slumping, "they don't have alibis. The arresting officers who took them in broke half a dozen laws, and I know for a fact the scene's been wiped clean, but they're still being held. The judge already signed off on a transfer downtown tomorrow morning."

His eyes find mine again, still looking like a shark stuck on a blood trail. I don't flinch, letting him see the storm of anguish swirling inside of me. Tempest squeezes my hand, loaning me her strength as I roll back my shoulders.

"I have a plan."

32

EVIE

Tempest wastes no time driving us to the precinct, despite the late hour. The hum of motorcycle engines trails close behind as we pull into the nearly vacant lot. A brick building stretches before us, framed by swaying palm trees. A gentle, foreboding breeze sends a chill down my spine as I step out of the car and into the night.

Silence descends when Noctis, Bane, Adrian, and Dominic join us at the concrete stairs, all of us staring up at the looming windows veiled by closed blinds.

"Are you sure about this?" Tempest asks, but we both know there's no other option.

Without answering, I pad up the cracked steps and enter. Flickering fluorescent lights buzz overhead as I pass through the monotoned lobby toward the front desk, where two men are talking. A large screen with a rotating camera feed hangs on the wall behind them. I allow myself a moment to search, but find no trace of my demon among the holding cells.

The first man to look up is a middle-aged officer with a permanent sneer and a bald spot poorly concealed by a greasy combover. He nods along as the elderly man in front of him finishes speaking. The man's tailored black slacks and polished shoes spark a flicker of unease, tugging at something in the back of my mind.

"Father Michael?" I gasp, stomach twisting as recognition slams into me.

His sharp eyes snap to mine, shrewd and calculating. I wring my fingers as he rises, peering down at me. His once-dark hair has faded to grey around the temples, and his usual black jacket is replaced with a light blue polo, nearly the same shade as his eyes. A permanent orangey tan stains his skin, and there, embroidered on his left breast pocket, is the emblem of my family's church: a pair of hands raised in supplication toward a rising sun.

"What are you doing here?" I ask, more to break the staring contest than anything else.

"I could ask you the same, Evie." One bushy brow lifts just as the front door opens behind me, the soft tread of boots echoing across the tile. "It's a shame I missed you at lunch this past weekend. My son recently returned from his travels and was promised a meeting with a good, upstanding woman. Jonathan assured me you would be there."

Heat floods my cheeks as Father Michael's gaze drifts past me, nostrils flaring. I don't need to turn around to know what he's looking at. Behind me are four of the deadliest men in the city, clad in motorcycle gear and covered in tattoos. The epitome of everything Father Michael has spent the last nineteen years warning me against.

"Jonathan came to me for guidance," he continues, voice rising so the others can hear, his condemning gaze boring into mine. "He confided in me about your troubled past and is worried you're being led astray once more."

Shame pulses through my veins, each pump of my heart pushing more of the potent drug through my system. Because judging by the way Father Michael's gaze dips to my chest and lingers, trailing down my body with slow appraisal, I already know my pervert half-brother supplied proof of my "troubled past."

"There there, child," Father Michael coos, a cold smile twisting his face as tears sting my eyes. "Come with me. I'll return you to your father's keeping and then Jonathan and I will purge whatever sin you've indulged in."

"Get fucked, old man," Tempest seethes, stepping beside me.

"Watch your mouth," the officer snaps, pushing to his feet.

My gaze darts between Father Michael and the police officer, realizing just how weird it is to find a member of the church here. In a police precinct. Late at night.

I suck in a deep breath, not wanting to believe the obvious, but needing to speak the words aloud.

"Did Jonathan put you up to this?"

Father Michael's lips press into a thin line as he lifts his chin. The look alone is all the confirmation I need. A door to the back office opens, and three more police officers emerge, looking ready to brawl at the slightest provocation, but I don't shift my attention.

"He did, didn't he?" A harsh laugh scrapes my throat before cutting off. "It was Jonathan who told you to arrest Silas, Erik, and Mavros. Wasn't it?"

The last sentence is all fury, and I relish the way Father Michael recoils.

"Those filthy heathens deserve to be punished, just like them," he spits, lifting a bony finger past my shoulder. He tsks. "And as much as it pains me to say it, you too, Evie. You've strayed from heaven's light and plunged into darkness. What will your father say when he sees what you've become?"

"You can't keep them in prison," I say, chest heaving. And despite knowing Silas *did* kill Mark, the words don't feel like a lie when I say, "They didn't do anything wrong."

"Actually, we can," says the officer with the bad combover. "They don't have alibis, and the victim is still missing."

"That's circumstantial evidence at best," Noctis states, his words clipped but controlled.

"We have a witness who claims the victim and one of the suspects were involved with the same woman," another officer adds. "We believe it may have been a lover's quarrel."

The blood drains from my face. They're talking about me. Me and Silas—but also me and Mark.

Anyone could've seen us at the nightclub that first night. Dozens of people could've watched me leave with Mark, then seen him turn up the next day with a black eye. And me grinding on Silas.

As if called by thought, my gaze lifts to the camera monitors. One of the previously empty cells now holds three men. One of them cocks his head, almost like he can sense me watching. He stands, dark hair and thick lashes coming into view as he stares straight into the lens. Silas.

"Don't blame yourself, Evie," the first officer says, his tone growing more patronizing as he looks me over. Nausea threatens to upend my stomach as he finally drags his eyes away from my body and gestures for me to go with Father Michael. "These devils could bewitch anyone, but I sometimes join Jonathan when he's out saving lost souls. We'll set you right. Tell your father I said hello when you get home."

Father Michael extends his hand, expecting me to take it. I could. I could let him to take me back and accept whatever horrible punishment Jonathan comes up with, falling back in line with the future they've written for me. That's what I'm expected to do. And in some ways, it would be easier.

I've been raised in this life. Told time and time again that being a wife, serving my husband, and becoming a mother was the path to find meaning.

It's hard to recognize the grave when you're already buried in it.

But somewhere along the way, I started digging myself out. Silas, Tempest, the Seven—they've helped me through the last of it, lifting me above the rot clinging to my body, the lies weighing on my soul. But it's always been up to me to continue to fight. To choose to live.

"They were with me all night," I say, ignoring Father Michael and focusing on the officer. I'm proud of the steeled tone to my words, even if I'm trembling inside.

"Don't do this." Father Michael shakes his head. "Your father will have no choice but to punish you."

The combover is a lost cause, so I turn to the three officers who don't seem to know who I am and lift my chin.

"Silas, Erik, and Mavros are innocent. And I can prove it."

33

SILAS

"How do the police know about Mark?" Erik asks. His head is cradled between his hands, elbows resting on his knees.

We were stuck in some shitty hole-in-the-wall cell with no camera for hours. I kept expecting some fucker to show up and beat the shit out of us, but maybe Noctis is making progress. We've now been transferred to a holding cell with an overhead panel light and a camera with a small, blinking red dot. Practically a five-star hotel.

It's been years since I've been locked up, since they've had anything solid enough to land an inquiry. I'm curious what they even think we've done. We've been here for hours and no one's asked a single question. Almost like the cops picked us up as a favor.

Considering how the arrest went down and Noctis's legal prowess, I expected to be home within the hour, preferably with Evie's thighs wrapped around my face. But we're still here. That, coupled with the fact that I was denied a phone call, is a problem.

"This isn't a typical arrest," Mavros says, echoing my

thoughts. "Those involved in the southern circuit must be onto us. We did take out six of their men in the last two weeks."

I grunt my agreement, combing through all the pieces in my mind. "Evie is the only person outside of us who knew about Mark," Erik says, trying to sound casual, but the implication pricks nonetheless.

"She wouldn't betray me," I snap, not bothering to hide my irritation.

"We're closer than we've ever been to finding Morana and shutting the ring down," Mavros grunts, heedless of the warning look I shoot him. "Evie could've been a plant all along."

"Enough," I hiss. "Evie may have been leashed by her self-entitled family in the beginning, but she's different. Kinder. Darker. You fuckers might not get it, but every second she's spent with me has been her choice."

Erik's icy blue eyes flash as he leans back on the bare cot, stretching his legs out in front of him. "All signs point to her," he drawls, cutting me off before I can lash out. "But she may not have leaked Mark's location willingly."

"You think someone got to her?" Mavros asks.

"Not exactly," Erik continues, eyes returning to mine. "Didn't Noctis have to block a number from her phone? One of those fucked-up family members, right? Her stepbrother kept hounding her or some shit?"

"Half-brother," I correct, catching on to what he's getting at. "Noctis said the fucker has his claws in deep. Evie didn't have any form of social media or even the illusion of friends before she met us—because of him."

"And don't you think someone that controlling would freak the fuck out the moment the cage door was kicked open?"

"He tracked her," I whisper, fists flexing.

"Not physically," Mavros adds. "We cleared the area."

"Her phone," I ground out, pacing between the two of them.

"This has nothing to do with the Seven or the southern circuit and everything to do with Evie."

"Tempest said the half-brother is obsessed with her." Erik tilts his head, weighing his next words. "I think something happened when they were younger. Tempest hasn't said it outright, but she got this haunted look in her eyes."

My heart hammers against my ribs. I shake my head against the truth clawing its way out. I had Noctis run the standard background check on Evie before she moved in… but that was when I was only protecting Tempest. And again when he set up a forwarding number for Evie. I underestimated the danger her family posed. I should've dug deeper. *Fuck*, I should've scoured her past, combing the shadows for any creep who ever touched her.

My knuckles *crack* from how hard my fists clench. I want to rage against the bars, to scream and threaten and kill until my little fox is tucked in close to my side. But instead, Evie's dipshit brother had Daddy call in a favor, locking me in a cage and leaving her exposed.

"Shit," I breathe, dropping onto the edge of the cot beside Erik. "Tempest asked if Evie could stay with us rent-free. I assumed her parents were cutting her off."

"But you think it's something more now?" Mavros asks, biceps straining against his shirt as he crosses his arms.

"They're pulling her from school," Erik adds.

My eyes snap to his. "When? And how the fuck do you know that?"

He shrugs. "I don't know, brother. Tempest felt shitty airing out all of Evie's trauma. I didn't press for details, but she was worried, so I have to assume it's soon."

Adrenaline floods my veins, my mind spiraling with all the worst-case scenarios—everything that could be happening to Evie without me there to protect her.

But then a wash of calm settles in my chest.

She's here.

I'm not sure how, but I know Evie is near. Following the pulse of energy tugging at something deep in my bones, I tilt my head toward the camera and stand up, staring straight into the lens.

Are you out there, little fox?

I get my answer minutes later when the crisp *clip* of boots and a familiar air of pompousness fills the hallway. A stout man with a grotesque combover and weak jaw glares at us before swiping his badge over the lock. There's an audible *click* as the bar retracts.

"You three are free to go."

The words sound painful for him to say. Mavros grins, showing off his slightly too-long canines.

"We posted bail?" he asks.

"Hardly," the cop sneers. "Despite the good sense of Father Michael and her family, Evie provided all of you with concrete alibis."

Something warm blooms in my chest as I follow Erik and Mavros out of the cell. My ferocious little fox defied every expectation and proved her loyalty to us. To me. She should've never been questioned, but I can't stop the pulse of pride that surges at knowing she did it for me.

We reach the lobby. Mavros and Erik join my brothers and I'm just about to follow when I hear the cop with the shitty hair piece lean forward and mutter under his breath:

"The used-up, disgraceful slut will get what's coming to her."

34

SILAS

I almost turn around and put my fist through the fucker's face. My fingers flex as I stand in the open doorframe, already calculating which camera feeds I'd have to wipe and how many bodies I'd need to hide—but then I see her.

My sister has Erik in a tight hug, Mavros is welcomed by my brothers, but Evie stands there with her big brown eyes staring up at me. Waiting. Resurrecting the withered, useless organ inside my chest.

She's wearing a loose crop top paired with baggy sweats and sneakers. Her wine-colored hair is thrown up in a bun, wisps left loose to frame her face. The splash of freckles across her cheeks is amplified by the gorgeous-as-fuck blush spreading across them.

"Hi," she mumbles.

It takes me three steps to reach her. My hand wraps around her throat as my other weaves into the short curls at the back of her head, tugging until her neck arches and her pouty lips part on a gasp. I'm on her in the next breath, my tongue sweeping against hers, devouring her sweet taste, consuming the faint hint of wildflowers and rain that cling to her.

Her pulse quickens beneath my fingers, her heart fluttering as her knees weaken. A desperate growl rumbles in my chest just as someone clears their throat, and I temper my baser instincts enough to pull back. I'm rewarded with the sight of Evie's swollen lips and heavily lidded eyes.

Fuck, she's beautiful.

"Uhhh… guys?" Erik says, half teasing, half imploring. I catch faint grumbling from the officers, but my gaze stays locked on the gift in front of me. "I think you're about to be arrested for indecent exposure, and I'm pretty sure they separate the girls from the boys."

The sheepish smile that spreads across Evie's face has me grinning like a fool. For the first time in my life, I set my need for revenge aside and focus only on this moment.

"Let's go."

Gravel crunches under my boots, the engine thrums beneath my thighs, and Evie's small arms tighten around me. Noctis has already sent a team to retrieve the car Tempest and Evie left at the precinct, but there's no way in hell I'm letting either of them out of my sight until her family is dealt with.

"Where are we going?" Evie asks through her helmet as we fly past the exit for the house she's come to know. The road opens up before us, and my brothers bask in the light of the stars as we follow the freeway south.

"Home," I rumble.

"But—" Evie starts, before Tempest cuts her off.

"Remember how I said we've got you covered if your family turns out to be a bunch of dicks?" Tempest asks. She's a car length or so ahead of us, arms wrapped around Erik's waist.

"Yeah," Evie answers warily.

"That was a real promise," Tempest says as we turn off the highway and onto a winding road through the canyon. "We can't be showy about it, of course, or the feds would get suspicious, but every pervert we've put down ends up donating a small portion of their fortune to a group of rebels whose main purpose is ridding the filth from our streets."

A small breath escapes Evie as we pull into a long driveway. A Spanish estate comes into view. It sits atop the canyon, the low moon a backdrop as light spills from massive arched windows. Palm trees frame white columns along the sprawling adobe-style porch, the red-tiled roof and white stucco walls adorned with intricate details.

"This is our home," I say, pressing my hand over hers where it still grips my waist.

Motorcycle engines cut, and then my brothers and little sister make their way toward the large wooden door inset with elaborate designs. Tempest spares a brief smile for us before crossing the threshold and disappearing inside with the others.

Evie stays on the bike, legs wrapped around mine, hands clasped in front of me—refusing to let go.

"Are you okay, baby?"

I feel her stiffen. Hear the sharp intake of breath through the mic. Maybe this is all too much. Killing Mark, defying her family, seeing the house—the life we could have. She's finally realizing how deeply I've woven her into my world... and she's afraid.

Shit, I'm afraid. She must be terrified.

I'm prepared to beg—no, fuck that. I'm ready to throw her over my shoulder and toss her into my room, refusing to let her go until she understands how fucking right we are—when she speaks.

"I can never go back home." Her voice is soft, barely carrying through the speaker. "He'll be angry. So angry."

The fine hairs on the back of my arms prick at the tremor in her voice. My grip tightens on the handlebars as I fight to keep my breathing even.

"Who?"

"Jonathan." She sniffles. "My half-brother. My mother and

father will be upset too, but… I'm almost twenty, and Jonathan set up this lunch for me to meet his friend, Father Michael's son, and I know—*I know*—he wants me to marry him."

I turn, plucking her from the back of my motorcycle like the little fox she is, and slide her around until she settles on my lap. Her legs straddle me as I remove our helmets—hers first, then mine—until I can stare into her big brown eyes, ringed in red and glistening with unshed tears.

"You are mine, Evie," I say gently, cradling her head in my hands. "You are safe. Whatever that piece-of-shit half-brother did to you. It's over. He can't reach you anymore."

I thought my words would calm her, ease the tension radiating across her shoulders, but something in her gaze cracks. Sobs rake her chest as the tears she's held so carefully at bay fall. Evie presses into my chest, and I wrap her in my arms.

She's breaking. And I can do nothing but whisper words of comfort as I hold her tight. On the outside, I'm soothing and calm, a peaceful refuge for her.

But inside?

My blood is boiling. This isn't some passing slight or sibling spat dressed in religious trauma. Evie's entire body is shaking. The perfect mask she's been forced to wear is splintering, like the first crack in an overflowing damn, and now water is rushing, bursting through all the lies.

I feel her pain as acutely as if it were my own. Worse.

Because I accepted my fate a long time ago. I've willingly sacrificed any hope for a peaceful future to ensure Morana is found and Tempest is safe.

But Evie?

Fuck, Evie never had a chance.

One thing is certain: I'm going to hunt down that motherfucker—half-brother or not.

And when I find him, I'm going to make what happened to Mark look like child's play.

35

SILAS

We stay there, under the stars in the driveway of my ridiculously expensive home. Tempest insisted on a place Morana would love, ensuring the property had enough space for the Seven to stay whenever they want. It's always felt too big. Hollow. But as I hold Evie, watching her tears dry and her breathing even out, I wonder if the home might feel brighter with her in it.

"We should probably go inside," Evie says, glancing toward the illuminated windows practically vibrating with music. I can already see Dominic, Adrian, and Bane raiding the liquor cabinet as they string together a party, but I don't feel like a crowd tonight.

"We could go in with the others," I start. "Or…"

"Or?" she whispers, licking her lips as her gaze dips to my mouth.

"My studio is to the left." I tilt my head toward the small path off the driveway tucked between gnarled olive trees.

My studio. The one place I can sit and think. Breathe without worrying. Even with my brothers, I'm vigilant. Always watching. Forever assessing as I wait for the next attack. The subsequent sliver of information that will inevitably lead to another person I need to hunt down and kill.

I'm always angry. Endlessly envious of my brothers' easy conversations and their ability to live while all I do is exist. It feels like I'm caught in an endless torrent of revenge and rage, unable to form relationships like a normal fucking person.

Until her.

"I'd like that." Evie's words are soft and dripping with kindness. She's never asked to see my art. Not after that night. And maybe that's why I want to show her. That, and everything she's just shared with me. She didn't speak. She didn't need to. The type of tears she shed were potent. Purging.

Still, I have every intention of asking Noctis to report on every fucking second of Jonathan's life. But right now, I want to stay in this moment, drinking in the feel of her body next to mine.

Evie's warmth thaws the plates of ice around my heart, exposing the ragged, fleshy organ beneath. The bands of muscle burn under the scrutiny of her light—flames licking the tendons and sinew—but instead of running, of searching for a way to put out the raging fire, I'm basking in the inferno, sending a prayer to the fates, or gods, or whatever the fuck is out there, that this hellish torment never ends.

The room is dark when I open the door. My boots echo in the large space as I kick them off and stride across the floor, eclipsing the softer pad of Evie's footsteps behind me. She lingers barefoot by the door like a stranger, as if she's not reflected in the dozens of canvases strung about the room.

"If you run, I'll catch you," I warn in a deceptively soft voice a moment before my finger flips the switch.

"Why would I..."

The buzz of electricity hums, illuminating the specialized lights. They're designed to replicate the sun on a cloudy day, providing the perfect blend of light and shadow while I work.

Little did I realize, all those years ago when I constructed my artistic haven, that I'd prefer to paint in the dim glow of cheap tea lights crisscrossing the wooden beams overhead.

I watch my little fox as words fail her, noting the way her eyes widen and her beautiful fucking lips part—like she's been led into Hades's realm only to discover the Underworld is more holy than any place promised to her before.

"Silas, this is—it's..."

"You," I say, the warmth of my breath causing gooseflesh to erupt on the back of her neck. She shivers as I wrap my arms around her waist, slipping one palm beneath the edge of her hoodie to rest on the soft curve of her stomach. I glide my other hand up, feeling the frantic beating of her heart beneath the swell of her breast. "I meant it when I said there's no escaping me, Evie. Not now. Not ever."

"You can't say things like that," she whispers, but her pulse races and she makes no move to leave, even as she starts to look away.

"Oh, but I can." Leaving one palm on her chest, I move the other to her throat, gripping the edge of her jaw as I force her gaze back up. "Look what you've done to me."

I turn her until she's facing the bleakest pieces—the small squares coated in smears of black and varying shades of grey, with only the briefest hints of emerald green.

"This is what I was before. Consumed with revenge for my sister. With envy for something other than the resounding nothingness gnawing away at me. And then, there you were, muttering to yourself on the steps of my home."

Her throat bobs beneath my fingers as I fix her gaze to the slash of yellow within the darkness. The paint is thick, layers rising in massive swatches of depression, split open by the riot of color at the center.

I know she feels the anger in that single slice. The small gasp from her lips as she studies the ripped edges curled back from the wound, the hitch in her breath as she marvels at the spray of paint reaching the edge of the canvas—so much like blood from a knife wound—tells me Evie realizes this was the moment her light forced its way through my realm of blackness. And the two of us were nothing but casualties in fate's war.

That crater of yellow, of deep reds and russet browns, stretches, shifting across the white canvas, growing until it's the same shade as her eyes. Until there's no doubt it's her lips I've painted, parted and gasping for breath, her cheeks flushed with need as my fingers tighten around her throat.

Just as they are now.

"There are dozens," Evie breathes, spotting the cluster of white and reds hung above the large bed in the corner. White silk sheets and matching pillowcases appear sleek among the haphazard paintings. Various-sized canvases are propped against the edge of the room, clustered together with what I couldn't fit on the walls.

"Yes," I say, guiding us toward the bed. The paintings here are splashes of her porcelain skin, her rose-tinted blush, and then a deep scarlet. I cup her sex, stroking the edge of her underwear as I arch her neck against my chest, licking over the spot where her pulse flutters. "These are you, my Evie. Flashes of what you'll look like once I've taken what's mine."

A small whimper escapes her parted lips as I slip two fingers through her wetness. "Silas…"

"Are you ready to be fucked, little fox?" I murmur, grinding my palm against her clit. She bucks against me, shaking her head, even as the slickness between her thighs builds. "I think you are. I think you want me to force you to take my cock. To hold this pretty pussy open for me while I split you in half."

Evie arches her back further, but she still hasn't answered. She's shaking her head no, and while I like our game of cat and mouse, of the serpent ensnaring his little fox, I need her to want me too. To need me just as desperately as I need her.

"If you say the word 'red,' we stop," I say, pressing a kiss beneath her ear as my fingers slow, just enough to be sure she's focused and understands. "Anything else, I'll keep going. If you want to leave—to end this—now's your chance. Because once I have you, no amount of begging will set you free."

She nods.

"I need to hear you say it, love. Say you want me to fuck you."

"No," she breathes, her ass rubbing against my cock. I hiss as she grinds. My grip tightens around her throat as her fingers slip between us, palming me through my jeans. "Let me go."

"Never," I growl, pressing two fingers inside her, pumping ruthlessly as I restrict her breathing, just enough for her to call this off if she wants to. Her fingers find mine, clawing at me for freedom, but she doesn't utter a word.

"Such a good little slut," I purr, my cock straining against my pants at her needy little cries. And, god, I love the way her pussy clenches around my fingers.

I kick her feet apart, spreading her legs with my knee as I add a third, holding her on the edge of orgasm. I savor the way she relinquishes control, how her hands drop away from mine. Any pretense of fighting is forgotten as she writhes in my grasp, desperate for that sweet release.

"Do you want to come?" I ask, kissing along the curve of her neck.

"Yes," she whimpers.

My lips curls into a hungry grin, my teeth scraping at the soft flesh over her hammering pulse.

"Beg me."

Evie bites her lip, brows pinching in that defiant way that makes my balls draw up.

"You're so fucking cute when you disobey." Maintaining my hold around her neck, I withdraw my fingers and shove her pants down until they pool around her ankles. I do the same to mine, stepping out of the fabric and kicking them to the side.

"Shirt off, little fox."

With trembling fingers, Evie lifts the edge of her sweatshirt, exposing the pale skin of her ribs, her soft curves, and the faint splatter of freckles across her shoulders. I drag a knuckle along the slope of her breast, still shrouded in thin white fabric. They're full, lifting and falling with each breath.

"Off."

Evie licks her lips, turning her head to look into my eyes. I brush a strand of hair from her face, twirling the wine-colored strands between my fingers as the scrap of cotton falls away. Her nipples are hard, peaked and waiting for me. The scent of arousal is thick in the air as I circle, marveling at my Evie—at her perfect fucking body and gorgeous mind. At the way her light and sins dance so gracefully with my demons.

"So fucking beautiful."

A needy whimper falls from her lips as I flick my thumb over one of her peaked tips, repressing the urge to drop to my knees and capture them between my teeth.

"Silas, please," Evie pleads, her eyes dropping to my mouth. "I need you."

"Soon," I rumble, slipping behind her until the full curves of her ass are before me. "But first, your punishment."

36

EVIE

I gasp as Silas shoves my head down, the cool white sheets pressing into my cheek. His feet kick mine further apart, exposing all of me to his assessing gaze.

"Hands stretched in front."

My heart pounds as I do what he says, every beat sending a rush of heat surging through my veins. Shame pricks at me as that small, mocking voice whispers that this is wrong, that I'm nothing if I let Silas fuck me. But then his firm hands are on my ass, caressing the soft curves before there's a sharp slap.

"Did you forget your last punishment so quickly?" Silas is already there, rubbing away the sting as I cry out, but his words are punctuated with another slap, this one on my other cheek.

"No," I pant, gripping the sheets as I remember the way he forced Mark's head into my pussy, angling his mouth around my clit as he gasped for breath—and then murdered him for touching me.

"Did you like using him?" Silas asks.

My pussy clenches as his palm lands a third slap across my sore flesh, and god, it feels like I'm flying. Like the heady mix of pain and pleasure is distorting reality, pulling me into that cherished in-between.

Slap.

"Tell me the truth, Evie."

"Yes!" I cry out, shame heating my face with self-loathing—knowing, and not quite caring, that it's probably as red as my ass. "I enjoyed the way you forced him to fuck me with his mouth. How you controlled my orgasm, even when you weren't touching me."

I press my face into the sheets before he can see the tears fall. Because that's the worst of it. My dark dirty secret. Jonathan forced me to take those photos when I was younger, forced me to suck on bananas or other phallic-shaped things before I knew what people paid for on the dark web. And worse. So much worse.

I'd been innocent then. A child. As much as I hate to admit it, Jonathan scared me, changing some intrinsic part of me forever. I know I wasn't to blame then—but right now, in this moment, I like the way Silas uses me.

It feels wrong to crave Silas's control when some people would consider his dominance similar to the pain I suffered… but it's different. And I think I'm finally understanding why. Silas is harsh and brutal, but he'd go to hell and back to find me. To keep me safe.

"Shh," Silas coos, shifting as he drops to his knees behind me, pressing soft kisses to the red marks his hand left. "There's nothing to be ashamed of."

"You killed him," I whisper, which only punctuates how seriously fucked up I am. But my voice isn't shaking for Mark. No, I'm trembling for a different reason as Silas's hands grip my ass, his fingers grazing over the slickness between my thighs.

"Yes. Does that bother you? Does the fact that I'd kill anyone for touching you make you want to run?"

"No," I confess. His movements still, and then his thumbs are spreading me, parting my ass to expose everything. Warm breath trails along my inner thigh, fanning over my pussy as he speaks.

"No," he agrees, licking up my center, teasing my aching core. "Because you're fucking mine, Evie. From now until forever, you're mine. It's time to show you what that means."

A half-moan, half-gasp slips from my lips as Silas holds me open, licking and sucking and nipping everywhere. Never have I been so exposed—so completely seen, body and soul—and it feels so good, so fucking good, not to hide. To arch into his ravenous feasting, unashamed. Free.

Before I know what's happening, I'm flipped over, thighs spread around Silas's face. The subtle scrape of his stubble teases my skin as he dives back in, sucking my clit, causing that delicious tension inside me to coil tighter.

"Oh god," I pant, arching into him, needing more. "I'm so close."

"You taste so good, baby," Silas says between licks. "I could stay between your legs forever, feasting on your sweet cunt."

Three fingers push into me, pumping as he presses a soft kiss to my throbbing clit. I buck beneath the stretch, moaning—begging for things I don't yet understand, for experiences I haven't had but ache for. Need.

"I'm going to fuck this virgin pussy, Evie." Silas spreads his fingers as they work, making me grip the sheets as he toys with my body. "It's going to be rough and painful, but you're going to love every minute of it, aren't you?"

My knees fall open, desperate for more. So close—so fucking close—but Silas keeps me on the edge, his other hand pressing down on my lower belly, stopping me from getting that last bit of friction I need.

"Say it," he commands.

"Yes," I growl. "I want you to fuck me, Silas. Hard. I want to bleed and hurt. I want every piece of my soul to shatter and be reborn in your image."

"That's my good fucking girl," he rumbles, holding my gaze as he lowers his head. "And good girls get to come."

His mouth closes over my clit, sucking hard as the fingers inside me curl, stroking that sensitive spot. The orgasm hits, brutal in its intensity. It feels like I'm floating, soaring above this reality and into the next, but his fingers slip free too soon, the last waves of pleasure still pulsing through me as my body is shifted. I feel the softness of a pillow beneath my head, the dip of the bed as Silas climbs between my legs.

"Eyes open, little fox."

I blink through the haze of satiated desire, eyes widening as a new pressure builds between my thighs. Silas waits for me to come back down, to realize that the velvet thickness sliding along the evidence of my arousal is his cock.

He grins wickedly before gripping my hips and thrusting forward, sheathing himself in one punishing motion. I cry out at the invasion, tears pricking my eyes, nails raking across his chest. Still, he moves, pulling out just enough to grant a moment of relief before splitting me open all over again.

"Fuck, Evie," Silas growls, leaning over me as I whimper, adjusting to his thickness.

I look through the tears, staring into his blazing green eyes as he continues his slow, torturous rhythm. His gaze softens as he takes me in, his hips moving steadily, easing the pain as pleasure begins to take root. His tongue licks the tears from my cheek as he cups my face, cradling me. Holding me through it.

"You're doing so well, baby. Bleeding all over my cock like a good little whore." Silas hovers over me, staring down, silently asking if I'm okay. And that, more than anything, has me leaning into him.

I capture his lips with mine, my hands threading into his

hair. He tastes like leather and spice. Like dreams I'd long forgotten.

Silas paints me like I'm the light between us, but it's been him all along. He found me when I'd already given up, brought me back to life in a way I never thought possible. Loving him has never been a choice. I've been his since the moment he cornered me on that stairwell.

I push back against him, deepening the connection of our bodies—the joining of our souls.

"I'm yours," I breathe. The look in his eyes when I whisper those words—desire, longing, disbelief—it's enough to make me believe in something greater than this world. "And you're mine."

"Yes," he growls, sucking my nipple into his mouth, nipping at the sensitive peak before abusing the other. Heat gathers low, pleasure coiling and twisting as his hips buck. All softness id forgotten as Silas's pace quickens, his hips slamming into me.

He shifts back, his hand pressing my legs apart to watch where he splits me. I stare down at the blood coating my thighs, glistening on his lower stomach, the ruby stains marring the white silk sheets beneath us. I'm a fucking mess—destroyed—just like I begged him to do.

"Fucking yes," Silas snarls, pulling out just long enough to flip me onto my stomach. He hooks an arm around my hips, dragging me back onto his bloody cock. I cry out as he takes me roughly, this angle leaving me at his mercy.

"You bleed so fucking beautifully, Evie. Does it hurt, baby?"

I whimper as his fingers dig into the meat of my ass, unable to separate the pain from the mounting pleasure. Silas must sense it, because his thrusts grow harsher, the sound of skin slapping and heavy breathing clashing with my moans and cries.

"Oh god," I groan as Silas finds a spot deep within, fucking me with ruthless abandon. The scent of sex, blood, and lingering traces of paint invade my senses as I catch glimpses of the paintings—an entire fucking gallery dedicated to me. "Oh my fucking god."

"That's it, baby." Silas's hand dips between my legs, stroking my clit as he drives hard. "Come for me."

But I'm already there, diving off the edge. The stretch of his cock inside me, the slick mix of blood and arousal between my thighs, the pinch of his fingers on my clit—I cry out as Silas tenses behind me. He thrusts deep into my clenching pussy, pumping his orgasm into mine. I let him, each drag of his length leaving more of him inside me, marking me as his.

When he pulls out, he keeps me there, bent over and ruined, my ass and pussy on display as his cum leaks from my bruised center. Two fingers trail up my thigh, gathering his seed before shoving it back inside.

I whimper at the invasion, but Silas already has me flipped over, his lips capturing the sound as his hand rubs soothing circles over my clit.

"Shh, brave girl. Don't cry. We're just getting started."

37

SILAS

My tongue licks at the soft skin over Evie's thrumming pulse, my cock twitching as she shivers. The sun has been up for an hour now, but her eyes are closed, lashes fluttering with dreams I wish I could see. I took her rough last night. And this morning. The blood from her sweet little cunt is everywhere, staining the sheets, smearing her thighs, her breasts, the beautiful fucking curves of her ass I'm staring at now.

There are bruises too. Most from my teeth, but some from where I held her down, open for me as I fucked and filled her up with my cum over and over again until even my orgasms were painful. One of her legs is bent as she sleeps on her stomach, exposing the sticky mix of our orgasms. It slicks the inside of her thighs even now, her hair mussed and wild around her shoulders.

I draw back, returning to the canvas I've set up at the foot of the bed, and settle on a rose-colored pink. The gentle highlight will contrast with the scarlet smears while bringing out the purples on her skin, revealing every place my mouth touched last night. Normally, I'd spend days on a single painting, but I want to capture this moment—to sear every sacred second into a tangible piece of art I can cherish forever.

Switching brushes, my motions grow more frenzied. Pale creams blend into the perfect curve of her spine; dark burgundies and deep reds twist and weave into the picture of her hair. Streaks of white, soiled by red, represent the sheets beneath my little fox. The gentle slope of her nose, the splash of freckles across her skin, the thick lashes and dried tears along her cheeks—and then it's time to finish my masterpiece.

A new color is needed. I crawl over her, running my fingers along the maimed flesh of her beautiful ass before thrusting them into her used cunt. Her back arches as she whimpers, lifting her ass as I pump my fingers, curling them before pulling back. Unable to help myself, I lean down, licking up the fresh mess I made before pressing a gentle kiss to her pussy.

"Soon, my love. But you can sleep for a little longer."

Her eyes stay closed, breathing steady, as I add the pink tint of her bleeding pussy to my palette. I reach for the tube of rich scarlet, squeezing a heavy amount onto the tray and mix it with her blood and cum. Indigo and a deep blue are next, then the brush is moving again, layering her porcelain skin with my touch. With bites and bruises, with hickeys and blood smears—in crazed, careful strokes.

It's almost like I'm there again, thrusting between her thighs, pulling her hair, gripping her throat as I rocked on top of her. Fucked her without mercy, just the way she likes.

I'm panting by the time it's done, startled out of my frenzied state by Evie's soft voice.

"It's beautiful," she murmurs, her eyes still glazed with sleep. She's pushed herself into a sitting position, not bothering to cover her chest with the sheet, and I realize I like her like this. Love that she feels comfortable enough not to hide.

That word rattles around in my mind, knocking down walls

I'd long since built. *Crash, crash, crash* goes my sanity. My invincibility. Relinquished at the feet of the woman in front of me.

"You're beautiful," I say. Setting the brush down, I wipe the splatter of paint from my fingers onto my sweats before closing the distance between us to capture her swollen lips in a kiss. "Good morning, little fox. How did you sleep?"

Such a mundane question, and yet I want to know. Because I want to know everything about her.

"Wonderful," she says, her bright eyes peering up at me before pulling me down for another brush of our lips.

"How are you feeling?" I ask, running my hand down her back, the pads of my fingers tracing patterns along the outside of her hip.

"Sore," she admits with a sheepish shrug. "But I think that's normal after everything, right?"

"Nothing about last night was normal, Evie." A sinister chuckle rumbles in my chest as I lean down, trailing kisses over each and every bruise. My mouth closes around her nipple, lapping gently as she sucks in a breath before I sink to my knees, following the trail of carnage down her stomach.

"Nothing between us will ever be *normal*." Taking my time, I part her legs, kissing every injury on her battered skin until she's shivering.

"What are you doing?" she asks, squirming when I reach the soft curls between her thighs.

I allow my tongue to graze her clit, flicking across the sensitive flesh with lazy licks, as if I have all the time in the world to explore her. Only when her breasts are swollen, nipples hard with want, do I answer.

"Taking my breakfast in bed. Lay back, little fox. I'm starving."

38

EVIE

Silas makes me come twice more before carrying me to the en suite. He sets me down on the shower bench and turns on the water, waiting for it to warm. Only when the air is steaming around us, does he angle the spout, allowing for the gentle patter of water to soothe my aching body.

"There's a bath inside the house," he says, dragging a sponge that smells like him across my breasts as he kneels on the tiles. That wicked smirk of his is back, tugging at my heart. "But I thought you'd want to wash before we risk running into anyone."

"Yes," I confirm with my own shy smile, watching as he wipes away a particularly heavy smear of blood across my lower stomach. Dried blood that confirms I'm no longer a virgin.

I thought I'd feel different. Like I'd sense my soul being slotted for eternal damnation, or that God would send a lightning bolt and strike me down for all to see. In my darkest nightmares, I dreamed a branded letter would appear on my breast, probably from that book where the townspeople revolted ostracized an unwed woman for getting pregnant. But as I watch Silas—his dark hair wet, his toned skin beaded with water and branded with tattoos as he cleans me with something akin to worship—I know I'll never regret last night.

I'd choose to lay my body down for him again and again. To submit to his will, his rule, because Silas's devotion to me is absolute. Maybe I did sell my soul to the devil, but if the promised heaven doesn't have him by my side, I don't want it.

So I choose this life—this eternity—of love and delicious, beautiful darkness.

I hiss when the sponge dips lower, parting my thighs for Silas's ministrations. He's gentle as he works, but I can see how his eyes dilate, how his cock is still hard from licking me earlier.

"You need rest," he says, more to himself than to me. "You're sore."

Setting my now clean legs down, Silas stands. Water pings across his shoulders, running down the murals of tattoos covering his hard stomach and thick-veined forearms. And his hands—god, his hands—have been everywhere. On me. In me. Shoving cum back into my swollen core before forcing their way into my mouth, coating my tongue with the sweet, bitter tang of our pleasure.

I grab his hand as he starts to turn, letting myself admire the crisp black lines across his knuckles before looking up. He must see something in my eyes, because his body goes still, cock twitching, the thick length just inches from my lips.

I meet his gaze, emerald flecks striking against the deep green tiles behind us, as I guide his hand to my head, adjusting my position until my lips hover over him.

"My mouth isn't."

Only once all the cum is cleaned from my face and neck, and my hair is brushed, do I exit the washroom. There's a pair of Silas's sweatpants and a T-shirt waiting for me, along with a new toothbrush still in its packaging, and my favorite toothpaste and floss set beside it on the counter. With minty-fresh breath and a subtle ache between my thighs, I step into the main studio and find Silas seated at a fresh canvas, still naked.

A forest-green towel is wrapped around his waist as he perches on his stool, but the edges have fallen low, revealing the top curves of his ass. The hard muscles across his back flex as his paintbrush flies across the canvas, and I realize what he's rendering.

The large rectangle set on the easel is a mixture of pearl and eggshell whites, twisted with flashes of scarlet. Most would assume it's impressionistic or perhaps modern with its bold strokes, but all I see is the backdrop of the bed Silas stares at as his hand moves.

"You're painting the sheets?" I ask, padding toward him.

"Yes and no," he says, tilting his head toward me, though his eyes never stray from the silk sheets—marred forever with my ruin—until the last splash of red is added to the canvas and his brush falls still. "I'm painting you. Us. Just in another form."

He tugs me to his side, pressing his head into my stomach, and I inhale the masculine scent of him. I run my fingers through his still-damp hair, my heart thrumming at how vulnerable he looks right now. How open he is with me—only me.

"I have this need to tell you I love you," Silas whispers, pressing a kiss to my navel. My breath hitches as he holds me there, staring up at me. "But that word isn't strong enough. I love you, and my soul is yours as much as it is mine."

His fingers tug on the drawstring holding my pants up, and

the loose waistband slips down, leaving me in nothing but his oversized shirt.

"I love you, and I would gladly worship at the altar of your body for eternity."

He lifts the hem of the fabric, sending sparks of electricity across my skin as he exposes my nakedness. Silas's fingers tease my core with gentle strokes, just enough to have me slick with need, despite the lingering soreness. And god above, I already want him again.

He pushes the towel from his lap, tugging me forward until the most sensitive part of me is poised over his straining cock, the velvety head sliding through my slick folds.

"I love you, and I would erase any threat." Gripping my thighs, he slams me down, impaling me on his length before lifting me again. This position draws him so deep I swear it feels like he's etching ownership into my bones. "Punish anyone foolish enough to hurt you."

His words are punctuated with another deep thrust, and I cry out from the sharp pleasure. He captures the sound with his mouth as he sets the rhythm, moving me with ease, as though I weigh nothing. Our bodies writhe together, desire already smoldering into a raging inferno of need and want and love.

Silas sucks hard on a nipple, and I cradle his head to me as his teeth find the other.

"I love you," he pants, his grip on my back tightening with his release just as mine crashes into me.

"And I'd destroy the world to keep you."

39

SILAS

"To help the ache," I murmur low enough for only Evie to hear as I slide three tablets and a glass of water across the kitchen counter.

"Thanks," she says, faint traces of pink stealing across her cheeks. I love the way she blushes, knowing she's thinking of all the ways I bent, fucked, and used her last night. And this morning.

Tempest pads into the kitchen, reaching for a coffee mug as she takes a seat beside Evie. I give her a smile before turning, finding Erik. His blonde hair is a mess, bite marks covering his chest and neck, and he's tying the drawstring on a pair of grey sweatpants like he only just remembered to put on clothes. Odd that he's coming from the east wing when his room's on the opposite end. They must've invited people over after all.

I catch a glimpse of Noctis in a teal-blue T-shirt and jeans, his put-together ensemble and wide awake gaze completely opposite of Erik. He's perched on the edge of a built-in lounge beneath the three large windows overlooking the canyon, his computer open and already humming. A pair of French doors lead out to the backyard, the combined light bringing life to the colorful Spanish tiles and wooden accents throughout the house.

One day, I'll get to Spain. Morana will be found, the trafficking circuits destroyed, and I can fucking run to the Mediterranean Sea with Evie at my side. I'd planned on Italy, but Evie mentioned wanting to see Spain, something in a book that caught her eye. And just like that, my dreams of Italy were replaced. Made better. Fuller. More whole with my little fox beside me.

I take a seat next to Noctis, waiting while he types. He looks peaceful, but I need to make sure Evie's dickwad of a brother gets what's coming to him.

"Robert's been taken care of," Noctis says, fingers flying over the keyboard. "Shane's still working that shitty above-the-table job. No signs of the circuit contacting him yet, but I still don't believe our little vacation downtown in the holding cells was all because of Jonathan—"

He stills, the clicking of keys going silent as his gaze shifts to Evie. She's peeling an orange beside Tempest, leaning in close as she hangs on every word my sister says. Another piece of my armor melts, knowing just how long Tempest has waited for a friend like her.

"She seems to think it is," I say slowly, watching my little fox. Her mouth closes around a slice, a bead of juice catching on her lip just before her tongue licks it clean. I adjust my pants, and force myself to focus. "That's actually what I wanted to talk to you about. You forwarded his calls to a ghost number, right?"

Noctis nods. "Yep. That motherfucker's definitely obsessed in a creepy sort of way. The mailbox I linked to it filled in a day."

My knuckles *crack* as I flex my hands, wishing I had his face in front of me to pummel. His bones to break. "Has anyone listened to the messages yet? Evie's afraid of that fucker, which already makes him a problem in need of solving."

"No, but I've done a full sweep on him. He's an entitled prick hiding behind the guise of the church, but he's clean. Never even had a parking violation."

"He wouldn't, though, would he?" I ask, meeting Noctis's skeptical stare. "Not if the cops are on his side. Not if his daddy's rich and the church thinks he's a golden boy."

Noctis starts to shake his head, then pauses. "I'll go through the voicemails and see what I can find. Between what Erik said about Tempest feeling uneasy with Evie's family, and the possibility of her brother having enough influence to get us arrested, it's worth another look. But I still feel like we're missing something."

"Something new?" I ask after a moment. "We've closed all leads. Unless you think Shane—"

"No," Noctis cuts in. "Mavros and I were reviewing recent reports of missing women, including the ones that fit the southern circuit's profile, and a lot of shit is pointing to someone sounding a lot like Mark."

It takes me a second, but when it clicks, I have to fight to keep my voice low. "Mark, as in the asshole whose brain I put a bullet through weeks ago?"

After I used his short bout of suffocation to get Evie off. That motherfucker was granted the best last minutes of his life, buried so deep in my girl's pussy he couldn't breathe. My jaw clenches as the familiar tendrils of jealousy claw up my spine.

"Maybe I just want it to be him." Noctis sighs, shaking his head as his eyes dart across the screen. "It would mean we already took care of the leak."

"But that wouldn't explain why the cops were bold enough to make a move on us with no evidence," I counter.

Noctis nods, frustration tightening his features. He doesn't care how long it takes. Once he's caught the scent of something, he'll track it until the trail ends in a kill.

"Maybe look into Evie's parents. And their church," I add

after a beat, eyes narrowing as Erik takes a seat beside Tempest and Evie.

There's nothing wrong with the way he's speaking to them, but something about the exchange, about the way Evie smiles fondly when looking between Erik and my sister, or maybe the way Tempest laughs, bright and open over her freshly refilled coffee mug that sends pricks of alarm vibrating beneath my skin. Not envy or even concern… but a protectiveness, all the same.

"Sure thing," Noctis says just as Evie's phone lights up next to her.

The laughter in her eyes dims. Her beautiful lips, tilted in a soft smile moments ago, tug down as she swipes to read the message.

And then her eyes find mine.

40

EVIE

I don't know why Dean Whitehouser would request a meeting with me. I'm even less sure how he got my personal number, but here I am, backpack slung over my shoulders, phone tucked into the pocket of a new pair of jeans. I considered wearing my family approved skirt-and-blouse combo, but I figure this probably has something to do with my parents not paying tuition. I might as well start embracing this new chapter of my life head-on.

"It's abuse of power," Tempest says, keeping stride with me as we pass the turtle pond and head toward the library. "The dean texting you. He can't just access your person information like that. Silas already has Noctis on it."

"I'm sure he does," I reply, a huffed laugh breaking through my worry. "Along with a full investigation into my family, my ex-church, and probably the first celebrity I ever had a crush on."

Tempest raises a brow. "I thought you weren't allowed to watch television, let alone movies with celebrities hot enough to crush on."

"Ralph is pretty hot." I shrug, my lips quirking into a grin. "I think it's the way he's allowed to wreck things, and everyone still loves him for it. Or maybe it's the large hands."

"The cartoon character?" Tempest laughs.

My grin widens. "Like you said, I had to work with what I had."

She draws me into a hug as the administrative office comes into view. "I've got your tuition covered for next semester. Adrian already approved the liquidation of assets and is setting up an account for you to use."

"Only as a loan," I insist, already feeling the bite of shame.

Why is accepting help seen as a bad thing? I have so many negative associations with it—shame, pity—but Tempest isn't pushing any of that. I want to know I've earned my degree on my own, but what percentage of students at Grace University were born into generations of wealth? I'm one of them—was one of them—and I'm only now beginning to understand how deep inherited privilege and systemic injustice go.

So, I'll accept help where I can. And maybe one day, I'll be the one extending a hand.

"Only a loan," Tempest agrees, turning down the path toward her next class. "Now get in there and show the dean you're not going anywhere."

Clouds roll in overhead, bringing a chill with them as I cross in front of the small chapel and reach for the door. The lobby is filled with bored students waiting in stiff chairs to be called back. I approach the receptionist behind the desk. His long blonde hair falls forward as he focuses on his phone. An awkward smile twists my lips as I wait for him to acknowledge me.

"Transcripts, degree planning, or financial aid?" he asks, still not looking up.

"Oh, um, Dean Whitehouser wanted to meet with me."

He lifts a perfectly manicured brow, his gaze sweeping over me. He takes in the frame of my body, color of my eyes, and shape of my face before something in his expression shifts.

"Yes, I heard something about that," he says, pushing back from the desk. Something about his gentle, almost pitying tone makes my spine stiffen. "I'll take you myself."

"That's not necessary," I start, but he's already moving.

I do my best to catch up, vaguely noting the fruity perfume lingering in the hallway. It's sharp and oppressive, the kind of scent that triggers the beginning of a headache—and flashes of familiarity I can't quite place. The smell only grows stronger as we enter a separate wing, the grey walls giving way to an open space that might be lovely if the floor-length windows weren't hidden behind thick blinds.

A thin woman with dark hair and glasses sits at a small desk in the center of the wide room, blocking what appears to be a large office. Wooden doors, lacquered in a deep tint, are shut—a clear signal to stay the fuck away. But the blonde receptionist pays no mind.

"Sorry about this, Sloane," he says, winking as he strides past the girl, who looks to be maybe a year or two older than me. I assume she's the dean's secretary because her eyes widen, panic flashing bright in her gaze.

"Ash, wait," Sloane calls, scrambling after him as I hover awkwardly near her desk.

"You were going to quit anyway, right?" Ash tosses over his shoulder with a shrug.

"You couldn't give me a fucking heads-up?" Sloane glances between us, shaking her head as she snatches her bag and hurries for the door. "Good luck, Evie. I'm sorry you had to find out like this."

My brows furrow, lips parting with a question, but she's already gone.

"Are you ready?" Ash asks, his voice gentle as his fingers hover over the handle.

"Ready for what?" I ask, flinching as another wave of that suffocating orange blossom perfume hits me. God above, I haven't had a migraine come on this fast since I was stuck in our hotel room while Mother met with someone from church.

I blink. My heart stutters, then starts to race as I recognize the perfume.

Ash gives a sympathetic shake of his head a second before opening the office door.

And exposes my mother—bent over the dean's desk, with her skirt bunched around her waist as Dean Whitehouser drives into her from behind.

41

EVIE

E*w. Ew. Fucking ew.* I'm not sure if the words actually leave my lips, but they blare through my mind as my mother throws her head back in what is obviously a fake moan, oblivious to me standing here in horror.

"Christ," Dean Whitehouser curses, his eyes wide with mirrored shock.

The sight of them, coupled with the scent of my mother's cloying perfume, sends nausea twisting through my stomach as my headache spikes to new heights. As if on autopilot, I'm sprinting for the door, desperately wishing the loud pounding of my heartbeat would drown out the sounds of bodies shifting and a belt hastily being adjusted.

"We thought you should know about the affair," Sloane says as I burst into the lobby. I glance back to find her seated behind the desk, looking sheepish but composed. "Dominic, Adrian, and Bane helped us out of a tough situation. I know this isn't usually something they concern themselves with, but they've mentioned how happy Silas is with you, and once I heard your mom trying to force us to kick you out, I thought this might help you stay. I wasn't expecting you walk in on anything that... overwhelming."

"Thank you." I swallow, my eyes darting toward the hallway behind us at the sound of rushed footsteps.

"Ask about tuition," Sloane mutters as I start for the door. My brows knit together, but the faintest whiff of chemical orange hits me again and I'm out of the office before I can ask what she means.

Pricks of bitter rain ping against me as I duck my head and keep moving, stuck in a half-walk, half-run even as I hear my mother call my name.

What the actual fuck did I just see?

My mother. The woman who's always demanded compliance, who preached quiet servitude to my father, half-brother, and every man in my life simply because I was born a woman. Because of some supposed sin recorded eons ago that had nothing to do with me. A curse I was meant to carry. And the whole time—the whole fucking time—everything she's said has been a lie.

"Sweetie, please let us explain."

The deep tenor of Dean Whitehouser's voice has me stopping in my tracks. Rain howls around us, soaking through my thin jacket and drenching my jeans, but I turn to face him with a viciousness I'm proud of.

"Do. Not. Call me that." The words are a growl as much as a promise. Of what, I'm not sure, but suddenly the image of Silas with a Glock in his hand and blood splattered across the canyon doesn't seem so scary. "Who the fuck do you think you are?"

Dean Whitehouser stands there, glancing back to where my adulterous mother huddles beneath the administration building's overhang, avoiding the worst of the storm. Because of course she is.

"This isn't how we wanted to do this," he says, shifting on his feet.

"We?" I snap. "How long has this been going on?"

I'm not sure why I ask, only that I expect the question to hurt him. And I want it to. I want my mother's shame, but I'll settle for his. And then his eyes soften.

"A little over twenty years. It started as a friendship. The early days of her marriage to Roy and having to be a stepmother to Jonathan were tough. I was there for her. Platonically at first, but then one thing led to another and… Trisha became pregnant."

I blink as the silence stretches between us, fat raindrops hammering the concrete.

"With you," he adds, searching my face, studying me with eyes the same color as my own.

"No," I whisper, waiting for him to laugh or to explain that this is all some kind of twisted prank, but he just stands there with an idiotic smile on his face. Like he expects me to run into his waiting arms.

"Yes, sweetie," he says, and just like that, the lens through which I view the world shatters. A cold sweat breaks out across my forehead, but he doesn't seem to notice. Or maybe he doesn't care because he keeps talking, keeps unraveling my reality.

"I'm your biological father. Your mother and I discussed the possibility of raising you together, but there was the whole thing with Roy and Jonathan… and well, I don't exactly have a lot of free time. Being the dean of a prestigious university is a significant commitment. Parenting would've been a burden."

I flinch as if he slapped me.

"I have to go," I mumble, needing to get out of here.

"Of course," he says, keeping pace with me for a few steps. "But now that it's out in the open, I'm happy to cover your costs of attendance. Tuition, room and board. Just send me the bill. It's the least I can do."

Numbly, I nod, holding on to the last shreds of my dignity

until he turns away, joining my mother at the edge of the building.

I keep it together until I'm out of sight.

Then I run, splashing through murky puddles and muddy sidewalks. The rain has softened to a hazy mist, but the vast doors of the cathedral rise through the grey ahead.

It's the time of day where morning services have ended and afternoon ones haven't begun, which means no one is there to see the mess I've become as I crash through the doors—rain and grime and heartbreak clinging to my heels.

Rows of pews stretch before me. Dark stained glass looms overhead, judging me. Weighing my battered heart and finding it wanting.

"Am I being punished?" I ask the flickering candles and silent saints.

Thunder rolls a few moments later, as if in answer.

I drop to my knees, my soaked jeans pressing against the cold floor, my wet hair clinging to my face. And cry.

42

EVIE

I'm not sure how long I stay there with my knees pressing into the marbled floor of the cathedral, but it's long enough for a puddle of tears and rainwater to form. My cheeks have dried, but I continue to stare at the reflection beneath me. The storm must have passed because the light streaming in through the stained-glass windows brightens the cavernous space.

There's a resounding silence, filled only with the faint trickle of water and the rhythm of my now steady breathing. Focusing on the light, I drag myself upright. My legs are sore and stiff, joints aching, but I raise my head and close my eyes, basking in the warmth of the sun's rays as I process all that's happened.

Dean Whitehouser may be delusional, but we have the same shades of brown in our eyes and a similar upturn to our noses. While accepting him as my biological father is difficult, it means I'm nothing like Roy, who isn't my father but my stepfather. More importantly, I share nothing—absolutely fucking nothing—with Jonathan.

The tormentor of my childhood. The nightmare parading as

a righteous protector and the evil lurking beneath the façade of a golden halo. Not one drop of my blood is related to him.

A sharp buzzing cuts through the torrent of my thoughts. I blink and pull my phone from my pocket. I'm surprised to find it still working despite the cold, wet fabric clinging to my thighs. But then my mother's face flashes across the screen.

I groan, silencing the call. It rings again.

I should turn it off or reject the call. Block her number. Do anything but answer it, but anger has a grip on me now. A part of me wants to hear her apologize, to understand her reasoning for being such a horrible person. So, I grit my teeth and answer.

She isn't even looking at the screen. She's seated at what appears to be the dean's desk, fixing her makeup in a compact off to the side as she starts speaking.

"Jonathan and your father are already livid about your lack of commitment to this family. I've arranged for lunch this weekend and taken the liberty of inviting Jonathan's friend, Jameson."

Disbelief ripples through me at her nonchalance, as if the last hour never happened. As if I'm suppose to just forget she's a hypocritical liar and my entire life has been a lie.

"Jonathan seems to think Jameson will still consider marrying you. If you repent for your wayward ways and return to the church."

"Are you fucking serious?"

Her eyes finally lift, locking with mine through the screen. There's so much rage. And all of it is directed at me.

The crescendo of my heart picks up, cold fear sliding down my spine. My mother has never been particularly loving, but I'd always thought of her as a buffer of sorts between Jonathan and my father—Roy. Not quite a wall, because god knows she's let plenty of things through, but a small form of defense nonetheless. But now… now I realize how wrong I've been.

"It's all been for you," I say, hating the prick of tears that comes with my dawning clarity. "You didn't want me to speak out because it would reflect poorly on you. Even college. When I thought you'd finally done something selfless, risked father—Roy's anger and Jonathan's irritation… I thought it was to support me. But it wasn't, was it?"

She lifts her chin, every trace of tenderness vanishing as I press on.

"You paid for school so you could fuck the dean whenever you wanted. And if your husband ever questioned where you were, you could blame me."

"Watch your mouth when you speak to me. I am your mother."

My voice cracks around a harsh laugh.

"Stop crying," she snaps, looking down her nose at me. "It's unbecoming and makes your face look splotchy. And I can't believe you're wearing jeans. Honestly, Evie. If you don't at least try to maintain a shred of decency, even our family name won't be enough to get you a husband. Is that what you want? To end up ugly and alone?"

A tear drops onto my screen, but my voice is surprisingly steady when I speak. "I won't marry him."

Her eyes narrow. "You'll marry whoever will have you. Whoever your brother deems appropriate."

"He's not my brother," I retort, leaning into the fury rising inside me. "All this time I've been told I'm broken. That I need to beg for forgiveness. As if what he did to me was my fault."

"It was," she spits, nostrils flaring. "It *is*. You're constantly tempting them. Flaunting your body in front of your father and brother when I'm not there."

"You're delusional," I breathe, shaking my head.

"Lie all you like," she sneers. "But I know a whore when I see one."

I hate that I flinch. Hate that she sees it. That she finds satisfaction in the way I hurt. My stomach knots as a smug grin curls across her face. And it's in that moment I realize how much I'm willing to give up to never see her again.

It's not a choice, really. More a truth that settles into my bones with terrifying clarity. To them, I'll only ever be a piece on a game board. A pawn they can use and discard.

"Goodbye, Mother."

I end the call.

With mechanical precision, I pull up her contact and block the number before she can call back. Then I do the same to the people I once called "brother" and "father."

When it's done, I collapse into the nearest pew, tilt my head toward the marble figure above the alter, and allow myself to purge all the pent up emotions I've held onto.

The rain is back, battering against the ancient stone outside these walls. Clouds hang heavy beyond the stained glass, and for a moment, I let myself pretend I'm in another place.

I imagine a distant bell tolling, picturing Spain, like I'm in one of Hemingway's novels. If only time could reverse and transport me there. I'd be dropped into the middle of a world where lives are claimed and souls are reaped, but I would have a family who loves me. When the great bell sounds from the Spanish church, signaling the end of a life—a returning of a soul to the great void—I would know that I'm connected to that life. To the afterlife and the millions of souls surrounding me.

That's what religion is supposed to feel like, I think.

It's a deep-rooted instinct of knowing I'm not alone. That there's a cosmic power, a lifeline connecting us all. Electric. Awakening. And I've never felt more alive, more at peace with myself and the world around me than when I'm with...

"Silas."

His name is a whispered prayer. Before I even realize what I'm doing, I reach for my phone, needing to hear the sound of his voice in my ear, missing the feel of his breath on my skin.

I hit call, and something in my chest loosens the moment the line begins to ring.

"Your mother was right, you know."

A deep voice sounds from behind me, slicing through the quiet and nearly making me drop my phone. I jump, starting to turn toward the sound—but he's already there.

Arms cage me from behind, locking me in place as a bitter, chemical-soaked cloth presses against my face. The sharp, acrid scent burns my eyes. My head begins to swim, but I fight it, clawing at his arm and clutching my phone with every ounce of strength I have.

The third ring cuts off.

Then connects.

"Hey, baby. Out of class early?"

Silas's voice—familiar and grounding—breaks through just as I try to scream. My lips move. My throat strains. But my muscles are failing, sluggish and numb despite the frantic beating of my heart.

"Evie?"

Black spots bloom at the edge of my vision, and my knees give out. The phone slips from my fingers, clattering to the ground as more of the poison seeps into my lungs. I can just make out Silas's threats, muffled and distant, as reality slips further and further away.

"You've been acting like a whore for far too long, Evie. It's time to repent."

43

SILAS

"Evie!"

I hear the muffled sounds of a struggle on the other end, then a loud *bang*. The phone must've dropped, but the silence that follows is quickly cut short by heavy breathing.

Someone is listening.

"You're dead, motherfucker. You hear me? You're fucking—"

"This is your fault."

The fine hairs on the back of my neck prick as his voice rushes over me. I grind my teeth together, stepping away from my half-finished easel, and use every ounce of self-control I have to keep quiet. The confidence in his voice doesn't belong to someone who's easily intimidated. No, this asshole thinks he has it all figured out.

"How is this my fault?" I bite out, slipping into my boots. I don't give a fuck about his answer, but I need to keep him talking.

I tap the speaker icon and send an SOS message to the Seven as I finish getting dressed. Noctis responds instantly, syncing with my phone to trace the call. That small difference of knowing I have the full force of my brothers behind me gives me the slightest edge of hope.

Hope that we'll find her before it's too late.

Because if they take her, if Evie ends up trapped in the same fucking nightmare as Morana… if I lose them both—

"Evie had been doing so well," the voice drawls. I can hear the subtle patter of boots over stone. He's pacing. "Sure, she had a rough childhood. Needed to be disciplined often, but she finally stopped fighting us. Until you found her."

"She's no longer your problem," I say, trying to keep my tone neutral. Arguing won't work, not with someone like him, but maybe if he thinks she's beyond saving he'll give up.

I mute the call briefly as I step into the rain and start my motorcycle, making sure the call connects to the comm in my helmet before I unmute. "You said yourself, she's fallen into sin."

Evie had a meeting with the dean this morning. I'd already planned on visiting him after he abused his power by texting her. But now, that creepy fucker just became my number one suspect.

For a moment, I think the man on the other end of the call realizes I'm on my way, but then he speaks.

"That's true. Sometimes I wonder why we try to save them, why we taint our bodies with theirs, but then I remember everyone must make sacrifices for the greater good."

My nostrils flare as I pull onto the highway. I hear the *crack* of thunder over the call seconds before it echoes around me.

"And there's no greater good than saving a soul destined for hell." His tone grows smug. "Besides, despite her namesake accepting the poisoned fruit and turning her back on heaven's glory, Evie here still ran to the church when she was in need."

A bell tolls in the background.

My eyes widen.

The cathedral.

I push my bike harder, splitting lanes, heading straight for the offramp that will take me to her.

"Don't follow, Silas," the voice purrs—silk over daggers. "You've already lost one sister. And I'm sure you wouldn't want me looking too closely into Tempest's moral state, now would you?"

"Don't you fucking dare—"

The line goes dead.

44

EVIE

The first thing I notice is the suffocating scent of orange blossoms and the grating of my mother's voice in my head. Garbled pieces of conversation reach my altered mind, but everything is so dark.

"Take her and let me go. I won't say anything, I swear."

It feels like an ice pick is splitting my skull in two, making it impossible to focus on the world around me. But my heart is racing, doing everything it can to pierce the thick fog clouding my mind. There's a painful numbness in my hands and fingers, an aching stretch in my shoulders—and then I realize they're drawn overhead, suspending me just enough that the soles of my feet barely brush the ground.

"There she is," a deep voice says, just as a sharp slap lands across my cheek, jerking my head to the side. Chains rattle, the sting of the hit reverberating through my skull as the faint echo of retreating footsteps fades. I blink, trying to open my eyes as the scattered puzzle pieces begin to rearrange.

Mother is next to me, standing in heels with her wrists bound, suspended from a large hook over head.

I remember finding her with the dean. The cathedral. And then…

"You drugged me." My mouth is dry, and there's a lingering bitter taste coating my tongue.

"If I drugged you, I wouldn't be here beside you." She rolls her eyes, leaning away from me. "For god's sake, stand up. You look ridiculous."

Shame burns through some of the lingering fog in my veins as I find my footing, easing some of the tension in my shoulders. Blood rushes painfully back into my fingers as I wiggle them and realize my eyes have started to close.

"Then who?" I rasp, trying to recall what happened.

A dank, moldy smell clings to the air. Worn brick pillars curve up to support a low ceiling. Wooden crates are piled along the edges, and a single suspended bulb swings overhead, casting a morbid yellow glow. Pale shards spill over the top of one, looking a lot like bones.

Swallowing against the dryness in my throat, I shift my gaze, searching the room for clues. Two doors sit on opposite walls, flanking a raised dais and crumbling alcove.

"Why are we in the basement of a church?" My tongue scrapes over my lips like sandpaper as I swing my gaze back to my mother. "I spoke with you, and then—"

Fingers grip my chin from behind, yanking my attention to the third presence in the room. Cold, familiar eyes scan my face, narrowing as he tilts my head from side to side.

Oh god. It can't be.

His cocky smirk is gone, replaced by a sneer. His blue eyes are lighter than his cousin's, his light brown hair darker and longer than Mark's. But the tattoos lacing his forearms, the arrogance gleaming in his eyes—it's the same.

"Not Mark," I croak, brows furrowing as I try to recall. It was months ago. A night of dancing. A back alley. Silas knocking Mark out. Tempest trying to leave with…

"Jameson?"

"Might've overdone it with the chloroform," he says with a shrug. "Heat of the moment and all that. Your mother didn't seem worried."

Accusation flares through my gaze as the effects of the drug continue to ebb.

"I had no idea you'd lose your mind and capture me as well," Mother snaps. Her glare is sharp, lips curled in disgust as she flexes her bound wrists. "I thought you were going to teach your future wife a lesson."

"Wife?" I hiss, but Jameson only tilts his head, his icy blue gaze dragging over my body—so disturbingly similar to Jonathan that my stomach churns.

"You're Father Michael's son."

"Finally connecting the pieces?" Jameson grins. "That's okay, Evie. No one expects you to be smart."

Once, I let people like him shape me, to mold and use me… but that's not quite right, is it? I was never asked. They took my identity, who I am in my truest, rawest form. And once I'd been reduced to a shell—hollowed and vacant—they made me believe it was for my own good.

If it had happened quickly, maybe I could've fought back. Maybe I would've remembered who I was before. But how could I when I never had the chance to become her?

"I'll never marry you," I spit, ignoring the tears coating my cheeks.

"Too late," Jameson says, withdrawing a sheet of paper from his pocket. He unfolds it slowly, holding the fine print up to my face. "Already done. It has your signature and everything."

A dull ringing grows in my ears as I stare at the forged signature, signed and sealed by Father Michael and Roy.

"You can't do this," I whisper, even as he tucks the marriage license away. But the words feel frail even to my own ears. It's already done. My life, my independence… gone.

"Enough with the dramatics, Evie," Mother chides. "Father Michael told me about the bikers you've been spending time with—"

"Yes," Jameson's harsh voice cuts through, his attention locked on me despite my mother's outburst. There's a shift in his eyes, a clearing of all emotion that sends dread sliding down my spine. "And he told me about you letting the filth out of prison too. Another reason why you'll earn redemption before I allow you to be seen at my side."

Fear grips me like a vise, locking my muscles. My heart hammers against my ribs so hard it feels like they might bruise from the inside out.

"Of course she will," Mother says, oblivious to the danger we're both in. But I feel it—feel the sick change in the air. I've had enough horrible men look at me the way Jameson is looking at me now. Like I'm not a person, but an object he's already decided to break.

"That's the entire point of this. Jonathan said you agreed to take her off our hands."

My breath hitches, eyes going wide. "You're the man he wanted me to meet for lunch?"

Jameson grins, his expression cracking the calm façade he's been wearing.

"Surprise. After your second unexcused absence, Mommy Dearest told me where to find you. Imagine my shock when I found out about your meeting with the dean. Or should I say... Daddy?"

My chest heaves, each breath of anger expelling more of the poison clouding my system. A flicker of strength stirs in my limbs, and I grip it tightly, trying to hold on as fear threatens to unravel me. But I need more time for it to wear off. So, I lift my chin and dare to meet Jameson's eyes.

"My family decided I'm a disappointment and wanted me punished. I understand them," I say, jerking my head toward my mother. “But you. What’s your excuse? You’re, what? Angry Tempest never called you back?”

The back of his hand whips across my face, splitting my lip. Blood floods my mouth as Jameson flexes his hand, then wipes the smear of red from his knuckles, like the sight of my blood disgusts him.

“You know damn well this has nothing to do with that bitch and everything to do with Mark.”

“Mark?” I ask, feigning confusion, because of course I know this is about his cousin. About the bullet that shattered his skull. But Silas and the Seven handled it. Jameson doesn’t have proof. He can’t. Or Silas never would’ve walked out of that cell.

“Oh, you mean the guy I danced with twice? He was your cousin, right?” I try for casual, but I can’t stop the cruel undercurrent lacing my words.

He closes his fist this time, the force of the blow taking me by surprise. Stars dance across my vision as my body sways. The skin across my cheek feels damp, the tissue beneath my eye already swelling. Fresh blood pools in my mouth, and I catch Jameson scrubbing his hand clean again.

I wait until he’s done, until the moment he thinks he’s rid himself of all traces of me, and then I spit.

Scarlet flies from my lips, splattering his face. It collects in his light brown strands, dripping down his face, his neck. For one glorious second, I reveal in the shocked horror consuming him before those hollow eyes find mine.

“Shit,” I breathe. *Maybe that wasn’t the best idea.*

The chains binding my wrists rattle as I instinctively try to pull away.

“Stop.”

Jameson halts, nostrils flaring as slow, deliberate footsteps echo from the far end of the room. My gaze shoots to the dark doors across the church basement. *No. It can’t be.*

But then he’s there—my nightmares brought to life—and I

wish, for one terrible moment, that Jameson had knocked me out. That I could rewind time and dig the knife a little deeper across my forearms or swallowed the seed from the *Cerebra odollam* blossom I once held in my palm.

Anything to avoid this.

Because I know Silas is looking for me. He's out there, right now, hunting. And as much as I want to believe he'll burst through those doors and slay the monsters at my feet, the truth is—he's not here.

Not now.

Time has run out.

The beasts are stalking toward me, intent on revenge, and I'm alone. With no way to stop them from tearing me apart.

45

SILAS

"You sure about this?" I growl as the seven of us prowl up to the administration building.

"Yes," Noctis replies, body humming with pent-up energy. It's the same manic vibrations he gets when he's closing in on a secret. Not that it matters. The cathedral was empty except for Evie's busted phone.

"The whole thing is pretty fucked," Erik chimes in. "I'll admit my ego gets the best of me sometimes, but the dean thinking he can just drop into Evie's life now and claim fatherhood is next level delusional."

Mavros grunts in agreement as we push through the door into the lobby. A blonde-haired receptionist quirks a brow at us, then nods.

"The dean is down the hall, to the right, and all the way back," he says, unfazed. "Just follow Sloane's tears."

Eric and I exchange a look before he shrugs and starts forward. The doors open, revealing a dark-haired girl with puffy eyes and a pink-tipped nose. A box of meager belongings is clutched in her arms as she stalks past us, desperately trying to stop the tears when she catches sight of my brothers.

Dominic, Bane, and Adrian offer to help, and for a moment, something nearly tangible passes between them, like a force drawing them together. But the woman—who I assume is Sloane—politely declines, leaving us with a quiet "good luck" as she walks away.

I turn to the open office door where Dean Whitehouser fidgets behind his desk. Erik hisses a warning, but I stride forward until I'm looming over him.

"Silas," Erik warns under his breath, but I ignore him.

"Do you know who we are?" I ask, my tone calm but steel-edged. The dean nods frantically, eyes wide.

"Good," Mavros says, cracking his knuckles. "When did you last see Evie?"

The dean's gaze sweeps through us once more before settling on me. "Oh, you're the biker gang Trisha warned me about."

"Club," Noctis corrects. "Biker club."

Low chuckles sound from my brothers, but I'm not amused. "When?"

"Right after I spoke with her," the dean says. "I planned it as a nice surprise. I was going to tell her Roy stopped paying tuition, but that her real father has sway with the university—her real father being me." He winks as if something he's said is clever, but the ghost of a smile fades when he meets my glare.

He clears his throat and continues. "Then Trisha showed up, wanting me to hide the truth from Evie after I'd waited years. I should've known. I *did* have to threaten to expose our relationship to Roy if she didn't let Evie attend university, but it was part of our agreement."

"What agreement?" Erik asks, narrowing his eyes.

"Shared custody," the dean replies matter-of-factly. "Trisha raises Evie with Roy. She keeps her marriage and image in the church. I get Evie for her young-adult life at Grace University."

"That is the most fucked-up custody agreement I've ever heard," Bane grunts as Dominic lets out a low whistle.

"It was a great plan," Dean Whitehouser says defiantly. "But then Evie walked in on us—well, you know—and ran away. I followed her into the rain, I might add."

"Dad of the year," Erik mutters.

"I told her who I am and offered to cover her expenses while attending Grace University, which she took pretty well. Then she sauntered off toward the heart of campus."

My gaze flicks to Noctis. *To the cathedral.*

"Was anyone with her?" I ask, feeling like I'm tugging on the final threads of a spool, only to find the ends frayed. "Did anyone follow her?"

"No," he answers, but his brows furrow. "Trisha was talking to someone outside the administration building when I returned. She denied it. Said I was seeing things, and that she was just using the camera to fix her hair, but I recognized him. The young man frequents campus, despite not being a student. Light brown hair, blue eyes. He's been reported half-a-dozen times by female students for inappropriate behavior."

"Inappropriate as in assault?" Erik asks, jaw clenching.

The dean gives a guilty shrug. "I've banned him from campus, but it's not like I can enforce it. Besides, the cops say he's harmless. Just visiting from out of state."

Mavros shifts his glare from the pathetic sack of bones in front of us to me, mirroring my suspicions.

It can't be. I killed him.

"Mark?" Erik asks, the purple lion across his leather gloves flexing.

"No." The dean waves his hand vaguely. "The other one who joins Jonathan at church. Shaggy hair, tattoos. His cousin—Jameson."

"Shit," Noctis mutters, already typing furiously on his phone.

"Shit is right," Erik agrees, catching my eye. "You think this is revenge for Evie..."

"Rejecting Mark?" Noctis finishes, eyes flashing. We can't afford anything incriminating getting out.

Do you think Jameson is avenging Mark's death? I ask silently, conveying everything I need to with a glance.

"No," Noctis says, thumbs flying across the screen. "I don't. Dean Whitehouser said he recognized Jameson from Trisha's church. Isn't that right?"

"Yes, I always hated that place." The dean nods. "Creepy. Trisha invited me once. Huge party, but I saw the prostitutes in the back of the cars. There was probably a dozen of them. I have my faults, but paying for sex from women who barely looked legal isn't one of them."

My stomach twists, my body registering the meaning behind his words before my mind fully catches up.

"I've found Jonah," Noctis says, snapping my attention to him. "It's all here. The last piece of the puzzle. The Blue Lagoon. Mark's claim that someone else took over the circuit. Shane's drop point. Even the holier-than-fuck descriptions. It all points to one person—Jonah. Only we know him by another name."

My pulse spikes, my body tensing and already preparing for a fight miles away.

"They weren't prostitutes," Noctis mutters, his voice heartbreakingly soft. He turns the phone toward me, the screen zoomed in on a grainy satellite image. It's blurry, the poor pixilation distorting it, but I know the girl before he says her name.

Her dark hair is longer than I remember. Her body is thin, too thin, despite the years that have passed. Her chin is tipped back, eyes turned toward the sky like she's praying for deliverance—searching for her wayward guardian angel to finally appear.

"Morana." Her name is a choked sob, causing my brothers to take a collective sharp breath.

"And beside her…" Noctis says, dragging the frame over.

"Jameson," I bite out, rage searing through my veins.

But Noctis keeps shifting the image until a third figure appears—grinning like the smug little shit he is, arm slung around Mark's cousin.

Jonathan.

46

EVIE

"Looks like I arrived just in time." Jonathan steps from the shadows, all pretense of the upstanding citizen erased as he surveys the forgotten space and meets my eyes. "I thought this was fitting, meeting in the basement of our church. Lord knows you're too filled with sin to set foot among the pews. Isn't that right, sister?"

My fingers grasp the chains suspending me, my breath coming in short, ragged gulps as I try to find a way out of this. But there's nothing—*nothing*.

And I've wasted so much time. Years trying to fit into their version of what is right, that I forgot there's more than this city —than the family I was born into. Tempest, the Seven, Silas— they're my family. The ones who see all of me and choose to support me. To pick me up when I've been kicked down.

"Thank heavens you're here, Jonathan."

Mother's gentle coo pulls his attention, gifting me a moment of reprieve from his stare. He's always acted for her, insisted on giving her the version of him she expects. Hope bolsters my failing limbs, keeping me afloat in a sea of despair. Maybe this isn't as bad as I think. Maybe kidnapping and physical assault are Jonathan's way of 'purging my soul of sin'.

"I'm afraid Jameson got confused," Mother says. The smile she offers Jonathan is forced, too tight around the edges, and there's a slight wobble to her words. "Would you mind releasing me, dear?"

"Jameson did as instructed, Trisha," a deep voice tsks from behind Jonathan. I crane my neck, looking toward the far end of the room, where the man I've called "father" my entire life steps from the shadows. "As did Jonathan."

He strolls forward, around the messy stack of barrels, past Jonathan, and stops once he's directly before my mother.

"Roy." She makes a choking sound, something between a gasp and a sob, before schooling her features. "Thank goodness. You're just the man I need. Help me down from here and we'll go home. I had Maria marinate steak for tonight's dinner. It should be ready soon."

There's a moment when I think she's gotten him. That Roy will unbind her wrists and they'll walk hand in hand up the steps. And I'll be here, left bleeding and alone for Jonathan and Jameson to toy with.

"You almost had me, Trisha." Roy starts pacing before her, his mannerisms eerily similar to Jonathan's when he first discovered he could lock me in a room with a camera. "All this time I thought I'd found the one woman who complied with the Lord's teachings. Women are weaker. Dumber. And meant to *serve*."

The last word is a paralyzing growl delivered inches from her face. Spit flies across her cheek, tears pooling in her eyes for the first time.

"Jonathan warned me about Evie." My stepfather's cold, haunting eyes swing to me, dragging down the length of my body in a way that has bile searing the back of my throat. "He showed me pictures she took like a slut, meant to tempt even the best of us."

"She's fallen into sin," my mother spits, matching his fury as she tries to redirect the fallout. "Punish her, Roy. Marry her off. Sell her. Do whatever you need to, but don't place blame on the mother for the actions of the daughter."

Hope is just as deadly as despair. And far more painful. Because the hatred staring back at me from my mother's eyes hurts more than it should. She's already shown her hand, waving the cards in my face, and yet I still want to believe there's a part of her that loves me. That wants to see me safe. But this…

"Yes," Roy drawls. "I thought surely I'd be able to beat back the talons of hell in my own child. I would ensure a daughter of my blood would be fit to marry and breed, despite her constant flirtations."

"I told you, she needs the opportunity to atone for her sins," Jonathan says, shaking his head. "The darkness is too deep. Evie needs to beg for forgiveness, like the rest of them."

My stomach twists.

"And now that we know she's not your daughter," Jameson adds, flanking the other two as they train their hungry gazes on me, "or your sister, you two can join in the cleansing of her soul."

"What do you mean?" My mother's confusion rings in her voice, but I don't dare look away from the three monsters before me. "Surely you can't mean to beat her any further. Think of the cost of the surgeries it would take to make her presentable again."

"Us," my stepfather corrects, withdrawing a gun from his pocket.

Mother's eyes go wide, her chest heaving, but she schools her expression, tilting her chin up even as he lifts the barrel to her chest.

"You meant to say 'us' instead of 'her,' Trisha," Roy says. His voice pitches, the wild gleam in his eyes half-hunger, half-deranged fury. He scratches his chin with the gun, shaking his head as he starts to pace. "Because you're just as guilty. All these years and the little bitch isn't even mine."

Roy points the gun at me, but Jonathan steps in front of him, tilting it down. "We must give them a chance to repent first."

My mouth runs dry at the exchange. They really believe this shit. That they're doing the right thing by abducting and torturing us. And the others. The other women they've alluded to. What happened to them?

"In need of saving," Roy murmurs, his gaze settling on Mother's suspended form. "If you can't find absolution through us, then we'll have no choice but to send you through the circuit. But I have faith it won't come to that."

"We'll use your bodies for as long as it takes," Jonathan says in the same casual tone someone might use to remark on the weather. My blood turns to ice, nausea churning as I fight off a wave of dizziness. He catches the large swallow, the shiver raking down my spine, and steps forward.

"Shh, little sister," he coos, a distorted mockery of concern. His fingers pinch my face hard, drawing fresh blood from the gash on my lip as I recoil from his touch. "It's for your own good. Only when you've seen the error of your choices can you return to the light and pray for forgiveness in the next life. I'm sacrificing my body for your soul, just as the Holy Son did for us. I'm not going to enjoy this." Jonathan's lips twitch, self-righteous glee flashing in his gaze as he angles my mouth toward his. "Well, maybe just a little."

The thunderous beat of my heart nearly drowns out the *crack* of a gun being fired.

47

EVIE

"Get the fuck away from her," Silas growls, dashing forward as Jonathan's knee explodes.

Jonathan screams as bits of bone and sinew splatter, coating my jeans, my shoes, spraying across the dirt floor as he crumples. Blood pools around the wound, his mangled knee listing at an unnatural angle.

Adrenaline surges through my veins, my lungs gulping air as forgotten strength floods my limbs. Because he's here.

My serpent.

Silas tears across the dimly lit crypt, looking like an avenging demon intent on enacting swift and brutal justice. Those deep green eyes zero in on the cuts marring my face and the bruise no doubt blooming beneath my eye. He rushes toward me, and I hear the thunder of boots behind him. The Seven.

Jameson gawks at my stepbrother's distorted leg for all of a heartbeat before wrapping one arm around my throat. Silas slows, his gaze bouncing from the way I'm working blood back into my swollen fingers to Jonathan writhing in agony at my feet, calculating how best to get us out of this—just as Mavros and Noctis burst into view.

The rest of the Seven charge. Jameson jerks me against him, wrenching my already sore shoulders. I cry out, the strain unbearable, but Silas takes advantage of the distraction and darts forward. Blinking through tears, I see he's within reach, only a few paces away—and my stepfather turning.

Oh god.

Silas is too focused on saving me to notice the barrel of the gun until it's pointing at his chest.

Time slows. Each second stretching. I catch the startled surprise flashing across Silas's face. Feel the shift of Jameson's grip as he cowers behind my body, tugging down on my torso to use me as a shield. The chains bite into my wrists, blood trickling down my suspended arms, but then he gives me just enough slack to pull up, biceps flexing as I kick out.

A guttural cry bellows from me as the chains swing and I throw my body forward. My shoe connects with Roy's shoulder just as he pulls the trigger, sending the shot wide. I whip backward, crashing into Jameson and sending him tumbling into Jonathan's hunched form.

Jonathan howls, but Jameson is already up, racing for the doors. Dominic corners him, Glock raised with Bane and Adrian at his back.

"Don't do anything stupid," Dominic warns, voice calm and cold.

But Jameson is already reaching for the gun tucked into his waistband.

"Watch out!" I scream.

Dominic fires.

Jameson stumbles back, bloody fingers clutching at his chest. His expression goes slack, dazed, before his knees buckle and he collapses.

"Roy, please stop this," my mother cries, tears streaming

freely now. I've never seen her like this. As anything other than perfect—yet mascara streaks down her cheeks, black trails running down her neck. Even her flawless blonde hair and tanned skin look frail, faded by a bone-deep weariness.

"Me?" my stepfather snarls. He scrambles to his knees with the gun still gripped in his hand, finger on the trigger as he levels the barrel at my mother. "This is your fault."

"No!" I cry, knowing Roy's too far away for me to reach with the chains still holding me in place.

There's a flash of dark hair and a glint of green. Silas collides with Roy just as the gun goes off. His shoulders crash into my stepfather's chest, slamming the evil bastard's face into the worn brick.

Roy fights back, the two of them brawling as leather jackets each embossed with a different sin rush forward, blocking my view of the one person I can't lose.

I scream when a second shot fires, vibrating the ground beneath my feet. A dull buzzing rings in my ears. The harsh intake of breath and my racing heartbeat are all I can hear as Silas stumbles, his back toward me. And there, at his feet, is Roy with shaking hands pressed over a wound in his gut.

"Silas?" Erik calls, voice low as he stands poised over Jonathan with his gun raised. "Tell me you didn't let that preppy asshole get you?"

"Not today." Silas grins, his emerald-flecked eyes finding mine. "Roy has a gunshot wound to the abdomen, and he's bleeding a lot. May have nicked his liver. Jonathan doesn't look much better in terms of blood loss, and the other fucker is already gone. We need at least one of them stable for questioning. Take your pick, boys."

He leaves them to it. And then he's in front of me, lifting the chain binding my wrists off the hook and sweeping my legs out from under me. Pain lances through my limbs as the pressure eases across my shoulders, soothing and aching at the same time.

"Evie," Silas breathes, cradling me as he scours my face, chest, arms, legs—cataloging every inch of me.

"There's no bullet wound," I say, fingers resting against his heart. I can feel the strength of it through his shirt, reassuring me that he's safe too.

"You're safe," Silas says, voice cracking. "Dom, get these cuffs off her."

"I'm fine," I rasp, tasting the lie and lingering metallic tang of blood. Dominic appears moments later with a key, unlocking the cuffs around my wrists. "My mother will need..."

My voice trails off as my eyes land on Bane and Adrian lifting her and carefully setting her down on the cold floor. A gasping, gurgling sound wheezes from her chest, drowning out the rest of the murmurs in the room. Blood coats her face and chest, splattered across her in bright scarlet streaks. Her skin is ashen, eyes wide and vacant as the wound in her chest expels more blood with every rapid beat of her heart.

"Baby, look at me." It's Silas, his palm grazing my cheek, willing me to return to him. But I can't tear my eyes away from her.

"I thought it was him," I say in a low, detached voice so at odds with the chaos inside me. "The harsh scrape of air. I thought it was Roy, but..."

"She has a gunshot wound to the chest," Erik confirms, examining the entry wound. "I'd guess punctured lung and possible rib fracture based on her breathing, but I'm still only pre-med. If we want any of them to have a chance at surviving, we need to get them to the hospital."

"Looks like it's too late for this one," Adrian muses at Roy's side. He cocks his head, a coin flipping in the air before he catches it. Russet brows lift above golden eyes as he reads the result on the back of his hand.

A ragged, wheezing cackle escapes Roy's chest. And then he stills.

"Yep," Adrian says, pocketing his coin as he strolls over. "Definitely too late for him."

"Evie," Silas calls, his voice almost afraid. Judging by his searching gaze and the frown tugging at his lips, I get the impression it isn't the first time he's called my name.

"It's now or never," Erik says, pressing on the wound in my mother's chest.

I realize what they've been waiting for. What all of them expect me to decide: whether we try to save her… or let her die.

"Save her," I hear myself say, knowing she wouldn't have done the same for me, but also knowing this is the only way I'll be able to live with myself.

The seven of them exchange a look, each turning to Noctis for confirmation. For one horrible moment, I think they won't listen, but then Noctis presses a button and holds the phone to his ear.

"Not a clean," Noctis explains, surveying the scene with almost mechanical detachment. "An augmentation. Two dead. Two injured."

There's murmuring on the other end, something that causes his gaze to flick from Jonathan huddled on the ground at his feet to me before he responds.

"One."

48

SILAS

Evie doesn't understand what Noctis's phone call signifies, but I do. *One.* As in one body to take to the hospital—and one to pin this on.

"Be quick," Noctis says, tucking his phone into his pocket. "They'll be here in six minutes. The ambulance in ten."

"What is he talking about?" Evie asks, tearing her red-ringed gaze away from her mother's unconscious form. My face softens when she looks at me, her heart in her eyes. My little fox has been through a lot in the last hour—too much—but I won't keep the truth from her. This has to be done.

"Have you heard the name Jonah before?" I ask her. My brothers move, the five of them shifting to circle Jonathan while Erik keeps Evie's piece-of-shit mother as stable as possible.

"No." Evie shakes her head, then pauses, her breath catching as her eyes cut to her stepbrother. "Only the story."

"Story?" I press.

"*Jonah and the Whale* was Jonathan's favorite story when we were little."

"Shut the fuck up, Evie," Jonathan growls. His face is coated in a sheen of sweat, skin pale, and even from here I can see his pulse is rapid and shallow. But he doesn't get to talk to her like that.

"Bad fucking idea making that the first thing you say."

My voice is lethal as Evie eases from my arms, standing on her own with a hand still braced on my chest for support. She holds me there, asking an unspoken question. I nod, allowing her to step toward the bastard.

"You don't scare me anymore," Evie says. Despite the trembling of her split lip and unsteady legs, she lifts her chin, letting that dark part of herself out to play. And fucking hell, it's beautiful. "You're nothing, Jonathan. You don't control me anymore."

"A person named Jonah has been using the Blue Lagoon as a drop point," I explain, not wanting to hurt her but needing Evie to understand what's at stake. Her brows furrow as I continue. "The same one frequented by your family. Curiously enough, the church we're standing in is also set up as a point to traffick women and children."

Evie sucks in a sharp breath, but there's no surprise in her eyes. Only crushing sorrow.

"Based on condemning evidence, including pictures and correspondence to known criminals," Noctis says, "we believe Jonathan is the connection to the entire southern circuit. All of which I've ensured is established on his personal devices."

"Go to hell," Jonathan spits.

"Already there," I growl, prowling forward. "I've been living in hell since the day my sister was taken. Dragged away kicking and screaming by assholes just like you."

"No hitting," Noctis chides, seeing my fists flex. "It won't match the story."

"Come on," Mavros whines, shoulders slumping. "Just once? What if we avoid the face?"

"No," Noctis says, rolling his eyes at Mavros's pout. "But his knee *is* already fucked. Can't see that being a problem."

Perfect.

My foot connects with the twisted joint, sending Jonathan curling up on his side, writhing in agony. His screams soothe the vacancy in my heart—the one left when Morana was taken. I crush the ragged, bleeding tissue beneath the sole of my boot, pressing until he loses consciousness from the pain.

I wait until he wakes, until I catch the flash of fear staring back at me, before I start again. "One month ago, there was a group of women at this church. Ones you piled into the back of a white van. Where are they?"

There's a moment where he considers lying to me, but a single glance at his shredded limb has him reconsidering.

"Some have been sold, but most are being held downtown at a place called the Devil's Lair."

Noctis has his phone back out, thumbs flying across the screen. "Got it," he confirms, eyes bouncing over the information. A few seconds later, his movements slow, the hope flitting across his face fading. A heartbeat later, I know why.

"Is this woman at the Devil's Lair?" Noctis asks, flipping his phone to show Jonathan a picture of Morana.

"I should've known this was about that bitch." A sneer twists his face as he looks away, but I'm there, pinching his chin between my leather gloves.

"Is that a yes?"

"Yes," he grits out, a haunting smile tilting his lips. "Unless the boss changed his mind. She was in Vegas not too long ago. Rumor has it, she's his favorite. Off-limits to everyone else."

Erik and Mavros are at my side in an instant, waiting for me to lead the charge. It's always been the plan: find Morana and kill as many of the bastards as we can. The three of us were the first to start this hunt—but then I catch sight of Evie. Of the memories flashing through her eyes from tormented nights long ago. And I know I can't take this death away from her.

"Go," I order, catching the flicker of confusion in Erik's

stormy eyes. "Mavros, Noctis, go with Erik. Proceed cautiously. I don't trust this asshole, but if she *is* there, if she's alive—"

"We'll do whatever it takes to bring her home safely," Erik finishes, clapping my shoulder. "I promise you, brother."

I nod as footsteps sound behind us. We don't flinch, every one of us familiar with the cadence of the cleaners by now.

"Can I use a knife?" I ask the cleaners, my voice steady as Dominic, Bane, and Adrian move to my side, letting them get to work.

"A gun would be better," one of the crew says, already positioning Jameson's limp body at the appropriate angle to Jonathan.

"Here," Dominic says, stepping forward. "Use mine."

"No," Jonathan says, eyes cutting to Evie. "You can't let them kill me. I'm your brother."

Evie stands there, silent and stoic, staring at the person who's haunted her dreams for years. Swallowing down the urge to end his life right then, I take a step back, holding out the handle of the Glock for her to take.

"I'll enjoy killing him," I murmur, searching her beautiful brown eyes. "But his death is yours to take, if you want it."

To my surprise, she spares only a glance for her parents, seeing one of the crew tending to her mother as others drag her stepfather's body into a position better suited for their cover story. And then she prowls forward and takes the gun.

"Why the story of Jonah?" she asks, cocking her head as she looks down at her abuser. "You were always fascinated by him, but his pride led him down the wrong path. He was literally swallowed by a whale, and only then did he ask to be forgiven."

"That's what I'm doing," Jonathan says, chest heaving.

There's so much blood around him. Too much. I must've hit one of those deep veins in his leg. At this point, I'm not sure another bullet is necessary, but Evie deserves to claim this.

"I'm the whale," Jonathan pants, sounding as self-righteous

as ever. "I'm the trial each sinner must face, and in so doing, I gift them the chance to return to God. To meet their Lord with a clear conscience. What I did to you, Evie, was just the beginning."

My blood boils, fury igniting in a raging inferno.

"Those pictures," he rushes on, sensing the end is near. "The videos. I helped you purge the sin—"

Fuck it. I know I should let Evie handle it, but this bastard deserves to experience every ounce of pain I can wring from him.

But then my little fox raises the gun.

A red hole appears in the center of Jonathan's forehead a heartbeat before I process the ringing of the shot.

49

SILAS

My brothers still. Even the cleaners, busy wiping evidence and planting new ones, freeze. Chunks of Jonathan's brain arc behind him in scarlet spray, coating the lower half of the wall and floor as his lifeless body tumbles forward. The faint wail of sirens breaks the haunted silence, bringing reality crashing down around us.

"Shit," one of the cleaners says, springing into action. The others follow, mopping up Jonathan's mess while dragging Jameson forward.

"I'll take that," Dominic says gently, plucking his gun from Evie's trembling, outstretched hand.

"Time to go," Bane calls.

Evie is still paralyzed, watching wide-eyed as one of the cleaners places a gun in Jameson's limp hand while the other presses the barrel to the bullet hole in Jonathan's skull, still trying to find the perfect angle for the bodies.

I catch her when her knees buckle, carrying her toward the exit after my brothers. She looks so fragile curled into my chest, her lashes closed over damp cheeks splattered with blood. Staring down at the swollen cuts across her perfect face, feeling the hitch in her breath that signals silent tears, and knowing what happened here today will only add to her nightmares—I wonder if I've done enough.

If you'd asked me a year ago, the answer would've been easy. Apart from sacrificing Tempest and my brothers, I would've let the world burn to save my sister—I have. I still would. But things don't seem as clear as they once were.

I've been trapped in an endless cycle of punishing while still hurting. Plagued by the knowledge that for every few I save, there are thousands still out there. Suffering. My heart hammers against my ribs, spurred on by fear—and worst of all, hope—that this could be the day that changes everything.

Morana could be safe in just a few hours.

Returned home at last.

We reach the stairs when the shot rings out behind us, blending with the blare of nearby sirens. I glance over my shoulder, clutching Evie tighter as I catch the fresh spray of brain matter and blood, the mess cast in a perfect splatter to complete the story the cleaners have concocted.

And then they're with us, bounding up the back of the church and into a waiting van as I position Evie between my thighs and start my engine. Our motorcycles peel out, slipping down a small service road just as the ambulance pulls through the main gates.

We're miles down the highway when Evie speaks. "The smell will give it away. The cleaning supplies. And footprints. They'll know Jameson didn't kill him."

I hate the hollowness in her tone, knowing it's reflected in the depths of her eyes, shielded beneath the helmet. Maybe I should've killed the fucker for her. Or, better yet, insisted she leave the moment we found them.

"We have connections with the hospitals," I say instead. "It helps when we need to get rid of a body. Or two."

"And the cops?" she asks, her shoulders slumping. Seeing that small show of vulnerability has me wanting to scream.

"Father Michael was involved in this." I do my best to keep my voice even, trying not to startle my little fox, but it sounds like a growl anyway. "Noctis found plenty of evidence condemning many members of the church. It was easy once he knew where to look. Turns out a lot of them are tied to local police. Being that Noctis has already sent evidence to the FBI and the entire precinct is under investigation, I don't think they'll be bothering us anytime soon."

The reckless, headstrong part of me wants to ride with the others straight to Morana. To forget the recon part of this and burst in, guns blazing. But that'll only get us killed. Or worse, cause Morana's death.

I have to trust my brothers. They'll contact me the moment they have answers. As soon as we have a real shot at getting my sister to safety. For now, my focus needs to be on Evie.

"It'll be okay, little fox," I murmur, pressing her against my chest.

Evie gives a tight nod, but tension clings to her body the rest of the drive. Sparing one last glance at the motorcycles ahead, I take the exit that will bring us back to the solitude of my studio.

"Let's go home."

50

EVIE

I killed my brother.

Stepbrother, I remind myself, as if that makes it any better.

The scene keeps playing over and over again. I'm watching from above my body, seeing his face twisted in self-righteous anger. Like I'm the one failing him again by not understanding how his abuse was a good thing.

That's what decided it for me. Jonathan didn't feel remorse. He was proud of the torture he put me through, and was gloating about what was to come. About all the women who'd been taken before.

I don't remember pulling the trigger.

He was talking, and I was dying inside… And then he stopped.

Bits of his skull blasted away, coating the church basement, and a single drop of red dribbled from the entry wound. For a few moments, there was nothing but silence. I swear there were a few seconds where he was aware of what I'd done. Fleeting heartbeats where there was still enough oxygen and activity in his brain for him to realize I'd killed him.

"Evie."

The tenderness in Silas's voice brings me back from the swirling memories. He's always had this strength about him. When we fucked, when he confessed his feelings for me, there was a possessiveness, a power underlying it all.

But not now. Right now, his deep green eyes are looking at me as if I might run. Concern, admiration, and something resembling regret all mashed together.

"Come, little fox. The water is ready," Silas says, extending his hand. He's standing just outside the shower, nude and waiting for me to join him.

Swallowing, I stare down at my blood-soaked clothes, fingers gripping the edge of my shirt. I tug it off. Red stains are everywhere. Dried bits flake from my hands, matting pieces of my hair. I need to get it off. Need all traces of Jonathan gone. Scrubbed from my body. And *god*, my jeans are stuck. His blood hardening the fabric. And I'm trapped.

Suffocating.

"Breathe, Evie," Silas commands as he grips either side of the zipper and yanks. Fabric splits, freeing my legs, and I scramble out of my underwear next, chest heaving as I start to scratch at the lingering stains across my body.

Silas captures my hands, throwing me over his shoulder before my nails break skin. The sudden change shatters the spiraling panic, leaving me feeling more defeated than ever.

"I can wash myself," I start, but Silas gives my ass a sharp slap.

"I'm not leaving you alone, little fox. Don't insult me by asking."

Steam billows from the glass shower, the scent of eucalyptus filling the bright space.

The main house is different from Silas's studio. Grander in an overwhelming way. We went to the studio first, but after realizing how shaken I am—how detached—Silas thought this would be better than his small washroom.

Part of me still feels like I'm floating outside my body. Even as the two of us step into the large shower, complete with two overhead spouts and a bench in the center, it feels like a dream.

Tempest and the others are at the house by campus, closer to downtown as they wait for an update. We have the Spanish-style mansion all to ourselves. Thank fuck for that, because I can't seem to keep it together.

Silas brushes away a lock of damp hair matted with dried blood, his hand cupping my cheek as he presses a gentle kiss to my forehead. He pulls away only for a moment, returning with a sponge that smells like him. He scrubs across my breasts, my stomach, my legs, then moves my hair to the side as he washes my back, working soothing motions across my skin. Silas takes his time, massaging the tension from my shoulders, combing through the tangles in my hair, erasing the tarnish of the day with each stroke until my skin is pink and the water runs clean.

And I just stand there, staring into nothingness. Trying to find a way to connect my mind to my body.

Noctis confirmed they'd found the Devil's Lair while we were on the bikes earlier, but the place was empty. Silas hasn't let a moment of worry show as the others monitor the space, putting my needs first as he anxiously awaits news. But that calm demeanor of his is cracking now.

He stares down, shifting as steam rises around us, and the uncertainty in his eyes breaks me all over again.

"I don't want you to go," I say. I don't like the way Silas's shoulders tense, as if he doesn't believe me. I close the distance between us, burying myself in his chest, inhaling the spice-and-leather scent of him. "I need you, Silas. Need you to help me forget what I did. Or maybe remember who I am. I'm not sure. But I know I need you here. With me."

"I'm here, baby. I've got you." His arms come around me, the warmth of his palms thawing every inch of flesh they touch. "You did well, Evie." He presses a kiss to the top of my head, holding me close. "He got what he deserved."

"I don't regret it," I say, drawing back until I'm holding his gaze. Pieces of his dark hair have fallen forward, his large, tattooed body beaded with water, but he meets the challenge in my eyes unflinchingly.

"Killing Jonathan—I would do it again. I know I would, but everything just feels… off. Like I'm here but not really. This is my body, and I can feel you, but I'm also sort of floating and disconnected."

Silas tilts my chin up, his thumb brushing away the tears across my cheeks like evidence washed away by the shower. His lips meet mine, gentle and soothing. Sweet in a way I didn't think he was capable of.

Silas kisses me like I'm his first breath of life, like he's experiencing a miracle by sweeping his tongue across mine. Much too soon, he pulls back, fingers tangling in my hair.

"Let me bring you back."

51

EVIE

"You're mine, little fox." He presses teasing kisses along the curve of my neck, hands roaming my body. One cups my breast, teasing my nipple, while the other dips between my thighs. "This body belongs to me."

I whimper as his fingers slide along my core, stroking my entrance. His cock presses against the small of my back, and I arch into him, needing the spark of electricity his touch brings.

A low growl rumbles from him as he spins me, pinning me against the cool tile. Hot water cascades over him, trailing down his sculpted form. Silas holds himself just out of reach, gripping his length and stroking from root to tip.

"What are you waiting for?" I ask, swallowing. The sight alone has my thighs trembling, promising pleasure, but more importantly—connection.

"Remember how much I love you." Another stroke, the veins along his forearm flexing. "Because I'm about to fuck you like I don't."

My core tightens, nipples growing hard as I watch a bead of cum form at his tip. I lick my lips, craving the salty taste of him. Needing to get lost in this. In us.

"I'm going to fill your needy little cunt up until you're sore and swollen," he murmurs with all the tenderness of a lover. "Until you don't know where pain ends and pleasure begins. And when your pussy is overflowing with my cum, I'll fuck your face."

He gathers the bead of cum from his tip, bringing it to my lips. I open my mouth, closing my lips around the pad of his thumb, savoring this small glimpse of what's to come.

"And then your ass."

"Please," I whisper, my breasts heaving and aching for his touch. This is what I need, to be reminded I'm alive. I'm wanted and cherished and… safe.

Silas stares down at me, gentleness warring with his intrinsic need for dominance. His knuckles drag down my chest, grazing over the space between my breasts before continuing lower. He kicks my legs apart, thrusting three fingers into my core before I'm ready.

I gasp at the stretch, but his other hand is there, pinning my throat to the wall, holding me up as he fucks me with his fingers. The water from the shower mixes with the slickness between my thighs, and in a matter of moments I'm grinding against him, bucking as I seek more friction, craving the pain I know his cock can give me.

"Silas," I pant, but he's already flipping me around, pulling my hips up as he positions himself at my pussy. I expect him to pause, to give me time to prepare, but he slams into me, pelvis smacking against me as I moan.

His fingers dig into the meat of my ass, the scalding water pinging off our writhing bodies as my face presses into the cold tile.

"I'm going to fuck you until you can't walk without pain. Can't breathe without knowing who this body belongs to."

Silas is harsh and punishing, but his filthy words only spur me on, pushing me to the edge of ecstasy. And then one of his hands finds my clit, stroking and flicking in time with his thrusts.

"Silas." I moan his name as I fall, crashing over the edge. Pricks of electricity dance across my skin as pleasure quiets the racing of my mind. *Yes.* This is what I want. What I need.

"That's right, baby," Silas murmurs, picking up his pace as my body loosens, molding to his will. I'm so caught up in the post-orgasm haze that I don't tense when his hands part my cheeks.

I glance over my shoulder, finding his pupils blown wide as he stares at the place our bodies are joined, watching his cock pump in and out of my pussy. My core clenches at the raw hunger in his eyes, at the unbridled desire surging with each thrust of his hips.

"I'm going to fuck you here too, little fox." Silas circles my ass, testing the tight hole with the tip of his thumb.

My body tenses at the threat, and I feel him reach between our rocking bodies, coating his fingers in my arousal before returning to that forbidden place.

"Relax," he breaths, pressing against the ring of muscle as he angles his hips, hitting that delicious spot inside me that has my toes curling, my mind short-circuiting.

"Good girl," Silas says, his finger stretching me, working my ass in rhythm with our bodies. "Look how beautifully your ass takes my fingers." He presses in a second, the searing burn of it foreign and punishing. Hell and rapture all at once. "Look how this greedy little cunt clenches around my cock, begging me to fill it. Do you want my cum, Evie? Do you want me to fill you up like the good little slut you are?"

"Yes," I cry. My hands search for purchase on the slick tiles as Silas unleashes himself, fingers stretching my ass, hips splitting me in two, bringing me higher. Higher. And then I'm crashing again, that delicious coil low in my belly snapping as the world around me shatters.

Silas cries out, pressing deep inside me as his cock pulses, filling me up just like he promised. He slips out, his fingers gathering the cum leaking down my legs, pushing it back inside my aching pussy before cleaning off the rest of me.

I still feel like I'm floating as he turns off the water, wraps me in a towel, and sets me down on the silk sheets of his bed.

"Eyes open, baby," Silas says, spreading my legs apart again. He hikes my knees up, pushing them wide until my back rounds, the most intimate parts of me exposed for his stare. "Hold yourself open for me."

Swallowing, I do what he says, my hands replacing his on the backs of my thighs. His fingers caress my folds, sliding through my pussy before circling my ass.

"Did you like when I touched you here, little fox?" Silas uses his thumb to press against the sore flesh, and even as a hiss of pain escapes me, I'm nodding, wanting more. "Were you picturing my cock here?" He presses into me, his cock already hard again as I moan against his finger. "To be properly fucked and filled by me?"

"Yes," I breathe, looking down over my stomach to where he toys with me. "I want you everywhere," I confess, my voice trembling with desperate desire. *God,* I need him—crave his cum in my ass, my mouth, covering my breasts. I want him everywhere. Filling me. Covering me until I'm drenched in the scent of him. Until he is my world. My entire reality.

He must see the tortured need in my eyes, because he spreads my cheeks further, letting a string of spit fall from his mouth to my hole—and then the head of his cock replaces his fingers.

I gasp at the pain, doing my best to keep myself spread for him, wanting him to continue even when it feels like there's no way he'll fit.

"Fuck," he groans, gathering more of my slickness to coat his cock. "So fucking tight."

"Silas, I can't," I whimper, trying to relax. I'm about to tell him to stop when his fingers find my clit.

"Shh, I won't break you, baby." Silas flicks and teases just the way I like, his thumb working my clit as he slips a finger into my pussy. "You're my toy, baby. And I take good care of my toys."

I moan as he takes me higher, the delicious promise of an orgasm easing the tight ring of muscle enough for him to pull out and thrust in deeper. My fingers tighten on my thighs, nails digging into my skin as the pain begins to shift.

Silas groans as he seats himself fully, his hands replacing mine as he draws back to the tip—only to slam forward.

"Oh god," I pant, gripping the sheets as he picks up his pace. Then his fingers are back, pumping into my pussy as his cock takes my ass. I'm full, so fucking full. "Oh my fucking god."

"You're such a pretty mess for me, baby. Look. Look at how well you weep for me."

I press up, staring at where our bodies are joined—at the wetness coating my thighs and his fingers, coating the skin right above his cock. Sweat and cum and the scent of him swirl around us.

"Fuck," he growls. I'm seeing stars, my head falling back as his body tenses, his hips slapping, fingers gripping my ass. And then I'm following him into the abyss.

52

SILAS

The clock flashes 1:58 a.m. as I reach for my phone, answering the incoming call before it can wake Evie. I was true to my word. Fucking her in every way imaginable, using her lips last. I came all over her face, her breasts and chest, then dragged my fingers through the mess, shoving them between her lips until she cleaned every drop.

And she loved every fucking moment of it. My little fox has earned her sleep. I won't be able to breathe without feeling me, but there's been no update from my brothers. And I need a distraction. A better man would put his own needs aside, let Evie rest…

I tug the sheets back, groaning as Evie's perfect pussy comes into view. We didn't bother getting dressed after the third shower. I'm just about to start dessert when I catch the flash of a purple lion on my phone and slip from the bed.

"Do you have her?" I ask, tugging on a pair of sweats as I move into the hallway.

"Not yet," Erik answers, his voice buzzing with pent-up energy. Good energy. "But there's movement. A white van just pulled up. The same one from the church."

"Plates?"

"Confirmed," he says. "Silas, it has to be her. We're monitoring, but the moment there's an opening, we're going in."

"I'm on my way."

"I'll drop our location." He pauses, and I hear the hesitation in the quiet before he exhales. "I told Tempest."

"You what?" I hiss, trying to keep my voice down, but then I catch sight of Evie in the doorway, my shirt thrown over her shoulders, hanging to mid-thigh.

"She deserves to know," Erik snaps.

It's the first time he's sounded serious in years. "I got her to promise to stay put, but I couldn't keep her in the dark."

Evie holds my gaze as I bite my tongue about keeping Tempest safe. I won't survive the loss of another sister if she changes her mind and follows us. But judging by the lift of Evie's chin and the firm press of her lips, she's already guessed what this call is about. And she's on Erik's side.

"Okay," I grit out, cutting off Erik's lecture mid-sentence. "Evie is coming too."

I hear the sirens first.

"Hold on," I say into the mic. Evie braces, her back pressing against me as I speed down the abandoned street, weaving through back alleys until the Devil's Lair comes into view. Red and blue lights flash against downtown buildings as people in black with guns drawn cluster in front of our place of interest.

"What's happening?" I ask, slowing my bike as I find an outcropping a few streets up. I can't see the back alley, but I can at least monitor the cars from here. "Cops?"

"Maybe," Erik replies. I hear the purr of his engine spring to life. "We're not sure."

The sirens go quiet, wariness pricking along my spine. It must've been a sign, because the group scatters, swarming the building. I recognize their formations, groups fanning out to cover every exit. They're clean. Anyone watching would assume it's a standard police raid, but these men move like they've worked together for years.

"Mavros thinks they might be special ops," Erik says. "Noctis is checking and monitoring from the roof."

My gaze cuts to the building across the street. It's tucked in shadow, providing the perfect place for a sniper.

"The rest of us are headed your way," Dom adds.

The ground vibrates moments later as my brothers round the corner, switching their lights off to conceal their movements. Erik and Mavros pull up beside me, watching as a team of three men slip around the back of the building and vanish from view.

"Dom, Bane, Adrian," I say. I don't like the idea of splitting up, but I need eyes on every possible escape route.

"On it," they reply, slipping through the streets, keeping to the darkness. I scrutinize the movement of the so-called cops, brows furrowing as I realize the ammunition they're packing isn't standard issue.

"They're not local" I murmur, hoping someone will contradict me.

"No," Noctis confirms, and I know he's looking through his scope, cataloging every detail. "The cop cars have the same emblem as the uniforms. Most wouldn't notice, but they're wearing military grade gear complete with Kevlar jackets, silencers, the works."

"How many?" Mavros asks.

"At least a dozen," Noctis replies. "Maybe more if there are still soldiers in the cars."

"Too many," Dominic mutters. "There's an SUV in the back. Black, tinted, and filled with another half-dozen decorated the same."

"But they're against the people who have Morana," Evie says, her soft voice unsure as she speaks.

"She's right," Dominic replies. "They just busted a window—"

Gunshots ring out, silencers curbing the blasts.

"Shit," Dom curses, his voice muffled as engines roar in the background.

"What's going on?" I ask, leather gloves flexing around the handlebars, ready to move at a moment's notice. Lights flash in the garage windows. Two more blasts ring out, and then the garage door lifts, revealing half a dozen men sprinting toward the cop cars—one carrying a thin woman with dark brown hair thrown over his shoulder.

Morana.

My stomach flips. She's here. She's really fucking here. Her arm is outstretched, reaching for something or someone inside the building. Another wave of men follows, carrying an unconscious woman with golden blonde hair and bruises along her exposed arms and legs that are visible even from here.

"Don't lose her," Evie says, laying her hand over mine. "Not again."

Never again.

"Hold," Noctis calls, but I'm already moving.

53

SILAS

"You're going to get her killed," Erik growls. He flies past me, tires smoking as he cuts his bike across my path.

"Shit," I grit out, slamming the break. Evie shrieks, my arm wrapping around her waist to hold her steady in the seat. "Get out of my way, Erik."

"No, Sie," he says, flipping up his visor. "We can't take them here."

"We're outnumbered," Dominic calls, appearing a moment later with Adrian and Bane at his side.

"They've clearly scouted this place well in advance," Erik continues. "Judging by how clean that abduction was, they must've been studying their enemy for weeks."

"*Their* enemy," Mavros says, pointing toward the fake cop cars pulling off the street. "You don't know if they're ours."

"They took her," I growl, my body tensing as I fight the urge not to run Erik over. "It's happening again. They're taking her, and we're doing *nothing*."

"They're heading toward the fifteen," Noctis says, and I can hear the shuffling of metal as he packs up his rifle. "Follow them, but don't let them see you. If we're lucky, they'll head for the desert."

"He's right, Silas," Evie says gently. "Morana is safe. We didn't see them hurt her."

"Yet," I mutter, kicking my bike into gear and speeding past Erik.

He curses but falls into line, the six of us catching up to the cop cars quickly. Trailing at a decent distance, we follow as they leave the city. A half hour passes before they turn east onto I-15, following the highway as it snakes through the desert.

"There's no cover here," Noctis warns, having just caught up to us.

"There'll be less once dawn comes," Erik adds. "Even now, under the cover of the moon with our lights off, they've probably already seen us."

"Agreed," Mavros says. "This feels like a trap."

My jaw flexes as I study the black SUV and two cop cars ahead. They've kept the same pace since we left. Mavros is right. A team as thorough as theirs, one prepared enough to have false cop cars, matching uniforms, and high-quality weapons, would surely have lookouts for a tail.

"I agree," Dominic says, as if reading my mind. "Something feels off, and we can't rescue Morana if we're dead."

"What do you suggest?" I ask. Cursing, I ease off the gas, putting more distance between us and my sister. "Letting them get away won't help."

"Two tails," Bane suggests. "Two others fall behind them but within sight in case the tails need backup. The rest pull off and wait. With any luck, we'll follow them into the city and get a location."

Another location. Which means more scouting. More planning. And that's if we don't fucking lose them entirely.

"We'll tail," Evie says, pressing her back against my chest, her way of showing she trusts me. That she understands the seriousness of this and is unafraid. Of course she is. My little fox is fucking incredible.

"Uhhh, guys?" Erik interrupts as the early morning sky turns the darkest shade of purple with the promise of day. "They turned on their flashy lights."

The cop cars split, leaving the SUV on the road, one veering left and the other swerving right. Clouds of sand and dirt swirl as their wheels blaze through the desert, each making a U-turn.

"Shit," Noctis mutters as the cop cars switch directions and head straight for us. "They're surrounding us."

"Silas," Evie whispers, pressing further into me. Her voice wavers around my name, and I wish to my fucking core that I could shield her from all that's to come.

The cop cars zoom past, dust kicking up in their wake before they swing back onto the road. They race toward us from behind as the black SUV stops, blocking our path forward.

"We could split up," Dominic says as our group slows. "Bike into the desert until we find a way to lose them."

"No," I cut in as we ease to a stop, our group pinned between them. "It's flat for miles. We'll be too easy to pick off."

"They haven't shot us yet," Mavros chimes in, hand twitching like he's considering reaching for his gun.

"Best not to tempt them," Adrian murmurs, turning his bike to face the cop cars behind us. Dominic and Bane do the same. Erik, Noctis, and Mavros take the front. Leaving me in the middle. I don't like hiding behind my brothers, but Evie is safest here. And her life is more important than my ego.

"Movement," Dominic calls, snapping my attention to the car on the left.

"Maybe I spoke too soon," Adrian says. "Should we put our hands up or reach for our guns?"

"Morana is with them," I bite back, wishing just as badly as my brothers that this had gone a different way. "Don't draw your weapons unless forced to."

I switch the mic so only Evie can hear me, my hands clamping over hers. "If they open fire, you ride south until you hit Highway Forty. You take that back to the fifteen. Don't stop. Don't look back."

"I'm not leaving you," she protests, the conviction in her voice cracking something in my chest.

"I need you to, little fox." My tongue is heavy, emotion clogging my throat, but I force the words out. "I need you to run, because if anything happens to you, it's over for me. You are my purpose. My life. My entire fucking heart."

I hear the tears in her voice, and as much as it pains me not to be able to kiss her, to fuck her until she forgets all the horrible shit in this world, I'm glad for the helmet hiding her from view. Because it allows me to imagine her happy and whole. Which is the only fucking way I'm able to swing my leg off the bike and walk toward the two men stepping out of the SUV, their guns trained on me.

I flip up my visor as I switch my comm to include my brothers again, and lift my chin. I glare at the one closest, recognizing him as the same man who carried Morana out of that garage.

"You took my sister," I say, my voice dripping with the promise of blood. "I intend to take her back."

54

EVIE

I don't care what Silas says. If he's taken or shot, I'm riding straight for the bastards and doing as much damage as I can. My fingers flex over the throttle, sweat soaking my brow inside the helmet as I watch two men get out of the second cop car, joining the ones already aiming guns at Silas.

But they don't shoot, even after Silas issues his threat. Instead, they appear to be communicating through earpieces. It's a quick exchange, and then the one nearest Silas lowers his gun.

"If you're Arthur's men," the cop warns, "I'll bury you in the sand and leave only your heads exposed for the vultures and ants to feast on."

"Who the fuck is Arthur?" Erik asks through our mics.

"I don't know." Noctis's response is clipped, the tension in his voice mirrored in the white-knuckled grip on his handlebars.

Silas shakes his head. "I don't give a fuck who your little pissing contest is between. I want my sister returned. I want Morana."

The man in front holds Silas's gaze for a long moment,

seeming to stare right through him, before signaling to the others. They move instantly, opening the back door of the SUV. A short woman with dark curly hair hops out, shooting a glare at the nearest cop as she brushes off her stained nightgown. The fabric is torn, the once-silky material marred, but the confidence she carries herself with is that of a queen, not someone stepping out of captivity.

She's been gone for years, stolen and sold to the worst kinds of people, but toned muscle covers her body, hardening her small curves, and there's a healthy glow to her tanned skin. More than anything, her deep green eyes are warm. Not broken or hollow—but alive.

"Silas?" I ask, not sure if this is really her.

"Morana." His voice is a disbelieving whisper, the closest I've come to hearing him cry. He tugs off his helmet, letting it topple to the ground as she takes a few tentative steps forward and then launches into his arms.

The rest of the Seven tense, ready to draw their weapons at the first sign of Morana's abductors trying to stop her. But the cops don't move.

"They're discussing something," Noctis says. "The SUV is turning around."

I tear my gaze from a grinning Silas and Morana, catching sight of the SUV speeding down I-15, heading toward Vegas.

"They're leaving," I breathe. "If Morana is really in danger, why would they leave?"

"They wouldn't," Erik says, and I can hear the smile in his voice. "It looks like *she's* ordering *them* around."

I swing my gaze back to them, finding Silas's spine stiff, hands flexing at his sides as Morana says something to the cop. She points to the other car, and after another minute of arguing, the cop lowers his gun, releasing the others from their positions.

"What the fuck?" Mavros rasps. "She's in charge?"

Silas nods at something the cop tells him, looking like he's not sure if he wants to murder or thank the man before him. Then he reaches for his helmet. His voice comes through the speakers a moment later.

"Morana was taken from her... family. These men were sent to bring her back to Vegas. She's under their protection."

"She's free to leave?" Erik asks, skepticism dripping from every word.

"That's what they said," Silas replies, his tone just as sharp. "She won't say much, but it sounds like she caught the attention of someone high up. Possibly in the business."

"Someone who's been taking good care of her by the look of it," Erik bites out.

I see the way his words ripple through Silas, his shoulders bunching.

"The most important thing is she's safe and they're letting us go," I say, hoping to ease some of the tension. "Right?"

Silas gives a curt nod, his head following Morana as she stalks toward the second cop car and opens the door. The second woman who was taken climbs out. There are bruises covering her pale skin, the discoloration made harsher in the early morning light. Her golden blonde hair is dull and tangled, matted with grime. She stands on wobbly legs, helped to Silas's side by Morana.

He offers her his hand, but the girl flinches away, hiding behind Morana. The same thing happens when Erik tries to approach.

"She's afraid," Mavros snaps, slipping from his own bike to clasp Erik on the shoulder and draw him back.

"I get that, asshole," Erik grumbles, shaking him off. "We need to be calm. Show her we're not a threat."

"Do you feel comfortable riding with Erik?" Silas asks. His visor is flipped up, gaze pinned on Morana.

"Only if Serena trusts one of you enough to ride," Morana replies, the mic picking up her words. She doesn't let go of Serena's hand. "If not, the guys have offered to drive us back with you."

Even as she says the words, Serena tentatively shakes her head, glancing at the cops before peeking around Morana's shoulder to look at Mavros. Her blue eyes roam his large frame, noting the thickness of his thighs and bulk of his arms and chest. I expect her to cower, as most people do. Mavros is a beast, but Serena stands a little straighter.

She lets go of Morana's hand. Serena in a few inches shorter than Silas's sister and looks as if a strong breeze could blow her over, but she digs in her feet, lifting her chin as she studies the helmet with the growling red bear embossed on the side.

"Take your helmet off," she demands, voice trembling.

Without a word, Mavros does as she asks, slipping his helmet off and handing it to her, offering to keep her safe in more ways than one.

There's a silent exchange, one that feels too big for this moment, too heavy for all that's transpired. But Serena must find what she's looking for in Mavros's dark gaze because she takes the helmet.

"Don't drive like an idiot," she says, startling a laugh from him as she stalks past. She swings a leg over Mavros's bike, waiting for him to join her. "I don't want to worry about escaping those assholes just to die from an incompetent driver."

I think I hear Mavros's deep voice rumble a promise, but it's too low to make out.

"Glad that's settled," Erik says, holding his helmet out for Morana. "Long time no see, sis."

There's the briefest twitch along Morana's lips before she accepts Erik's helmet and climbs on.

That small flicker of hope loosens the constricting band

across my chest, cutting away some of the bindings that have been growing tighter with each passing moment since I pulled that trigger. These women have been through hell. So have I. But regardless of what we've been through, we're strong enough to climb our way out of the abyss.

The people who were meant to love me betrayed me. My support system was nothing but shackles, clamped around my ankles, dragging me down as water flooded my lungs. But I rose, clawing my way to the surface in spite of them.

Silas turns, removing his helmet as he closes the distance between us. I barely manage to remove my own helmet as he tugs me from the bike, gathering me in his arms. He kisses me deeply, holding me tight.

"I thought—" he starts, the words getting lost.

"I know," I murmur, leaning up to capture his lips again. Bikes roar to life around us, our circle waiting until the cop cars disappear over the horizon. "Take us home."

The scent of leather and spice banishes my worries as the heat of Silas's body settles behind mine. His warmth cuts through the crisp chill of the early morning air, and some intrinsic part of me knows everything will be all right.

Memories of a poisonous flower from another life surface, and I thank God or fate or whatever is out there that I didn't go through with it. Silas offers me comfort. Protection. Grants me infinite possibilities by simply believing in me. Seeing my strength even when I feel weak. Trusting in my courage when the only thing I want to do is hide. Silas's hand presses against my waist, holding me tight, reminding me that despite all the shit that's happened, I still have a family. Not the one I was born into, but a better one. A loving one.

"Are you okay?" I ask.

He takes a deep breath, pulling me closer. Morana sits behind Erik, Serena's small frame eclipsed by Mavros's giant form. The rest of the Seven fan out in front of us, light laughter and soft chatter ringing through the mics. The sun rises in the clear blue sky, and nothing but open road stretches before us.

"I will be, little fox. For the first time in a long time, I think I will be."

EPILOGUE: EVIE

One month later

The beeping monitors stop as the nurse disconnects the tangle of wires from my mother's hand. I've stayed away, not sure what I would say to her. Or if I even wanted to talk to her after everything that's happened. The investigation involving my stepfather and Jonathan's deaths closed last week—a murder-suicide between guilty members of the church involved in money laundering and sex trafficking.

The FBI arrested dozens of people, closing the church and the Blue Lagoon until further notice. This past week has felt like a dream. One filled with justice and relief, knowing sick assholes like them are off the streets. The judge only granted them a handful of years, but Silas assures me none of the perverts will be leaving prison alive.

With Roy and Jonathan officially having a cause of death, it also means it's time to settle the financial aspects of their wills, not that I want anything from either of them. Still, I need all ties connecting me to my old family cut. So, I'm here, sitting in Mother's hospital room.

"By all means, take your time," Mother snaps, glaring at the nurse as she unplugs the leads over her heart.

My spine stiffens, Silas's hand gripping mine for support. "The nurse has it under control," he says, pressing his lips to my cheek.

Sure enough, the nurse gives my mother a sanguine smile before ripping off the last adhesive with more force than necessary. Mother flinches, cursing, but the nurse gives me a wink on the way out, not bothering to conceal her smirk.

"I'll let the lawyer know you're ready."

"Trisha, darling," a familiar voice calls, making the fine hairs on the back of my neck rise.

"Breathe," Silas murmurs, thumb rubbing across the back of my hand as Dean Whitehouser—my biological father—precedes the lawyer into the room.

"I tried to come in sooner, but they wouldn't let me," he says, taking my mother's hand. "I'm here now, my sweet."

"Gross," I mutter, earning a curious glance from the lawyer.

She's young for someone in her profession, maybe mid-thirties, with dark blonde hair and kind, clever blue eyes.

"I'm Morgan and will be handling the distribution of assets today. Let's get started, shall we?" she says, handing my mother and me identical folders. "Inheritance can be a touchy subject for the recently deceased's family, especially when the contents of the will were altered so close to an untimely passing."

My brows furrow as I glance up to find my mother glaring at me with suspicion.

"A delay was needed to verify said documents," Morgan

continues. "But now that cause of death, fault of death, and all legal matters are settled, we can proceed."

Mother sits straighter in the hospital bed, plastering on the expression that's earned her a running tab of condolences.

"Either way," Silas whispers to me as the lawyer continues to speak, his fingers gently tilting my chin until I meet his gaze, "I've got you covered. School, housing, if you want to drop out and travel. Anything. You're set."

The green of his eyes simmers with warmth, something I've come to learn is just for me. We've discussed our future at length. I appreciate that Silas wants to care for me in every way he can. It'd be foolish not to take him up on his offer. I know it's genuine. No catch. No hidden ties that would come back to strangle me. But a part of me is still holding on to the hope that I'll be able to take my place beside him. As an equal.

"Henceforth," Morgan says, seeming to wait for us to tune back in, "the funds will be dispersed as such—to my wife, I leave our main residence, the San Diego estate, with a monthly stipend to maintain staff and other expenses."

Morgan hands a paper attached to a clipboard and pen to Mother. "Sign on the highlighted line."

She does. Morgan tucks the document into a folder before turning to me.

"To my daughter—"

"Wait," Mother cuts in. "That's it? What about the villa in Italy? The vacation home in Florida, Spain, or the one in Brazil? They're rightfully mine."

"I'm aware this can be difficult," Morgan says, not sounding sorry in the least. "Feel free to take a moment to process, but I must continue.

"To my daughter, I entrust your husband to care for and protect you in the case of my passing. As such, he shall take ownership over your allotment."

I blink, a weight sinking in my stomach. "He cut me out of the will?"

"It would seem that was his intent," Morgan says, true sympathy shining through as she passes me a document to sign.

"Serves you right." Mother's bark of a laugh is like a slap in the face. Dean Whitehouser shoots her a reproachful look but doesn't say anything. I banish the tears threatening to spill as I sign, grateful for Silas's strong hand on my thigh.

"Congratulations on your wedding," Morgan presses on, flipping through her folder to withdraw a thick stack of papers.

Silas inhales sharply as my brows furrow, looking to him for answers. His jaw flexes, a harsh shake of his head telling me he doesn't know what she's talking about.

"And condolences," Morgan continues, a mischievous glint in her eyes. "Your father took it upon himself to have a copy of your marriage certificate to a Mr. Jameson Barns added to his will. As you know, Mr. Barns also tragically died on the same day, which means you inherit his portion of your father's wealth in its entirety."

My mouth falls open, staring at the large sum of funds listed on the front page of the stack Morgan slides my way.

"Details can be found on subsequent pages as noted by the color-coded tabs. The key is listed on the bottom of page one. This is your copy to keep."

"This is preposterous," Mother seethes, nostrils flaring as she cranes her neck to see. "Evie never married Jameson."

"Trisha, please," Dean Whitehouser chides, looking at the monitor and inflating cuff circling her arm. "Your blood pressure, dear."

"A legal marriage certificate was documented and signed. With you listed as a witness," Morgan says, seeming to enjoy the way Mother has to bite her tongue before she turns to me. "If you sign on this line, the inheritance is yours. Your legal marriage to Mr. Barns has already been signed by a judge and the required witnesses. And subsequently ended due to his death."

I glance at Silas, watching his fists clench, and knowing the idea of me being bound to another is torture.

"Sign it, little fox." He sighs. "As Morgan said, Mr. Barns is *dead*."

The extra emphasis on the last word has my lips quirking. I scrawl my name on the dotted line, realizing I'll be able to finish the school year without aid from Dean Whitehouser. Or Silas. Who knows, we might even be able to transfer to my dream college in Spain once Morana and Serena are settled.

They're processing as well as they can. Serena feels safest with Morana, but Tempest and I are growing on her. She's looking into school and careers and recently found a therapist she feels comfortable with.

Likewise, Morana is slowly opening up, sharing rare glimpses of her past when she feels up to it. Each person's trauma is their own, and while I don't expect Morana to tell us everything, I can't help but feel there's something she's hiding. It's in the way I catch her looking toward the horizon at sunrise, staring out across the desert as if envisioning someone coming for her. As if *wishing* to be found. Like she has a secret she's kept even from Serena.

Time will tell. Isn't that what they say? There's no use running from a past that's already happened or racing toward a future that has yet to unfold. Life is happening right now—all around us.

I set the pen down, relieved to find only love swirling in Silas's gaze. "Is that it?"

"One more thing," Morgan says. Even Mother stops her cursing long enough to watch as Morgan withdraws a second, equally thick stack. "Jonathan died without a will, meaning all his assets revert to his next of kin."

"Me," Mother declares, her grin as warm as an icy shard.

"Actually, no." Morgan's smile is triumphant. "Being that you're not his biological mother, according to the state's succession law, Evie's status as half-sister affords her his claim. Sign here, please."

Mother opens her mouth, no doubt ready to tell the world that I'm not related to Jonathan, but Dean Whitehouser stops her. With the investigation and nearly everyone from the church ending up in jail, Mother has had to be careful what she admits to. Wanting to cover up an affair is motivation enough, but if she tests me on this, I'll tell the entire world how she supported Roy. How she offered to sell her own daughter.

I don't blink, holding her gaze as I wait to see what she'll do. With effort she swallows and turns away.

Laughing, I scrawl my name across the bottom as fast as I can. Silas and I push to stand, accepting a copy of the paperwork before rushing from the room.

"I'll be in contact shortly to help with dispersal of funds," Morgan calls, waving farewell as she heads for the elevator.

"Damn, baby." Silas chuckles as we step outside the hospital. Light clouds drift lazily across the blue sky, palm trees swaying in a cool breeze. Hints of salt coat the air, the gentle caw of seagulls humming in the distance. "Looks like you're taking me out to lunch. Where should we go?"

Anywhere, I think as a smile splits my face. We can go anywhere. Do anything. Spain doesn't have to stay a dream. Silas dedicating himself to his art and me, free to study at leisure, becoming a professor so I never have to stop learning. We can do it all.

Weaving my fingers through his, I press up on my toes, capturing his lips in a crushing kiss. Silas groans, fingers tangling in my hair, tugging hard enough to have my thighs clenching in anticipation.

"Fuck, Evie," Silas pants, his cock twitching as I press my body against his.

"What do you say about eating in?"

His palms trail down my back, brushing over the curves of my ass as he licks his lips, the sight alone sending a pulse of heat straight to my core. I bite my lip, craving the feel of his hands on my body, of his mouth and lips and tongue worshiping me.

As if reading my thoughts, his hand cups my pussy through the fabric of my dress.

"Are you asking me to eat this sweet pussy of yours, little fox?"

"Yes," I breathe, nipples pebbling as his pupils dilate. It's only been hours since he was last between my thighs, but I want more. God, I hope this never ends—this incessant yearning for him. For the serpent who's stolen my heart and made it his own. "Once we get back."

Silas groans, throwing his head back as if the thought of having to wait is torture.

"You're going to feel my cock pressing into your back the whole ride home," he purrs, practically dragging me toward his bike.

"You say that like it's a bad thing." I grin, arching my back and leaning forward as he starts the engine.

"Christ," Silas curses, gripping my waist and dragging my ass against his hard length. "Keep doing that and I'm going to fuck you here, Evie. Fill this tight hole up with my cum as you scream my name."

"Promise?" I ask, my voice breathy.

A rumbling growl is his only response as Silas guides us through the streets, heading for the winding canyon road that will take us home.

Home.

For the first time in my life, I've found a home. Not the house Silas and I live in, or the sheets we sleep on, but us. Him. We may be a little fucked up, but the splintered pieces of our lives match, clicking together like a twisted puzzle.

"I hope you're ready, baby." Silas angles his bike left, heading down the driveway toward his studio, to our place of comfort. "Because now that I have you, now that your last excuse for not being mine is gone, I'm never letting you go."

An elated laugh escapes me as Silas throws me over his shoulder, slapping my ass as he races through the door. He's right. A part of me was still holding back, so scared of being dependent on another person, even if that person was Silas. But now…

Silas tosses me onto the bed, the silk sheets dipping as I sit up.

"So many promises today," I murmur, sliding over to the edge. He lifts a brow at my ministrations, eyes growing hooded as I let my knees fall open. "I hope you plan on keeping them."

The look he gives me is feral, all want and hunger and something softer. Deeper. Silas kneels, hiking the hem of my dress up as he spreads my thighs. A low growl hums against my panties as he presses an intimate kiss over the soaked fabric. My head falls back, eyes closing—only for him to pull away.

I blink, finding Silas on one knee between my legs, holding a small box. My eyes widen as he swallows, the dark flecks of his emerald eyes brimming with love and nervous anticipation.

"I love you, Evie," Silas says, as if him loving me is a fact—a requirement for life. "You are the light in the darkness. The brilliant splash of color illuminating a grey canvas. I vow to worship every inch of your body. To keep your heart safe. To learn and cherish your beautiful fucking mind."

Tears stream around my smile as he flashes that devilish grin of his.

"You're mine already, little fox. But I still want my ring on your finger. My name attached to yours." He opens the black velvet box, revealing a large teardrop diamond surrounded by glimmering emeralds. "Will you marry me?"

"Yes!" I cry, launching into his waiting arms. He slides the ring onto my finger, securing our promise, and I think my heart might explode from happiness.

All of the torment, the pain and suffering, the bleakest moments when I couldn't see a future—I'd do it all again to find him. His lips crash into mine, licking and nipping between smiles. I squeal as his hands trail up my thighs, his mouth grazing the edge of my collarbone as he sets me back on the bed.

"Lay back, my Evie," Silas purrs, gazing at me as if I'm the most precious thing in the world. "I want to enjoy my first meal as an engaged man. And I'm starving."

ACKNOWLEDGMENTS

Thank you.

Thank you to my amazing editor and friend Samantha Peirce at Radiant Editorial. Envy was a lot for both of us. Thank you for being my sounding board and safe place while we took this story to where it needed to go. I don't know how I survived this long without you! Bookish sister wives forever.

Thank you to everyone at Artscandare Book Cover Design for making an incredible cover image, and delivering on everything I imagined. I love it!

To my wonderful narrators Rylee Kuberra and Christian J. Gilliland, thank you for bringing theses characters to life. Envy asked a lot, and you both rose to the challenge beautifully.

To the readers who have been with me from the beginning and the ones we've picked up along the way, your energy is everything. I can't express enough how every message, post, repost, like, share, or interaction brightens up my day. You are so deeply appreciated. And hang in there. We're just starting to enter the Dark Romance Era.

Thank you to my husband for reading the trigger warnings and not being phased. You once told me I can't write anything to scare you away. Challenge accepted.

And to my girls: Amelia, Juliet, and Ellie. I love you more then you will ever understand. You are every happy moment. Every bright sun. I'm so lucky I get to be your mommy.

ABOUT THE AUTHOR

C.L. Briar is a believer that books are normally better than reality and one of the biggest offenses a person can commit is interrupting reading time. When she is not busy dreaming up dark worlds and plotting destruction, she can be found drinking coffee in her backyard with her husband, three young daughters, and hound dog.

ALSO BY C. L. BRIAR

<u>Sinful Seasons</u>

Spring's Descent

Summer's Seduction

Morpheus & Thanatos: A Novella

<u>Storm of Chaos and Shadows Series</u>

Storm of Chaos and Shadows

Storm of Blood and Vengeance

Storm of Death and Darkness

Storm of Mist and Monsters

<u>The Seven Princes</u>

Envy

www.ingramcontent.com/pod-product-compliance
Lightning Source LLC
Chambersburg PA
CBHW020336310726
48979CB00015B/2391/J

9781956829303